Shadows on the Shore

Annie Seaton

A Bec Whitfield Mystery:2

Shadows on the Shore

This is a work of fiction. Characters, institutions and organisations mentioned in this novel are either the product of the author's imagination or, if real, used fictitiously without any intent to describe actual conduct.

The moral right of the author to be identified as the author of this work has been asserted.

ISBN 978-1-7641263-2-8

Prologue

Two humans move about the deck with purpose, their voices rising and falling in sharp bursts, too tense for comfort. The man—tall, lean, with dark hair—works jerkily at the stern, frequently stopping to gesture angrily at the woman. His movements grow increasingly erratic as he repeatedly repositions the weights. The slender woman stands rigid beside the weighted bundle on the deck, her posture defiant as she sweeps the surrounding waters with binoculars, deliberately turning her back to him when he approaches.

The tropical air hangs thick with moisture, heavy with unspoken menace; a weather pattern the tern knows will drive it to shelter before morning. But for now, it watches, transfixed, as the humans handle their task with forced efficiency, the bundle briefly fought over when the man snatches it from the woman, who attempts to adjust the positioning herself.

The tern tilts its head, black eye fixed on the scene below. It has seen humans dispose of fish guts, empty containers, sometimes themselves when storms or drink take them. But this is different. The random movements and the way they interfere with each other suggest conflict.

The woman speaks sharply, jabbing a finger at the man's chest, her voice carrying across the water with cold fury. The man shoves her hand away, finishes securing the rope with angry tugs, and then steps back. Together, they lift the bundle to the rail.

A dull splash breaks the evening stillness. The bundle disappears beneath the surface, chains pulling it down into depths where even the tern's keen eyes cannot reach. Bubbles rise, then nothing. The humans stand at the rail, the man glancing repeatedly at the woman, she refusing to meet his eyes, both watching the water with a detachment that fails to mask their underlying hostility.

The bird watches as the man turns away first, moving to clean the deck with aggressive, forceful strokes. The woman stands straight and still, staring at the spot where the sea has swallowed their cargo.

There was nothing more to see. As the tern launches itself into the air, the woman looks up, tracking its flight. For a moment, their eyes meet—human and bird. The woman's gaze is hard. Then the tern banks sharply, catching the offshore breeze that will carry it towards the mainland, towards shelter from the coming storm.

Behind it, the yacht's anchor light flickers on, a small beacon in the gathering darkness that emphasises the blackness surrounding it. The humans have begun to argue again, their voices carrying across the water, sharp and accusatory, but the tern pays them no mind. Like all creatures of the wild, it is driven by survival and keeps its own counsel.

The sea conceals their secret in its depths.

For now.

Annie Seaton

The Arrivals

Shadows on the Shore

August 2024 - Sally and Amanda.

The fluorescent lights of Sydney Kingsford Smith Airport buzzed overhead as Sally Walker bounced on her toes in the customs queue, her excitement barely contained within her petite frame. Her short, curly brunette hair shone under the light as she craned her neck to peer around the dozens of travellers ahead of them, her brown eyes sparkling with anticipation.

'God, Amanda, can you believe we're actually here?' Sally whispered, though her voice carried enough enthusiasm to draw glances from nearby passengers. 'A whole year in Australia! Twelve months of beaches, sunshine, and...' she waggled her eyebrows suggestively, 'gorgeous Australian men with those sexy Down Under accents.'

Amanda Priestley shifted her weight from one foot to the other, carefully adjusting the strap of her carry-on bag. Where Sally vibrated with barely contained energy, Amanda's composure spoke of calm. Her olive-toned skin, inherited from her Welsh grandmother's Romany heritage, seemed to glow under the harsh airport lighting, and her striking green eyes swept the customs hall with an analytical gaze.

'Sally, keep your voice down,' Amanda murmured, though a small smile tugged at the corner of her mouth. 'We haven't even cleared customs yet, and you're already planning your romantic conquests.'

'Oh, come on!' Sally nudged her friend with her elbow, the gesture emphasising the curves beneath her fitted travel T-shirt. 'We're twenty-one, we're in one of the most beautiful countries in the world, and we have absolutely no responsibilities. When will we ever get another chance like this?'

'Ah?' Amanda put a finger to her lips. 'Responsibilities? We have to get jobs to support our good times, so our money doesn't run out.'

'Actually, we don't have to work at all if we don't want to,' Sally said, scrolling through her phone. 'I was reading about it last night. They changed the rules for us Brits in July. We used to have to do three months of farm work to get a second-year visa, but not anymore. We can just apply again and stay for up to three years without doing any of that rural work stuff.' She looked up with a grin. 'So, we can just travel and party the whole time if we want. Though I suppose working might be fun too— meet some locals, earn some spending money for the touristy tours and stuff.'

I have to get a job, Amanda thought. It was easier for Sally; her family was wealthy and would subsidise her trip if she needed more money. Sally was a sweetheart; she never bragged about her wealthy family. If anything, she watched her money almost as closely as Amanda did.

The queue shuffled forward, bringing them closer to the stern-faced customs officers who were methodically checking passports and asking questions. Amanda pulled out their documentation, her movements precise. Everything about Amanda spoke of someone who planned ahead, who researched thoroughly, and approached life with caution.

'I'm excited too,' Amanda said, her voice softer now, more genuine. 'It's just... this is a big step, Sal. We're on the other side of the world from everything we know. Our families, our friends, our entire support system.'

Sally's expression softened as she recognised the slight tremor of nerves in her friend's voice. Despite their different approaches to life, they'd been inseparable since their first year of primary school in their village of Northleach. Even when Sally went to boarding school at the end of their primary years. Sally's vivacious confidence balanced Amanda's thoughtful reserve, while Amanda's steady presence grounded Sally's often impulsive nature.

'Hey,' Sally reached over and squeezed Amanda's hand. 'We've got each other, right? Besides, you're the smartest person I know.'

'Next!' The customs officer's voice cut through their conversation.

They approached the window together, Amanda handling their passports and documentation while Sally tried to contain her excited fidgeting. The officer, a middle-aged woman with greying hair pulled back in a severe bun, examined their papers with professional thoroughness.

'Purpose of visit?' she asked in a clipped Australian accent.

'Holiday,' Amanda replied. 'We have working holiday visas for twelve months.'

The officer nodded, scanning their visa details on her screen. 'What kind of work are you planning to do?'

'Whatever we can find, really,' Sally jumped in enthusiastically. 'Fruit picking, waitressing, bar work; we want to travel around and see as much of Australia as possible.'

'Do you have sufficient funds to support yourselves?' the officer continued, her tone routine but thorough.

Amanda produced their bank statements and travel insurance documents. 'Yes, we have the required funds, plus our return flights are booked.'

'How long do you intend to stay in Sydney initially?'

'A few weeks to get our bearings,' Amanda explained, 'then we're planning to travel up the east coast. Sally wants to head to Darwin eventually, and I'm thinking about working in some of the rural areas – maybe fruit picking season in Queensland.'

The officer's expression softened slightly. 'Darwin, eh?' She glanced at Sally with what might have been amusement. 'Hope you're prepared for the heat, love. And the humidity. And the crocodiles.'

Sally's eyes widened with delight rather than concern. 'Crocodiles? Really? That's amazing!'

The officer smiled at them. 'Welcome to Australia, girls. Enjoy your stay and good luck with the job hunting.'

After they collected their passports and moved towards the baggage claim, Sally practically vibrated with renewed energy. 'Did you hear that? Crocodiles! This is going to be incredible!'

Amanda shook her head, but she was smiling now, caught up in her friend's infectious enthusiasm. 'Only you would be excited about dangerous reptiles, Sal.'

The baggage carousel was a chaos of travellers wrestling with oversized suitcases and anxious families waiting for arrivals. Sally and Amanda found a spot along the conveyor belt, joining the dance of airport baggage claim: the careful watching, the false alarms when someone else's similar suitcase appeared, the patient waiting.

'So,' Sally said, lowering her voice conspiratorially, 'have you given any thought to the romantic possibilities of this trip?'

Amanda shook her head. 'Sally...'

'I'm serious! You're gorgeous, you're brilliant, and you're

going to be working alongside rugged farm hands and charming baristas in the romantic Australian countryside. It's like something out of a romance novel!'

'I'm here to experience Australia and earn some money, not to find romance,' Amanda protested, but her tone lacked conviction.

'Why can't you do both?' Sally's brown eyes danced with mischief. 'I fully intend to make the most of every opportunity this year presents. Life's too short to spend it all worrying.'

Their bags finally appeared, and they manoeuvred through the crowd to retrieve them. Sally's case was covered in stickers from various countries—evidence of her family's frequent travels and her adventurous spirit. Amanda's was a soft backpack with wheels; she wondered how long Sally would last before she swapped to one.

As they wheeled their luggage towards the exit, the automatic doors slid open, and suddenly they were stepping out into Sydney. The humid air hit them immediately, carrying scents of coffee and car exhaust, and something indefinably foreign yet exciting. The early morning sun was already warming the concrete, promising a beautiful Australian day.

'Oh my God,' Sally breathed, stopping in her tracks to stare at the bustling scene before them. 'We're really here. We're actually in Sydney!'

The airport pickup area buzzed with activity. Passengers queued for taxis, families reunited with emotional embraces, and black-suited business travellers strode purposefully towards waiting hire cars. Tour buses idled nearby, their sides emblazoned with images of Sydney's iconic harbour and Opera House.

Amanda pulled out her phone to check their

accommodation details. 'Our hostel is in Bondi. The email says we take the Airport Link to Central, then transfer to Circular Quay, then catch Bus 333 directly to Bondi Beach. I think we should have followed the signs inside.'

'Bondi!' Sally's excitement ratcheted up another notch. 'Wait, this is where they film *Bondi Rescue*! I've watched every episode. Those lifeguards are so hot.'

They joined the flow of people heading towards the train station, their suitcase wheels clicking rhythmically against the pavement. The multicultural tapestry of Sydney was immediately evident; conversations in dozens of languages spoke of the city's international character.

'You know what I love already?' Sally said as they navigated through the crowd. 'The energy here. It's different from London. More relaxed but still exciting. And look at all these gorgeous people!'

She wasn't wrong. Sydney seemed populated by an unusually attractive cross-section of humanity: sun-bronzed surfers with bleached hair, elegant businesswomen striding in designer heels, ruggedly handsome tradesmen heading to work sites. The casual lifestyle was immediately apparent in the way people dressed, moved, and interacted.

'Sally,' Amanda warned, noticing her friend's appreciative glances at passing men, 'remember we're here as working holidaymakers. We need to maintain some level of professionalism when we're job hunting.'

'Being professional doesn't mean we can't have any fun, Amanda. Besides, look at them looking at us!'

And it was true. Sally's petite but curvaceous figure, highlighted by her well-fitted jeans and clingy T-shirt and the way her curly hair caught the morning light, was drawing appreciative glances from male passersby. Her natural vivacity and excitement radiated from her.

Amanda felt practically invisible beside her vibrant friend, and that suited her. While she knew she wasn't unattractive, her more reserved nature seemed to fade into the background against Sally's magnetism. She pulled her light cardigan a little tighter around herself, suddenly self-conscious about her practical travel clothes. Next to Sally's effortless charm, Amanda felt like the sensible, boring friend; the friend who was almost invisible to guys whose eyes skipped over to focus on the bubbly brunette beside her.

'I can't believe we're going to be here for a whole year,' Amanda said softly, and for the first time since their arrival, her voice carried wonder rather than nervousness.

'Three hundred and sixty-five days of adventure,' Sally agreed, slinging her arm around her friend's shoulders as they approached the train platform. 'Amanda Priestley, I have a feeling this is going to be the most incredible year of our lives.'

The train arrived smoothly, its doors sliding open with a gentle beep, and as they stepped aboard with their luggage, they grinned at each other. They were no longer the young women who had boarded a plane in London twenty-four hours earlier. They were adventurers, working holidaymakers on the threshold of wonderful experiences that would shape the rest of their lives.

Once they settled into their seats with their backpacks crammed against their legs, they smiled at each other and exchanged a triumphant high five.

June 2025 - Phillipa.

Phillipa Fairchild stood at the floor-to-ceiling windows of Sydney's international terminal, her blonde curls catching the early morning light as she gazed out at the tarmac where planes taxied one after the other. Not as busy as Heathrow or New York, but still constant. For the first time in months, she felt as though she could breathe properly. The family expectations, stepfamily hassles, and her father's disappointed lectures felt like they were on the other side of the world.

'They are,' she whispered to herself, pressing her palm against the cool glass. 'Finally.'

Behind her, the terminal buzzed with the chaos of international arrivals. Families reunited with tears and laughter, business travellers strode past in suits, and tour groups clustered around guides holding destination signs.

But Phillipa remained aloof from it all, revelling in the moment of transition between the life she was leaving behind and the unknown adventure ahead.

Her phone buzzed insistently in her designer handbag, a Hermès bag that had been a twenty-first birthday gift from her father, back when their relationship hadn't been poisoned by Glenys and her precious twins. Phillipa glanced at the screen and her stomach tightened. Three missed calls from Glenys and a curt message from her father that simply read: 'Call when you arrive. We need to discuss your financial arrangements.'

'Discuss my financial arrangements,' Phillipa muttered, shoving the phone back into her bag without responding. 'As if my trust fund is any of *her* business. As if those spoiled sixteen-year-old twins need protecting from me.'

She was well used to the bitterness that consumed her. *Three unbearable years.* Three years since Dad had remarried, bringing Glenys and her children into their previously peaceful house, and Phillipa now felt like an outsider in her own home. The twins, Marcus and Millicent, were lavished with attention, their every whim catered to, their substantial trust fund from their late father ensuring they wanted for nothing. Meanwhile, Phillipa found herself constantly defending her own needs, her place in the family hierarchy.

This trip was her declaration of independence, her escape from the unreasonable expectations that had made her childhood home feel like enemy territory. Her home had been taken over by the interlopers, and she knew that Glenys had only married her father because of his title and wealth money that Phillipa would one day inherit—if there was any left. Her mother's settlement had been substantial, but Dad hadn't learned anything from the divorce. He'd fallen for the same type again: a grasping, calculating woman who was determined to get as much as she could from him.

Phillipa and her mother had been estranged since her mother had left Dad for a bartender fifteen years her junior. Phillipa had been mortified by the ribbing she'd gotten at school when the news had spread like wildfire. The humiliation had been devastating; whispered conversations that stopped when she entered a room, pitying looks from teachers, and worst of all, the barely concealed amusement of her so-called friends. She would never forgive her mother for that public shame, and now she had to deal with Glenys and her ghastly little brats who treated her father's house like their own personal playground.

Small wonder I've fled to the other side of the world.

The memory of her last argument with her father still stung.

She'd been in his study, the same room where he'd once helped her with homework and listened to her dreams. But that warm, supportive father had disappeared when Glenys entered their lives, replaced by a man who seemed to view every request from Phillipa as an unreasonable demand.

'Phillipa, you're twenty-four years old,' he'd said, not even looking up from his laptop. 'Your trust fund provides you with a very comfortable income. Most people your age would be grateful for such financial security. I'm not funding this overseas jaunt. You can pay for it yourself.'

'Most people my age don't have to watch their stepmother redecorate their childhood home and install her precious twins in the best bedrooms,' she'd shot back, her frustration finally boiling over. 'Most people don't have to justify every expense while their stepsiblings buy whatever they want with their inheritance money.'

That's when her father had looked up, his expression cold in a way that still made her chest tighten. 'That inheritance was left to them by their father. It's not our family money, Phillipa. It's *theirs* by right.'

'And what about my rights?' she'd demanded. 'What about my place in this family? Ever since you married Glenys, I've felt unwelcome in my own home. A tolerated resident who's expected to be grateful for whatever scraps of attention I receive.'

The argument had escalated from there, with accusations and hurt feelings flying back and forth until Phillipa had stormed out, determined to prove that she could make her own way in the world. Australia had seemed like the perfect destination—far enough away to make a statement, exotic enough to satisfy her sense of adventure, and offering opportunities for the kind of independent experience her father claimed she needed.

Now, standing in Sydney's airport, Phillipa felt a complex mixture of emotions. Relief was paramount; the sheer joy of being away from the constant tension, the sideways glances from Glenys, the twins' entitled attitudes, the disappointed lectures from her father about financial responsibility. But underneath the relief was a deep hurt. She pushed it away, welcoming the current of anger that replaced it, motivating her to prove herself.

She'd lost Dad when he married Glenys; the father who had once been her champion now viewed her as a financial problem to be managed rather than a daughter to be cherished.

I hate him.

'Phillipa Fairchild to the information desk, please. Phillipa Fairchild.'

She approached the courtesy phone with trepidation, her heart pounding as she lifted the receiver. No one knew she was here.

'Miss Fairchild? This is Jennifer from the concierge service. I have a message for you from your travel agent regarding your accommodation in Sydney.'

The relief was so intense that Phillipa had to lean against the phone booth for support. Just travel arrangements, not family drama. Not her stepmother's manipulative concern or her father's lectures about responsibility.

'Yes, please go ahead,' she managed, her voice steadier than she felt.

'Your suite at the Hilton has been confirmed, and they've arranged for a car service to collect you. The driver should be waiting in the arrivals area with a sign bearing your name.'

'Thank you,' Phillipa said, though part of her wondered if

she should have chosen more modest accommodations. The Hilton was hardly the choice of someone trying to prove their financial independence. But old habits die hard, and she reasoned that starting her adventure in comfort would give her a better foundation for the challenges ahead.

She found her driver easily; a cheerful man in his fifties holding a sign with 'Miss P. Fairchild' written in block letters. As he led her towards the exit, chatting about Sydney's weather, relief filled her.

'First time in Sydney?' the driver asked as they loaded her luggage: three expensive suitcases that probably contained more clothes than she'd need for a year, but she'd been too flustered when packing to make rational decisions.

'Yes,' she replied, settling into the back seat of the luxury sedan. 'First time in Australia, actually.'

'You'll love it here,' he assured her, pulling into traffic. 'Sydney's got everything: beautiful harbour, great beaches, fantastic food scene. What brings you Down Under?'

What had brought her here?

Escape? Rebellion? A desperate need to prove herself? The need to find out who she was when she wasn't defined by family drama and financial dependence?

'Just a holiday,' she said finally, which was true enough without being too revealing.

As the car wound through Sydney's streets towards the harbour, Phillipa pressed her face to the window, taking in her first real glimpses of the city. The architecture was different from London: more modern, more casual, the streets meandering organically rather than following any imperial master plan. London plane trees lined some streets, their leafy branches swaying in the harbour breeze, and even in the early morning, people were jogging along waterfront paths, their faces already touched by the warm Australian winter sun.

Her phone buzzed again, and she pulled a face as she glanced down at it. A message from her father, this one more insistent. 'Phillipa, don't be childish. Call me and tell me where you're staying in Sydney so we can discuss your budget and your timeline for returning home.'

He must have talked to the travel agent? How dare he? Phillipa stared at the message for a long moment, then deliberately turned off her phone. Not powered down, but off. For the first time in her adult life, she was completely unreachable, completely free from Dad's expectations and Glenys' demands. She'd only stay one night at the Hilton, and then he wouldn't know where she was.

The harbour came into view, and Phillipa's breath caught in her throat. She'd seen pictures, of course, but nothing had prepared her for the reality of Sydney Harbour Bridge arching gracefully over the sparkling water, or the distinctive white sails of the Opera House gleaming in the morning sun. It was more beautiful than she'd imagined.

'Quite a sight, isn't it?' the driver said, noticing her amazement.

'It's incredible,' she breathed, and for the first time, she felt excited. Genuinely, purely excited about what lay ahead.

The uniformed doorman approached the car with a welcoming smile, and as Phillipa stepped out into the warm Sydney air, she felt like she was stepping into a new version of herself. One who was free to make mistakes and take risks.

April 2025 - Paulo.

Paulo Ramirez leaned against the bar at the Beach Hotel, his dark eyes conducting a leisurely survey of the talent at the bar. The outdoor venue buzzed with exactly the kind of energy he'd been hoping to find in Byron Bay: live music drifting from the stage, the salt tang of ocean air mixing with the scent of beer and barbecue, and most importantly, an impressive collection of beautiful young women scattered throughout the crowd.

He'd positioned himself strategically at the corner, giving him a clear view across the entire venue while projecting the kind of casual confidence that he knew would draw attention. Even after the journey up from Sydney and an afternoon settling into the backpacker resort, Paulo knew he looked effortlessly polished; his linen shirt fitted perfectly to emphasise his naturally athletic build, and his dark hair was tousled by the coastal breeze.

'Corona with lime,' he ordered, choosing a beer that would mark him as international without being pretentious. As he waited for his drink, his gaze continued to take in the crowd around him.

Near the door, a group of Scandinavian backpackers shared a large table, their blonde hair catching the lights as they laughed together. Attractive, certainly, but they had that slightly overwhelming group dynamic that could be challenging to navigate. Better to wait for one to separate from the pack.

At a high-top table closer to the bar, two sophisticated women in their late twenties nursed cocktails and conducted what appeared to be a serious conversation. City professionals on a weekend getaway, by the look of them. Interesting possibilities, but they seemed too focused on their discussion to welcome interruption.

But it was the petite brunette near the pool tables who caught his attention. She was laughing at something her companion had said, her curly hair bouncing with the movement, and even from across the crowded venue, Paulo could appreciate the curves beneath her fitted sundress. She had this bubbly energy that was pulling the guys in; a few were checking her out.

Paulo scanned the back of the bar as he finished his beer, and then he turned and ordered another one.

'Are you a local?'

The brunette with the curly hair had spotted him checking her out. Brown eyes looked up at him, sparkling with infectious enthusiasm. British, clearly, with that distinctive accent and the excited energy of someone discovering a new place. She was hot in that girl-next-door way: small and nicely built. Somehow, she'd approached without him noticing. Paulo prided himself on maintaining awareness of his surroundings, especially when attractive women were involved, but she'd quickly slipped past his radar. His smile was lazy; he was pleased she'd targeted him. He was more than willing.

'No. I have today arrived from Sydney,' he replied, allowing his Brazilian accent to add its exotic flavour to the words while giving her his most devastating smile. 'Paulo Ramirez, very pleased to meet you.'

'Sally,' she replied, extending her hand with a confidence that Paulo found refreshing. 'Let me guess? South American, definitely well-travelled, probably taking a gap year before settling down to some boring job?'

Her accuracy was startling, but Paulo maintained his

composure while simultaneously noting that this close, she was even more striking than he'd first thought. Brown eyes full of trouble, skin with cute freckles and just a hint of tan, and yeah, the kind of body that would definitely mess with a guy's head. Designer labels, if he wasn't mistaken. The clothes and the confidence spoke money.

'Pretty close, but not quite,' Paulo said. 'I'm just having some fun before I have to get serious about life. And yeah...' He shrugged casually. 'Let's just say I'm keeping my options open before I join the family business.'

'Me too.' Sally laughed, and when a few guys at nearby tables turned to check out what was so amusing, Paulo smoothly slipped his arm around her waist, a casual but possessive gesture that sent a clear message to anyone watching.

'I like that you're being honest. Most guys try to act all mysterious and important when really, they're just regular people.'

'What about you?' Paulo asked, surprised by how much he was enjoying talking to her. 'Are you figuring things out as you go, or do you already know what you want?'

'I'm on a working holiday from England,' Sally said with infectious enthusiasm. 'My friend Amanda and I have been in Australia for nine months now. We've been everywhere! Started in the Riverland in South Australia, fruit picking, then up to Darwin, where I worked in a bar and Amanda did some admin work. We even spent time in Tasmania, cold but pretty. Now we're ending our trip, leaving the best to last.'

'And where is the best?' His fingers ran lightly down her bare shoulder, and she moved closer.

'We're making our way up the east coast to Cairns. Best

decision I've ever made, honestly. The whole trip, that is.'

Her contentment was so genuine that Paulo felt a momentary stab of envy. When was the last time he'd felt that kind of satisfaction with his life? When had he ever known exactly what he wanted and felt confident he was living the life he wanted?

Probably when more family money had flowed in his direction. If it ever did. He knew his brothers were showing him up. They both went straight into the business after university, but Paulo had insisted on one last trip when he graduated.

'A working holiday,' Paulo repeated. 'That sounds incredibly liberating. What kind of work are you doing?'

Sally's eyes sparkled with amusement. 'Whatever pays the bills! I'm working at a surf shop here in Byron. I don't have to, but I love meeting people. And it makes Amanda feel better about having to work, I think.'

'In that case,' Paulo said, moving slightly closer and running his fingers just beneath her breasts. 'Sounds like you're doing it right. I'm keeping it simple too. I've got myself a Troop Carrier that I've kitted out for camping. Freedom to go wherever the road takes me. I think you are exactly the kind of person I need to meet. Someone who knows how to live.'

And someone who obviously has money, if she doesn't need to work.

As they continued talking, Paulo found himself enjoying the conversation more than he'd expected. Sally's energy was infectious, and he found himself smiling every time she spoke.

'So,' Sally was saying, 'if you want the real Byron Bay experience, you need to get up early and catch the sunrise from the lighthouse. Most tourists miss it because they're too hungover, but it's absolutely magical.'

'I'd love that,' Paulo replied, moving closer as the music got louder. 'When would be good for you?'

'Tomorrow morning?' Sally suggested with a grin, then paused as her phone buzzed. She glanced at it and laughed. 'Early start, but trust me, it's worth it. Though speaking of early starts...' She looked back towards a table where a taller woman with olive skin and striking green eyes was gathering her things.

'That's my friend Amanda,' Sally explained. 'She's brilliant but way more sensible than me. Looks like she's calling it a night, probably thinks I'm mental for staying out this late when we've got to check out of the hostel tomorrow.'

Paulo watched as Amanda stood up, clearly preparing to leave. 'Does that mean you have to go too?'

Sally bit her lip, glancing between Amanda and Paulo. 'Well... Amanda's got her own key, and she's perfectly capable of getting back to the hostel on her own. She's done it before when I've decided to extend my evening.' Her brown eyes sparkled with mischief. 'Besides, you haven't shown me where you're staying yet. I'm curious about this Troop Carrier you mentioned.'

'It's nothing fancy,' Paulo said, though his pulse quickened at the suggestion. 'But it's got everything I need, and it's parked right near the beach. Perfect for watching that sunrise you were talking about.'

'Sounds perfect,' Sally said, her decision made. She waved at Amanda, who rolled her eyes but smiled knowingly before heading towards the exit. 'Lead the way, Paulo Ramirez. Let's see if Brazilian hospitality lives up to its reputation.'

The evening had taken exactly the turn Paulo had been hoping for. Byron Bay was delivering on its promises, and as they made their way out of the venue together, Sally's hand finding his, he felt that familiar thrill of a conquest.

After all, he had eleven months of freedom left, and if tonight was any indication, Sally was going to provide him with exactly the kind of adventure—and money—he'd travelled halfway around the world to experience.

Victoria - July 2025.

Victoria Chandler spread the well-worn map of Queensland across the small table of the Brisbane hostel's common room, her fingers tracing the coastal route north from the city. Even in the late afternoon humidity that made most travellers wilt, she was energised and focused; she loved the short pixie haircut and knew it revealed the strong line of her jaw and the determined set of her blue eyes.

The past three weeks in Brisbane had been exactly what she'd needed: a chance to establish routines, find her rhythm, and prove to herself that she could thrive in this coastal environment. Every morning began with a five-kilometre run along the Brisbane River, followed by a workout at the local gym where her dedication had quickly earned the respect of the serious lifters who gathered there before dawn. Her body had adapted to the humid climate with surprising ease, her muscles growing leaner and more defined under the combination of consistent exercise and the active lifestyle that seemed to be the default setting for most Queenslanders.

But Brisbane had been just the beginning, a place to find her feet before launching into the real adventure. Now, as she studied the map with methodical attention, she was ready for the next phase of her visit.

'Noosa,' she murmured to herself, her finger settling on the coastal town about two hours north of Brisbane. She'd heard other travellers talking about it: pristine beaches, excellent surfing conditions, a laidback atmosphere that supposedly captured the essence of the Australian beach lifestyle. More importantly, it offered opportunities to meet the sort of company she was looking for.

Victoria observed the other travellers in the hostel with the same intensity she brought to everything else.

'Excuse me, are you using this?' A voice interrupted her planning, drawing her attention to a young German backpacker hovering hopefully near the table. The common room was filling up with travellers returning from their day's adventures, and space was at a premium.

'Just for a few more minutes,' Victoria replied. 'I'm planning my next destination.'

'Where to?' The German guy—tall, blond, with the kind of deep tan that spoke of months spent outdoors—glanced at her map with interest. 'Queensland is beautiful. I just came down from Cairns. Where are you thinking of going?'

'Noosa next, I think.'

'You are Australian?' he asked, checking her out more closely.

'Yes. Is it that obvious?'

He grinned at her and nodded. 'I have seen much of Australia. Where do you live?'

'You wouldn't have been there.'

'Try me.'

'Broken Hill.'

'I have visited there. I went to the Broken Heel Festival. It was a blast. Such fabulous costumes and high heels!' He chuckled.

'Well, if you've been to Noosa, you'll know why I want to go there,' she said. 'I want to try surfing, and I've heard it's good for beginners but still challenging enough to be worthwhile.'

The German's face lit up with enthusiasm. 'Noosa's fantastic! I spent three weeks there learning to surf. The waves at Noosa Main Beach are perfect for beginners, but if you're athletic, you'll pick it up quickly.'

Victoria felt a familiar spark of anticipation at the mention of a physical challenge. This was exactly what she'd been hoping to find. And the sort of personality that came with it.

'Any recommendations for accommodation?' she asked, pulling out her phone.

'There's a great hostel right near the beach—Noosa Backpackers. Clean, friendly, and you're walking distance of everything. Many travellers too, so it's easy to find people to surf with or explore with.'

Victoria made a note of the recommendation, though she'd had private accommodation until now. But she also knew she needed to connect with other travellers; it would give her a broader scope for finding the sort of person she was looking for.

'Are you travelling alone?' the German asked, and something in his tone suggested more than casual interest. Maybe she'd been wrong.

Victoria looked up from her notebook. He was attractive enough; fit, obviously adventurous, with the kind of easy confidence that came from successful travel experiences.

Maybe.

'I am,' she replied neutrally, neither encouraging nor discouraging his interest. 'I prefer the freedom of solo travel.'

'That's admirable,' he said, and his respect seemed genuine. Victoria smiled, the first genuine smile she'd offered since the conversation began. Compliments about her capabilities always pleased her more than comments about her appearance. 'Not many people have the confidence to travel alone, especially for extended periods. How long are you planning to travel?'

'Until the money runs out,' Victoria said. 'I want to see as much as possible, try everything I can and decide where I want to live.'

'Good plan. See it all.'

'That's the plan,' she said, standing and shouldering her new backpack with easy grace.

'Well, if you do end up in Noosa and want company for surfing or hiking, I'm Klaus,' the German said, extending his hand. 'I'll be up there in two weeks before heading west.'

Victoria shook his hand, noting the calluses that spoke of serious outdoor activity. 'Victoria. And thank you for the recommendations. Maybe I'll see you there.'

As she made her way back to her room, Victoria was ready to leave. Tomorrow, she would catch the bus to Noosa, continue her travels.

But tonight, she had research to do. Victoria pulled out her laptop and started work.

Part 1: The Mystery

Chapter 1

Monday, August 18.

Pandanus Point Police Station - Bec Whitfield.

The drive from Townsville had been spectacular—a reminder of why North Queensland pulled at something deep inside me despite my recent past. The highway curved through dense rainforest, occasionally revealing emerald paddocks and those heart-stopping coastal views of the impossibly blue Coral Sea.

Now, as I stepped out of the Land Cruiser and approached Pandanus Point Regional Police Station, I straightened my detective's shield. Stupid. As though perfect alignment would somehow make me feel qualified. After accelerated training in Townsville and completing detective competencies, I was starting at this remote station north of Mission Beach, only six months after my previous promotion to Bowen River. My quick advancement through the Detective Appointment Board had raised eyebrows, but Todd Davenport, my mentor and now Detective Inspector, insisted I'd earned it.

Humidity plastered my ironed shirt to my back within minutes of leaving my air-conditioned vehicle. Sweat beaded at my hairline, threatening the professional image I'd carefully constructed.

The station stood before me—a Queensland-style building with wide verandas and tropical landscaping. Once the area's first post office, it retained its heritage charm despite housing modern police technology, modest compared to Brisbane, but familiar after Bowen River. Behind it, towering rainforest pressed in—a wall of impossibly green vegetation that seemed to breathe in the heavy tropical air. Massive strangler figs and fan palms created a primeval backdrop that made the small station appear even more isolated, almost swallowed by wilderness.

The yard itself shocked me—overgrown and neglected, with tall grass nearly obscuring the walkway and paperbarks dropping debris across the cracked concrete. Two patrol vehicles sat at awkward angles, one with obvious mud caked on its undercarriage, the other sporting a spiderweb crack across its windscreen. This wasn't the meticulously maintained government property I'd expected.

Inside worked a team of five: a veteran Senior Sergeant, three constables, and now me—filling a detective position that couldn't keep occupants due to isolation. We covered a hundred kilometres of the Cassowary Coastline, handling everything from community policing to marine incidents, wildlife protection, tourist problems, and drug trafficking along the isolated shore.

I shouldn't be nervous. Todd's parting words echoed: 'Don't let jealous colleagues take the gloss off your achievement, Bec. Show them what you're made of.' The memory of our goodbye—his hand briefly finding mine before he pulled away—steadied me somehow. My chance to prove my promotion wasn't luck or favouritism. I squared my shoulders, adjusted my shield once more, and stepped inside.

Career first. Whatever had passed between Todd and me in that goodbye moment could wait. This was about proving myself. My thoughts quickly moved to the present as I stood at the desk of the station, and the reality of my new posting hit me.

Holy hell. The reception area was a disgrace. Reality dawned as I stood at the station's front desk. Files teetered everywhere, coffee rings marked the counter, and someone's half-eaten sandwich curled beside the radio. The air conditioning wheezed ineffectively against the heat, while mould, stale coffee, and something unidentifiable created an odour that forced me to breathe through my mouth.

'Yeah?' The young man at the desk flicked me a nervous look, his Adam's apple bobbing as he swallowed. His name badge identified him as Constable Tickle.

'Detective Whitfield. I'm reporting for duty.' I kept my voice steady, professional.

That got his attention. 'Oh. Right. Sorry. The new one.' His hand shook as he made a vague gesture to a corridor that seemed to recede into darkness. 'Sarge is in his office.'

Professional? Right. Welcome to Pandanus Point Police Station, serving the Cassowary Coast and operating by its own rules, apparently including a flexible approach to basic cleanliness. I walked down the hall, wondering if the station had ever seen a mop. If it were possible, Sergeant Keith Bradley's office was worse than reception. Papers covered every surface, his uniform strained at the buttons across his substantial belly, and he was smoking despite the prominent NO SMOKING sign on the wall directly behind his head. The stale smell reminded me of Gray after one of his big nights out—before I discovered what he was really up to. I didn't think about him much these days. He was a piece of my past I was determined to bury and forget.

'Whitfield?' He didn't stand or offer his hand. Just squinted at me through a haze of smoke, his bloodshot eyes giving me a once-over that made my skin crawl. 'Didn't ask for a bloody detective, but they sent you anyway. Your office is down the hall. Try not to get in anyone's way.'

My spine stiffened, but I kept my voice level. After surviving the head instructor in Townsville—a man who seemed to believe women belonged anywhere but law enforcement—Bradley was nothing. 'Thank you, Senior. I'm looking forward to working with the team.'

His laugh turned into a wet, phlegmy cough. 'Team. Yeah, good one.' He waved me away with a meaty hand splattered with liver spots. 'Morrison's off with his back again, Tanaka's on maternity leave, Tickle's as useless as tits on a bull, and regional command thinks a rookie detective is going to help. Just don't expect any red carpet, love.'

I could feel my carefully constructed professional façade threatening to crack at the casual dismissal, the deliberate belittling. This wasn't what I had imagined when Todd had called to tell me about the opening at Pandanus Point. 'It's a good spot for you, Bec,' he'd said. 'Small enough to make your mark, big enough to matter. I put in a word.'

Now I wondered if he'd been trying to get rid of me, push the awkward almost-something between us to a safe distance. But that wasn't Todd. He'd been my mentor since we'd worked Leanne Delaney's case in Bowen in autumn when I was still in uniform. He wouldn't have set me up to fail.

I turned on my heel, before I said anything I'd regret later. Even though I was a Detective Senior Constable, Bradley outranked me. As a detective, I'd work in specialised investigations, based at Pandanus Point but on rotation to other small stations as the need arose. but I still fell under the command structure of the station. No point making an enemy of my superior officer in the first five minutes.

The hallway reeked of stale coffee and the cigarette smoke that drifted from Bradley's office. Two constables were propped against the wall in the staffroom, whispering conspiratorially. They fell silent when they saw me, one expression shifting to poorly concealed disdain, the other, embarrassment. I might be a coward in relationships, but at work? Different story. The one next to the window looked me up and down, taking in my crisp white shirt and pressed trousers with the same expression I'd seen countless times before. That subtle assessment: female, early thirties, trying too hard. I'd been getting that look since I left Bowen River in my teens, determined to prove my father wrong about everything I could and couldn't be.

'The new detective,' she said, loud enough for me to hear, her lip curling slightly. 'Hope she knows how to make coffee.'

I stopped. Turned. Gave them a cold smile that never reached my eyes. 'Constable...?'

'Reeves.' Less cocky now. Late twenties, hard eyes, the chip on her shoulder obvious from fifty paces. She shifted her weight, trying to maintain her bravado.

'Constable Reeves. I make excellent coffee. For myself. You'll make your own. And while you're in the kitchen, you might want to wash those mugs in the sink. This station is a disgrace.'

Her mouth opened and closed like a stunned mullet.

The other constable—younger, Indigenous, with quick, intelligent eyes—bit her lip to suppress a smile. 'Welcome to Pandanus Point, Detective,' she said quietly.

'Thank you, Constable Fields,' I said, glancing at the name tag above her right breast pocket.

I walked back into the hall. They didn't bother me; it was

water off a duck's back these days. I'd dealt with worse. I'd survived a criminal partner and a religious zealot of a father who believed women should be silent in church and everywhere else. I could—and would—make mincemeat of a disrespectful junior who thought territorial pissing contests were the way to establish dominance.

The office they'd assigned me was small, barely more than a cupboard with a desk wedged inside, but at least it had a window overlooking a strip of rainforest that separated the station from the road. The glass was grimy, streaked with the residue of the last wet season and God knows how many before that. I set down my box of personal items I'd carried from the car: Mum and Dad's photo—Dad and I had made a tentative attempt at getting on since I turned up in Bowen River. My detective graduation picture with Todd, his arm around my shoulder, me smiling like I'd conquered the world. My favourite mug from Bowen River, a parting gift from the Lovatts—a reminder of my brief but happy time there. Bradley could certainly learn a few lessons from my previous boss, Sergeant Mark Lovatt at Bowen River Station.

As I unpacked, I thought about what I'd say at the first morning briefing. Firm but fair. No weakness. I hadn't fought my way from uniform to criminal investigation just to let a dysfunctional station knock me off course. I was Detective Senior Constable Rebecca Whitfield now, and I'd earned every inch of that title through sweat and sacrifice. I was arranging my few personal items on the desk when the radio in the front office crackled to life, cutting through my thoughts.

'Dispatch to Pandanus Point Station. We've got a report of an abandoned vessel at Garners Beach, north of Ninney Point. A resident walking his dog found it washed up on the shoreline. Over.'

As I walked down the hall, Constable Tickle reached for his handset, his voice surprisingly brisk. 'Unit four responding. Any details on the vessel? Over.'

'The caller spotted a catamaran drifting towards the beach about three nautical miles north of Pandanus Point. Appears to be a private yacht, no identification visible. Said he watched the tide bring it right to the beach. The caller reported no obvious persons on board or in the vicinity. Recommend caution.'

My pulse quickened. One of the reasons I was posted here was because of the suspected drug smuggling that was taking place along the coast. I reached out to Tickle to take the handset, my instincts immediately on alert.

'Detective Whitfield responding. Exact position, please?'

There was a moment of silence on the other end, then: 'Who?'

For God's sake. 'Detective Senior Constable Bec Whitfield. The vessel's position?'

'On the beach, a couple of kilometres north of Ninney Point.' The dispatcher's voice held a note of uncertainty, like he wasn't sure he should be talking to me, the new detective, a woman, an unknown.

Bradley appeared at the end of the hall, his substantial bulk blocking most of the light. For the first time since I'd arrived, he looked vaguely interested.

'You know boats, Whitfield?' he asked.

'I do.' I didn't elaborate. No need for him to know I had my Coxswain's certificate. Always better to keep something in reserve, especially with men like Bradley, who would use any information you gave them as ammunition later.

His lips twitched into something that might have been a smile on another face. 'Then you can handle this, princess. There's no road access to that beach. Tess and Reeves, you can go too. Fieldsy, you man the front desk.'

'Yes, sir.'

I wondered which one Tess was as Reeves appeared from around the corner; her earlier smirk replaced with reluctance. 'Sarge, I was about to—'

'Tess, take the Prado to the marina. Reeves, don't forget the keys to the boat.' His tone held no respect and left no room for argument. The casual use of 'princess' had my teeth on edge, but I kept my expression neutral. *Choose your battles, Bec.*

Tickle reached up to the board and grabbed a set of keys, his movements nervous but eager. Reeves' expression was sullen as she lifted another set of keys from a small board beside it and hurried after Bradley.

Tickle waited until Bradley clomped down the hall before he offered me a nervous smile, his eyes darting around to make sure no one else was listening.

'My name's Trevor.'

I raised my eyebrows as understanding dawned. *Tess Tickle.* My estimation of Bradley, already subterranean, sank even lower. I nodded and went back to my office for my waterproof jacket. Crisis had a way of cutting through all the crap; the station's bullying culture could wait. An abandoned yacht took priority.

Chapter 2

The call had come through just after nine-thirty.

Before I followed the two constables outside, I picked up the phone and dialled Cairns CIB. 'This is Detective Senior Constable Whitfield, Mission Beach station. We're responding to an abandoned vessel at Ninney Point. A catamaran with no response to radio contact. We're heading out to assess the scene now. If it turns out to be suspicious, we'll need forensics support.'

'Copy that, Detective,' came the response. 'We'll have a team on standby. Keep us posted.'

'Will do. Out.'

I grabbed my keys and headed for the door, then stopped as my phone beeped—a message from Todd Davenport.

Settling in ok? I glanced at the timestamp. He'd sent it an hour ago, probably not long after I'd arrived. I slipped it back into my pocket without answering. Later. When I had something worth reporting.

'Let's go,' I said to Trevor, my mind already turning to the abandoned vessel and what we might find there.

The police vehicle had the same lack of care as the rest of the station. Empty food wrappers and cigarette butts littered the floor. Dirty marks on the seat and a pervading smell from the rear of the wagon topped off the scene. Reeves was in the back; she'd obviously recognised my seniority.

The first heavy drops hit the windscreen as we pulled out of the station car park, fat splashes of rain that quickly became a torrent. The sky had transformed from tropical blue to solid grey in the two hours since I'd arrived. Some welcome to paradise, this was turning out to be.

Show them what you're made of. Todd's voice again in my head, a steadying presence even in his absence.

I intended to do exactly that.

Five minutes later, as we stood at Clump Point Marina, I stared at the patrol boat with disgust. The vessel sat neglected in its pen, bumping against the walkway without fenders. Deep scratches scarred one side, a testament to careless mooring. As I stepped aboard, my distaste for my new sergeant deepened further.

A large, once-white fish box dominated the rear deck. The cabin door hung unlocked, and inside, fishing rods and assorted gear lay scattered about in disarray. I turned to Trevor, who merely shrugged.

'Sarge likes his fishing.'

The keys dangled from the ignition—another display of slackness—but the worst revelation was yet to come. When I turned the key, the fuel gauge showed the tanks were nearly empty.

'For the love of God.' I couldn't believe what I was seeing. 'Constable, where's the fuel dock?'

After refuelling at the dock, we finally departed, though my impatience with the wasted time showed. The boat now bobbed precariously in the choppy water as I steered us out of Clump Point Marina. I checked the GPS screen and noted the destination coordinates. Rain lashed sideways against the cabin, sometimes driving through the semi-open window to strike my face despite my hood and the Perspex windscreen. Each drop stung like tiny needles.

I'd been grateful for the waterproof jacket when we set out, but the relentless wind kept forcing the hood back, leaving my hair plastered to my scalp and icy rivulets trickling down my neck and between my shoulder blades.

'You sure you know how to handle this thing?' Reeves called over the angry growl of the outboard motors and the violent slap of waves against the aluminium hull. Her face had taken on a greenish tinge, her knuckles white as she gripped the boat's side.

Years on my mate's fishing boat in Brisbane had taught me to handle conditions far worse than this. I loved being on the water and had even considered applying to join the water police, earning some marine qualifications in the process. Coastal weather could turn treacherous in seconds, so I'd made sure to learn how to handle myself in conditions far worse than this.

This seven-metre vessel was child's play, even in deteriorating conditions. I worked the throttles carefully, avoiding hitting any swell beam-on, mindful of the concerned look on Trevor's face. Reeves moved to the storage box at the stern, her expression sour beneath her rain jacket, eyes narrowed against the spray; her body language spoke volumes—resentment, discomfort, and something else I couldn't quite identify. Fresh-faced Trevor, at least, seemed willing to follow my lead without the attitude, though his complexion was growing more pallid by the minute.

As we rounded a headland and approached the beach north of Ninney Point, I throttled back, scanning the shoreline through the curtain of rain. There it was—the distinctive shape of a catamaran's twin hulls perched ominously on the sand just above the waterline like a beached whale.

'There she is,' I called, pointing towards the vessel. I navigated carefully through the small break, idling in before killing the engines at a safe distance from shore, where the water was still deep enough to keep us afloat. The sudden absence of the motor's noise made the hiss of rain and distant rumble of thunder more pronounced, lending an eerie quality to the scene.

'Trevor, take your shoes off and jump out to drag us up, please,' I said, gesturing towards the shallows.

He nodded without hesitation, unlacing his boots and rolling up his uniform trousers. Reeves visibly relaxed as she realised I hadn't selected her for the wet work.

'Reeves, you stay with the boat and make sure the tide doesn't take it out,' I instructed. 'We need to secure the scene properly before anyone boards that catamaran.'

'No, I don't want—' she began, a flash of resistance in her eyes.

'What did I say?' My voice cut through the sound of rain drumming against the hull. She fell silent immediately, the scowl deepening on her face.

Trevor splashed into the knee-deep water and gripped the bow rope. I stepped out, cold water seeping through my boots as I made my way towards shore.

As Trevor stood on the sand, Reeves tossed his boots to him. 'There you go, Tess.'

Trevor's face flamed red. I'd already connected the dots— a crude, juvenile pun that said everything about Bradley's leadership.

'Are you responsible for Constable Tickle's nickname, Reeves?' I asked.

'No, that's the Sarge.' She smirked, but something uncomfortable flickered in her eyes.

Another item for my growing list of Bradley's failings.

Together, Trevor and I trudged along the rock-strewn sand towards the catamaran.

'Lucky,' I commented, surveying the vessel's position with a professional eye. 'When the tide comes in and out again, it might have moved or been dragged back out to sea.'

'Might have sunk,' Trevor commented.

The catamaran sat awkwardly on the sand, its twin hulls preventing it from keeling over completely. Even from a distance, it looked expensive—sleek lines, well-maintained fibreglass gleaming dully in the grey light. Not the kind of vessel that should be abandoned on a remote beach. Not the kind of vessel whose owner would simply walk away.

'Some damage to the hull on the port side,' Trevor noted as we circled it, his voice steadier now that we were on solid ground. 'Looks like someone tried to scuttle it.'

I inspected the other side of the vessel where, despite the rain blurring my vision, I could just make out the name on the bow: *Lady Windward*.

From our position on the beach, I could just see dark stains on the deck near the cabin entrance. My pulse quickened—possibly blood, and substantial amounts of it.

I turned to Trevor, his previously ruddy complexion ashen. 'What's the mobile service like on the coast?'

'Good. Thirty-kilometre range. There are a lot of repeaters.'

I reached for my mobile and called Cairns again. 'This is Detective Senior Constable Whitfield at Ninney Point. I have visual on the abandoned vessel *Lady Windward*. I can see what appears to be blood evidence on the deck from here. We won't board until forensics arrive. Requesting immediate forensics response and senior officer attendance. Can you please advise

Sergeant Bradley at Pandanus Point too?'

'Copy that, Detective. We've been trying to contact Senior Sergeant Bradley for an update, but no response. Forensics team from Cairns on the way, ETA approximately three and a half hours. They're departing now.'

Trevor ran back to let Reeves know what was happening. When he returned, he looked uncomfortable.

'What did she say?' I asked.

'Um… exactly?'

I nodded.

'She wants to know why she has to sit out there getting rained on when she could be doing paperwork back at the station. Her exact words were, "This is bullshit. Tell the detective I didn't sign up to be a bloody sea anchor".'

Three and a half hours. I glanced at my watch—it was nearly ten-thirty. The forensics team wouldn't arrive until after two o'clock. In good conditions, the coastal run from Cairns to Mission Beach was about seventy-five nautical miles, and their boat would be pushing it at full speed.

'Understood. We'll maintain the scene until they arrive,' I responded.

'What do you reckon, boss?' Trevor asked.

'I think we've got a crime scene,' I said grimly. 'And thank God we did this properly. If we'd rushed aboard like I almost suggested, we could have compromised vital evidence. So, we'll treat this as a potential crime scene from this moment.'

'Three hours though,' Trevor muttered, looking at the grey sky. 'Hope the weather holds.'

'Go back and get the investigation kit from the patrol boat. I assume there is a kit there?' I said, thinking of the fish box and fishing rods.

He nodded. 'Yes, it's one of my jobs; I check the kits on the boat and the vehicles every week.'

'Good. We'll establish a perimeter while we wait. I'll get you to walk to each end of the beach and see if anything else has washed up after we've done that.'

The wait was frustrating but necessary. Trevor walked the beach, but found nothing. Reeves occasionally started the patrol boat and moved it as the tide came in. My phone finally buzzed with a text message about one-thirty.

Sarah Chen, forensics. I've got Constable Martinez on the boat, photographer Hollis, and evidence tech Thompson with me. We're fifteen minutes out.

When the forensics team arrived just before two o'clock, the morning's heavy rain had given way to patches of sunshine. Trevor helped pull the boat up, and they anchored close to the patrol boat. Sarah introduced herself and her team, and I briefed them from outside the secured perimeter, pointing out the visible stains and the yacht's position. Only then did we approach the vessel properly, with protective equipment and proper documentation in place.

'Good call not boarding initially,' she said as we suited up. 'I've seen too many crime scenes compromised by first responders who couldn't wait.'

'I nearly suggested it myself,' I admitted. 'But something about those stains on the deck looked wrong from the start.'

The metal rungs were slick with rain; I climbed aboard first, waiting for Sarah and her team to follow. The deck was slippery, but otherwise orderly—no signs of a struggle, no equipment strewn about. Everything was battened down properly, as if the captain had secured the vessel before... what?

Being forced to leave? Leaving voluntarily?

Making my way towards the saloon entrance, I drew my service weapon before pushing the door open. The interior was dim but dry, with the faint metallic smell that all boats seem to have—until another scent hit me, sickly sweet and unmistakable. The copper tang of blood.

'Watch your step,' I warned Sarah, reaching for the light switch. It clicked uselessly beneath my finger. 'Power's out. Use your torch.'

Our flashlights swept across the large cabin, casting grotesque shadows that danced across the walls as we moved. The living space revealed itself gradually in the narrow circles of light—tidy, well-appointed, with no signs of disturbance until we reached the galley at the far end. There, dark stains splashed across the small countertop and floor—unmistakably blood, and not a small amount. The bank of small windows looking out towards the bow caught our light briefly, reflecting it onto the twin stairways leading down to the cabins in each hull. I looked for a weapon, but there was no sign of one. There was nothing. Apart from the stains, there was nothing on the countertop or sink.

The beam of Sarah's torch landed on one big dark stain at the base of the stairs.

'It's blood?' I asked.

'I'd say so.'

I moved carefully, avoiding the stains as I checked the rest of the saloon.

My instincts proved correct, and I was pleased we had waited despite Reeves' whining from the patrol boat. The blood evidence was substantial—too much for a minor accident.

Whatever had happened aboard this vessel, it wasn't a simple breakdown or abandonment.

The signs all pointed to a hasty departure.

And no sign of any crew. No personal possessions, no clothes, no ID like wallets, no electronic devices, no plates in the sink, no food in the galley. The beds were stripped, but there was no sign of any bed linen or towels.

But why?

A closer inspection with the forensic tech had revealed the lack of a tender, which suggested that they hadn't simply gone overboard; they could have left in the boat that had been attached to the davits. The blood in the galley pointed to an incident of some sort, but the lack of anything in the vessel suggested a less hasty departure.

Again, why?

As I walked along the deck, a scrap of cloth on the wire along the port side had caught my attention. Rather than risking it blowing away, I carefully removed it. It looked as though it could be off a piece of clothing, a small square of floral cotton.

'Sarah, this needs bagging.' She nodded and took it from me.

The scene was eerie. Not only from the low mist that had rolled in again, but the complete absence of any trace that anyone had been on board, as if the crew had simply vanished into thin air, leaving only the blood behind to suggest something violent had happened.

'We'll need to arrange for the vessel to be towed to the impound dock,' I told Sarah as we prepared to leave. 'Can't leave it here with the tides.'

The trip back to the marina was tense. My mind raced as we cut through the angry sea, every detail from that bloodied galley replaying in sharp focus. The wind had picked up after the squall, sending spray over the bow, but I barely noticed the salt sting on my face—I was too busy piecing together what we'd seen, what it meant, what we'd missed.

The patrol boat pitched and rolled as we navigated the swells, each wave seeming to rock loose another question, another angle needing investigation. I gripped the wheel with steady hands, my jaw set with determination to solve this case.

By the time we reached the marina, the weather had cleared. Walking up the wharf, our clothes steamed in the afternoon warmth. My mind was already three steps ahead— evidence bags that the forensics team had taken, checking the boat registration and waiting for blood results.

Reeves had spent the entire trip back on her phone, pointedly ignoring my questions about local vessels. Inside the station, Sergeant Bradley looked up from his paperwork, his face a mask of boredom and indifference.

'All bloody day. Took your time,' he said, as if we'd been on a casual outing rather than processing a potential crime scene.

I bit back a sharp retort and forced respect into my voice.

As much as I didn't like it, he was still my senior.

'Sir, where are we with that catamaran registration Constable Tickle called in?'

He didn't even look up. 'Yeah, yeah, I haven't got to it yet.'

That lazy drawl made my jaw clench. 'When you can—'

'Look.' He gestured at the stack of files covering half his desk. 'I've got local cases stacked as tall as my coffee mug here, alright? Your boat's not going anywhere.'

'This isn't just some boat. Someone has been—'

'Has been, could be, might be, probably is.' He finally

glanced up with that infuriating smirk.

'We found blood, Sarge,' Reeves offered, eager to report. 'Forensics has processed the scene.'

He turned back to his screen, dismissing us. 'Look, I'll run your precious registration when I finish the Morrison break-in, okay? That's an actual crime with concerned locals who are calling me every five minutes.'

His phone started ringing. He picked it up without another glance my way.

I stood there for a moment, my hands balled into fists, before turning and walking away. 'I'll do it,' I muttered.

I called the water police and was about to chase up the vessel when Bradley appeared in my doorway.

'Look, Whitfield, we handle our own business here,' he said. His territorial posturing was textbook small-town policing—exactly what Todd had warned me about. 'So, tell me about it,' he grunted.

'Blood patterns consistent with assault, signs of a cleanup attempt, and no sign of any crew from the vessel.'

'It wouldn't be crew,' Reeves said, standing in the hall behind him. '*Lady Windward* is a charter vessel out of Cardwell.'

I could see her preening slightly, pleased to have information I didn't. Typical—helpful only when it made her look good in front of the boss. I held my temper and kept my expression bland. 'Is that so? You didn't think to mention that earlier, Constable Reeves?'

She shrugged, and the look Bradley exchanged with her spoke volumes.

'Welcome to paradise,' he said, a smirk pulling at the face I was beginning to dislike more every time he opened his mouth.

'Where tourists get drunk, hurt themselves, and abandon rental boats all the time. You'll soon learn. We've been policing these waters since before you got your shiny detective badge, Whitfield.' He leaned forward. 'Not everything needs to be by the big city book.'

I ignored him, my mouth set as I pushed away my temper, reconstructing the scene on the yacht, and going over what we'd seen on the vessel.

Once they'd both disappeared up the hall, I called Todd and reported what we'd found.

'I'll be down in the morning. Keep me informed.' His voice was distracted.

'Will do.'

I spent the next hour writing up my preliminary report, documenting every detail while it was fresh in my mind. The blood patterns, the missing tender, the complete absence of personal effects—it all painted a picture of deliberate concealment. Someone had taken great care to remove evidence of who had been aboard, but they couldn't scrub away the blood that told its own story.

Chapter 3

Edge Reef, Coral Sea.

Monday, August 18 - 4.00 p.m.

Twelve kilometres off Mission Beach, the *Hookers* fishing charter vessel bobbed in the thick, humid air, the water beneath them still as glass despite the gathering storm clouds overhead. The oppressive heat clung to everything—skin, clothing, the vinyl seats of the boat—making each breath feel like swallowing steam from a kettle.

'Hey, skipper, reckon my daughter's got something.'

Gerry Stone, owner of the charter and a man who'd spent forty years reading these waters, watched the little girl struggle with her rod. Her ponytail was plastered to her neck with sweat, her sunburned cheeks flushed with excitement as she wrestled with whatever had taken her line. Something in the way the rod bent—too stiff, too dead—sent a flicker of unease through his weathered frame.

The air was too still. The usual afternoon sea breeze that brought relief to tourists and locals alike had abandoned them today, leaving only the pressing weight of tropical moisture that made even seasoned fishermen like Gerry feel claustrophobic. Something about the day felt off—the birds had gone quiet hours ago, and the usual surface baitfish activity had disappeared hours ago.

'Doesn't look to be fighting much; might be snagged. I'll come and give you a hand,' he said with practised nonchalance, though a cold knot was forming in his gut.

He moved past his other clients—three sweating tourists

who looked ready to surrender to the heat and head back to their air-conditioned hotels—and gently took the rod from the small girl. Her innocent eyes shone with excitement, blissfully ignorant of the growing sense of dread prickling at the back of Gerry's neck.

'Let's see what you've hooked, sweetheart.' He pulled firmly on the rod, but the line remained stubbornly stuck. Another brisk tug, and he felt a hint of movement as his experienced hands felt something wrong through the taut fishing line—too heavy, too yielding in all the wrong ways.

'I think you've snagged a big lump of coral. Let's see if we can get it up without losing the gear.'

The rod buckled as he began slowly winding. Enough tackle had been lost to the reef already today—the underwater world seemed to be claiming more than its fair share—and he was keen to retrieve the hook and large sinker if possible. As he wound, there was no fight, no telltale jerking of something alive on the end of the line. Just dead weight. The kind of weight that settled in his stomach with a familiar dread he'd learned not to ignore over decades at sea.

Anxious eyes peered over the side of the boat as the others on board gathered to see what was on the line. The water was clear today, deceptively so, as if trying to conceal something by revealing everything. At twenty metres depth, visibility was usually poor this close to shore, but today the water was crystal clear—unnaturally so. Gerry could see to the bottom, where dark shapes moved with sinuous grace among the coral outcroppings.

A large, strangely coloured mass began to take shape in the clear water, rising like a spectre from the deep. Something about its movement wasn't right—too heavy, too swollen, too solid.

Gerry's sun-baked skin prickled with goosebumps despite the oppressive heat.

The little girl danced excitedly on the front deck, oblivious to the change in atmosphere, the way the adults had gone silent, the way her father's face had drained of colour. 'I think I've caught a mermaid! Look at the pretty colours!'

Gerry stopped winding; his weathered face suddenly pale despite his permanent tan. The heat pressed closer, the air growing heavier with each passing second. He turned to his young deckhand, keeping his voice calm but urgent.

'Hey, Spud, grab the gaff, mate. And a bit of rope too, please?'

He wound a few more metres, his movements now mechanical, already knowing what he'd find but needing to be sure. The shape below became clearer—mottled fabric, heavy with water, wrapped around something that shouldn't be there. He abruptly stopped winding; his knuckles were white against the black rod.

'Spud, take the others to the stern of the boat. Now, mate.' The uncharacteristic sharpness in his usually laconic tone conveyed the urgency more than any shouted command could have.

The deckhand, barely eighteen and still learning the routines of a fishing charter, hesitated, suddenly alert to the tension radiating from his boss. 'What's up, skipper?'

'Just bring me what I need and get them to the stern. Move the little one first.' His quiet voice carried more weight than a shout.

As Spud ushered the confused group to the back of the boat, Gerry kept his eyes on the water, watching the mass rotate slowly in the current. The humid air seemed to grow thicker, making it harder to breathe.

Spud returned, standing beside Gerry, looking over the side. The colour drained from the young man's face as he understood what he was seeing.

'Jesus.'

'See if you can reach down and hook that, will you? Don't pull it right up; just leave it hanging below the surface.' Gerry's voice was calm, belying the churning in his gut.

Spud carefully leant over the gunwale, the boat tilting slightly with his weight. He hooked the mass, and as it rolled on the edge of the large gaff, the truth revealed itself in the most horrific way possible. A badly decomposed human hand flopped from one side of what appeared to be a rolled-up tablecloth or sheet. The fabric, once white perhaps, was now stained with colours that had nothing to do with tropical fish or coral reefs.

'Bloody hell, is that what I think it is, skipper?' Spud's voice cracked, and he looked like he might be sick over the side.

'Yeah, reckon so.' Gerry's voice was steady, years of handling emergencies at sea taking over, even though he'd never pulled up a body before. 'Make sure you keep the kids away, right down the back. See if one of the adults is willing to help me secure this to the side; then I need to contact Gaz at the marine rescue base. And get on the radio to the Pandanus Point police.'

He paused, studying the mass more closely. Heavy anchor chain glinted dully over the fabric, and the way it was all bound together spoke of deliberate action, not accident.

'This isn't someone who fell overboard,' he muttered, more to himself than to Spud. 'You don't end up wrapped in a cloth with chains wound around you by accident.'

The storm clouds overhead finally made good on their threat, and as the first heavy drops of rain splattered on the deck, Gerry Stone heard the little girl asking her father why they couldn't keep the pretty mermaid. He hoped she'd never learn what she'd snagged that day, in the clear waters off Dunk Island.

Chapter 4

Monday - 4.00 p.m.

Pandanus Point Police Station.

By four o'clock, I was still wrestling with the registration details when I suddenly remembered my appointment with the real estate agent. Shit. The keys to my rental house. I grabbed my phone and quickly dialled the number.

'Mission Beach Realty, this is Debbie speaking.'

'Hi Debbie, it's Detective Whitfield. I was supposed to pick up my keys this afternoon, but I'm stuck on a job. Any chance you could drop them at the police station?'

'Oh, don't worry about that, love,' came the cheerful response. 'I'll be working late tonight anyway—got three more settlements to finish. No matter how late you are, I'll wait for you. These things happen in your line of work.'

'Are you sure? It could be quite late.'

'Absolutely. I'll leave the office light on. Just come when you can.'

'Thanks, Debbie. I really appreciate it.'

I'd barely hung up when the radio on my desk crackled to life, startling me from my thoughts.

'This is charter vessel *Hookers*. We've... we've found something. Need some assistance. Over.'

There was a tremor in the voice that made the fine hairs on my arms stand up. I reached for the handset, pulse already quickening. '*Hookers*, this is Detective Whitfield at Pandanus Point Station. Go ahead. Over.'

'We've recovered a body about three nautical miles northeast of Dunk Island.' The voice paused, struggling for professional detachment. 'Been in the water for a few days by the look of things. Over.'

My stomach tightened. The timing aligned with the abandoned catamaran, the location not far from where we'd found it. '*Hookers*, can you provide any identifying details? Over.'

A pause, then: 'Female, I think. Hard to tell much more. The body is... severely decomposed.' His voice dropped, as if trying to shield someone nearby from hearing. 'It's wrapped partially in some kind of fabric. And chains. Over.'

The last word hung in the air like a death knell. Wrapped in fabric. Chains. This wasn't an accidental drowning or even a suicide. This was deliberate. Someone had wanted to ensure that whoever this was stayed at the bottom of the ocean.

I grabbed my notebook, forcing my hand to remain steady. '*Hookers*, what's your current position and heading? Over.'

'We're heading back to Clump Point Marina. Should dock in about fifteen minutes. We have twelve passengers on board, including children. They're pretty shaken up. Over.'

The drive to the marina was tense, my mind racing through possibilities. The *Lady Windward* was registered to a Jeremy Winters from Sydney and hired out by Cassowary Charters in Cardwell. But who had been aboard? Who had bled in that galley? And whose was the body they'd found?

We arrived just as *Hookers* was tying up at the marina. I spotted the vessel easily—a 40-foot charter boat with "**BEST REEF FISHING**" emblazoned on the side in fading blue paint. A shaken-looking man with a grey ponytail stood at the stern, his weathered face grim as he waved us over. His T-shirt with the boat name and fish logo identified him as crew or owner.

'Detective Whitfield,' I said, showing my badge as I stepped onto the deck. 'You reported finding a body?'

'Gerry Stone. I own *Hookers*,' he replied, his weathered face grim. 'Yeah, not the catch we were after today. We were on our way back from a day trip to the reef when one of the kids hooked something. Thought it was a good fish at first, but...' he trailed off, gesturing towards the covered shape on the rear deck, his casual manner belied by the tightness around his eyes.

'I need to ask you some questions before we proceed,' I said. 'Can you estimate how long the body had been in the water?'

Stone ran a hand over his salt-stiffened hair. 'Hard to say exactly. Like I said, a few days, I reckon. Advanced decomposition, fair bit of marine life activity.' He swallowed hard. 'The face is... gone, basically.'

'And the exact location where you found it?' I kept my voice professional, detached, though my stomach churned at the mental image his words conjured.

'Marked it on the GPS. About three nautical miles northeast of Dunk Island, in the channel. There's a current there that could have carried it from further north.'

'You mentioned fabric wrapped around the body. Can you describe it?'

His face brightened slightly, relieved to focus on something less gruesome. 'Yeah, it has writing on it. In the corner, bit hard to read with the staining and all, but clear enough.'

My heart skipped. 'What does it say?'

'*Lady Windward.*' He watched my expression change,

suddenly alert. 'That ring any bells?'

'We found an abandoned catamaran by that name this morning. Blood in the galley.' I glanced towards the covered body, apprehension mingling with a grim satisfaction at finding a connection. 'I need to see the fabric.'

Stone hesitated. 'Detective—we have families on board. Kids. They didn't see much, but they know something's wrong.'

'Of course,' I said, nodding to Reeves, who for once seemed to read the situation correctly. 'Constable, can you please take the passengers up to the wharf? Get their details and arrange for victim support if needed. I'll handle this.'

As Reeves moved to the cabin, I followed Stone to the covered body. I immediately called the forensics team on my mobile.

'Sarah, it's Detective Whitfield. I know you've probably just made it back to Cairns, but we've got a body recovered from the water. It's connected to our Lady Windward case—the body is partially wrapped in fabric with the boat's name on it.'

There was a brief pause, then: 'Jesus. We're still about twenty minutes out of Cairns. Give me the location and we'll turn around. This changes everything.'

'Clump Point Marina. The charter boat, *Hookers* just brought it in. I'll secure the scene until you arrive.'

'On our way. Don't let anyone near that body.'

I ended the call and turned back to Stone. 'What exactly is the fabric?' I asked as we approached. 'A sail? Bedding?'

'It's a spinnaker,' Stone replied, technical knowledge momentarily overriding his unease. 'Lightweight sail used for downwind sailing. Distinctive pattern, usually colourful. This one's pretty torn up, but you can see the name embroidered here.' He pointed without touching.

Sure enough, there in blue thread against white fabric stained with unspeakable things: '*Lady Windward.*'

I nodded, my mind racing. The connection was undeniable now.

'Did you notice anything else unusual when you found it? Any other vessels in the area? Debris?'

'Nothing else floating nearby. The sea was pretty choppy with the weather system moving through this morning. Could have scattered anything else.'

I studied Stone's face—he was holding it together, but I could see the slight tremor in his hands, the way he kept swallowing as if fighting nausea.

'One more question, Captain—in your experience, could someone have fallen overboard in the conditions we've had over the past week? Accidentally?'

Stone considered this, his seafarer's knowledge evident in his thoughtful pause. 'The swell was up a little this morning with that squall, but not dangerous.'

'Would you call it deteriorating weather in the past few days?'

He looked surprised. 'No. Only this morning, when we had that rain squall. Up until then, it's been like a mill pond for a week or so. An experienced sailor wouldn't typically go overboard unless they were being careless or...' He didn't finish the thought, but he didn't need to.

'Or someone helped them over,' I completed quietly. 'And made sure they sank to the bottom.'

He nodded, the unspoken understanding passing between us.

I turned to watch as Reeves managed the passengers on the

wharf, then looked back at the covered shape. The partial wrapping of the spinnaker sail struck me as odd—not a deliberate shroud, more like they'd become entangled in the sail. With the level of decomposition, we'd need dental records or DNA for identification. Assuming we could even find out who was supposed to be aboard in the first place.

My phone buzzed—a text from Todd: **Update?**

I typed quickly: 'Body recovered off Dunk Island. Severely decomposed, gender uncertain, partially wrapped in a sail from *Lady Windward*. Connected to this morning's crime scene. Forensics turning around to come back.'

His response came immediately: 'Christ. Almost there. Don't let Bradley take the lead.'

Typical Todd—always worried about jurisdiction, but he had good cause with Bradley running the station. But Todd was right about one thing—this case had just escalated from an abandoned vessel to a definite homicide. Someone had bled out in that galley, and now we likely had our victim.

Or one of them, at least. According to the charter company I'd called earlier, *Lady Windward* had set sail with three people aboard. So where were the other two? And had one of them wrapped this poor soul in a sail and chains and consigned them to the deep? Or had someone else come on board, and there might be more bodies out there?

The forensics team arrived forty-five minutes later, their faces grim as they boarded the charter vessel. Sarah Chen looked exhausted—the day had started with processing the *Lady Windward*, and now they were back for what was clearly a related homicide.

'This is definitely connected to your boat?' she asked as she suited up again.

'The fabric around the body has the boat's name embroidered on it,' I confirmed. 'It's a spinnaker sail from the *Lady Windward.*'

She nodded grimly. 'Then we're looking at a linked crime scene. The blood in the galley, now a body wrapped in the boat's sail. The captain said there was a chain on the body that came off as they lifted it into the boat. Someone wanted this person to disappear permanently.'

As the forensic team worked to document and prepare the body for transport, I stood back and watched the evening light fade over the marina. What had started as a routine first day on a new posting had become something far more sinister. Somewhere out there, at least two other people from that charter boat were either victims or perpetrators—and I had no idea which.

The radio crackled from the patrol car: 'All units, this is Pandanus Point base. Senior Sergeant Bradley requesting immediate update on the Clump Point situation. Over.'

I grabbed the handset. 'Pandanus Point base, this is Detective Whitfield. Body recovery complete, forensics processing. Will return to station for full briefing within the hour. Over.'

'Copy that. Senior Sergeant Bradley says he'll be waiting. Over and out.'

I looked at the covered body being carefully lifted onto a stretcher, then at the forensics team packing their equipment with methodical precision. Twenty-four hours ago, I'd been looking forward to a quiet coastal posting. Now I was staring at what could be the most complex case of my career.

'Sarah,' I called as they prepared to transport the body.

'How long before we get preliminary results?'

'DNA will take weeks,' she replied, stripping off her gloves. 'But I might be able to give you some basic information within a few days. Gender confirmation, approximate age, cause of death if there's enough left to determine it.'

I nodded. 'The blood work from the boat?'

'Human, type O negative. Substantial loss—definitely consistent with a fatal injury.'

'Any match to missing persons reports?'

She shook her head. 'That's your department. But whoever this is, they've been in the water for at least a week, possibly longer.'

As the forensics team departed for the second time that day, I stood on the wharf with Reeves, watching their boat disappear into the gathering dusk. The marina was quiet now, just the gentle lapping of water against the hulls and the distant cry of seabirds settling for the night.

'What do you think happened out there?' Reeves asked, and for once there was no sarcasm in her voice, just genuine curiosity and perhaps a touch of unease.

I looked out towards the dark water, thinking of the abandoned catamaran we'd found that morning, the blood in the galley, and now this body wrapped in chains and sailcloth.

'I think someone wanted to make three people disappear,' I said quietly. 'And they almost succeeded.'

Chapter 5

Monday - 7 p.m.

Bec's house.

Just after seven, I pulled my Land Cruiser into a parking spot outside Cassowary Coast Real Estate, grateful for the brief respite of air conditioning before I had to face the wall of humidity again. The Mission Beach township was busier than I'd expected, tourists in bright holiday clothes meandering along the street, enjoying ice creams and the shade of the massive melaleuca trees that lined the foreshore.

The real estate office was mercifully cool, the receptionist's smile warmer than anyone I'd encountered at the station. 'Detective Whitfield? We've been expecting you.' She extended her hand. 'I'm Mel. Debbie will be with you in a moment.'

'You're working late too?'

'Always busy here,' she replied. 'It's normal for us both to be here until seven-thirty.'

I nodded, thankful for the interaction. No raised eyebrows, no assessment of whether I deserved my shield or had it through favouritism. Just another new resident picking up keys. It was refreshing, and I began to feel a whole lot better.

Debbie appeared minutes later, a fortysomething woman with a deep tan and blonde hair pulled back in a practical ponytail. 'Rebecca! Welcome to Mission Beach.' She pumped my hand enthusiastically. 'How was your first day in town?'

'Educational,' I replied diplomatically, which made her

laugh.

'Small towns,' she said with a knowing look. 'Don't worry, they'll warm up. Now, about your cottage—I know you took it sight unseen, but I promise you won't be disappointed.'

She produced a set of keys attached to a small wooden keychain shaped like a cassowary. 'Twenty-seven Hibiscus Drive. You've got absolute beachfront, and I mean absolute. Step off your back deck and your feet are on the sand.'

'Sounds perfect,' I said, trying not to let my relief show. Housing had been my biggest worry when accepting the posting. Todd had put me in touch with Debbie, vouching for her integrity. She worked at the Cairns office and had sourced his apartment for him a couple of months ago. 'The kitchen's fully equipped?'

'Everything you'll need,' Debbie confirmed, handing me a folder. 'Here's the inventory list, emergency contacts, and instructions for all the appliances. The previous tenant—a locum doctor from France, left everything immaculate; she was transferred to Brisbane quite suddenly. Her transfer was your gain.'

I tucked the folder under my arm and took the keys. 'Thank you. I appreciate you holding it for me.'

'Any friend of Todd's,' she said with a smile. I felt a familiar twinge in my chest. Was there anyone in North Queensland who didn't find Todd charming?

'Right,' I said briskly. 'I should get going. I'll have to do some shopping and get unpacked.'

'Of course.' She walked me to the door. 'Call if you need anything at all. And Rebecca?' She lowered her voice. 'Welcome to the community. Whatever's going on at the station—and we've all heard the whispers—don't let it get to you. We're not all like that. Mission Beach is a great place to live. Just ignore the local gossip and you'll settle in quickly.'

I nodded my thanks, oddly touched by her welcome.

The drive to Hibiscus Drive took less than ten minutes. After calling into the mini-mart in town and picking up a few essentials, I followed the main road back through the shopping centre, the blue sea flashing between palms and pandanus trees on my right. The cottage itself was at the end of a quiet cul-de-sac, each house screened from its neighbours by dense tropical vegetation. I pulled into the driveway of number twenty-seven, half-hidden behind a magnificent poinciana tree, with an umbrella of delicate green foliage.

The cottage was a weatherboard Queenslander, raised on stilts to catch the sea breeze. Painted a soft sea-green with white trim, it looked like it had grown organically from the landscape around it. The six front steps led to a small veranda wrapping around the side of the house. I climbed them, keys in hand, feeling a flutter of anticipation.

The door opened to a central living area, and I stopped in my tracks, momentarily stunned. The back wall of the cottage was almost entirely glass, sliding doors that framed a view straight out to the Coral Sea. It would be spectacular in the daytime.

'Oh,' I breathed, dropping the keys on the nearest surface. The interior was simple but tasteful—polished timber floors, white walls, and furniture in shades of blue and green that echoed the colours outside. A comfortable-looking couch faced the view rather than the small flat-screen television in the corner. A small dining table with four chairs sat adjacent to an open kitchen with white cabinetry and stone countertops.

I slid open one of the glass doors and stepped onto the back deck. The salt-laden breeze immediately tangled my hair, but I couldn't have cared less. The deck extended the width of the cottage, with steps leading directly down to a narrow band of grass that gave way to white sand. The beach was empty in both directions, save for a lone figure walking a dog in the distance.

For the first time since arriving in Mission Beach, the tension in my shoulders began to ease. This was what I'd expected of North Queensland. Not the politics of a small-town police station, but this—this wild beauty, this sense of space and freedom.

I returned inside to explore the rest of the cottage. A short hallway led to three bedrooms with a surprisingly modern bathroom adjacent to two of them. The main bedroom continued the ocean theme with a queen-sized bed dressed in crisp white linens with aqua accents. A door from this room also opened onto the back deck. The second bedroom was smaller but equally pleasant, with a double bed, and the third bedroom held a small desk positioned to catch the morning light.

Back in the kitchen, I opened cupboards to find them well-stocked with cookware, dishes, and even basic pantry staples—salt, pepper, olive oil, tea, and coffee. The refrigerator hummed quietly, empty but spotlessly clean.

I returned to my Land Cruiser and began the process of unloading my belongings. I hadn't brought much—clothes, books, my laptop, and a few personal items. Everything else had been sold or stored when I'd taken the posting at Bowen River. Six months of living in temporary accommodation had taught me to travel light.

As I carried the last box inside, my phone buzzed with a message. Todd.

Settled in yet? Baptism by fire. How's the new team?

I hesitated, then typed back:

Just got the keys to the cottage. It's perfect. Team is… shall we say… a work in progress. Yes, an unexpected first day.

His reply came quickly:

Give them time. You earned that shield, Bec. I'll see you tomorrow.

I smiled despite myself, setting the phone down as I began to unpack. It was good to get a personal message from Todd. Within an hour, my clothes were in drawers, books on shelves, and my laptop set up on the small desk in the third bedroom. I hung my one good piece of art—a watercolour of the Brisbane River that a friend had painted—on the living room wall and placed the framed photo of my parents on a side table. A small gesture towards healing.

The cottage already felt like mine, which was both surprising and deeply satisfying. After the upheaval of the past year—the situation with Gray, the posting and being thrown headfirst into a missing person case in Bowen River, dealing with my parents and then the intense training period in Townsville—having a space that was truly mine felt like an incredible luxury. I was already looking forward to buying some proper furniture and really setting up home. With a minimum two-year posting, I'd have time to make this place truly mine.

As the afternoon light began to soften, I made myself a cup of tea and took it out to the deck. The tide was coming in, waves gently lapping at the shore. A sea eagle soared overhead, riding the thermals with barely a wing movement. In the distance, clouds were building on the horizon—perhaps an evening storm brewing, typical for the tropics.

I pulled out my phone again, scrolling to Todd's last message. Before I could second-guess myself, I typed:

The cottage has a spare bedroom and bathroom. Once this case is sorted, you should come down for a welcome meal. You can stay overnight if the drive back to Cairns seems too much.

I hit send before I could change my mind, surprised by my own boldness, then set the phone face down on the table beside me. Whatever happened at the station tomorrow—however difficult my new colleagues made things—I had this place to return to. A slice of paradise where the endless sea met an endless sky.

My phone buzzed. I waited a full minute before turning it over to read Todd's reply:

Sounds perfect. Thanks.

I smiled, sipping my tea as the first hints of sunset began to colour the sky. Maybe Mission Beach was going to work out after all.

Chapter 6

Tuesday, August 12 - 2.00 p.m.
New Scotland Yard, London.

Lord Charles Fairchild burst through the doors of New Scotland Yard's Specialist Crime Division, his face ashen, expensive Oxfords clicking against the polished floor.

'I need to speak to someone urgently,' he said, his voice strained. 'Someone has taken my daughter.'

Detective Inspector Eleanor Morgan guided him to a quiet interview room, noting his tailored Savile Row suit and platinum Patek Philippe. Old money, and lots of it.

'Lord Fairchild, I'm Detective Inspector Morgan. Tell me exactly what's happened.'

Fairchild ran manicured hands over his thinning hair. 'I got a call about an hour ago. An international number. This man said he had Phillipa. Said she was fine for now, but that would change if I didn't follow his instructions.' His voice broke. 'He told me not to call the police and to transfer twenty thousand pounds to an account.'

'Have you transferred any money?'

'No. The sound was distorted, like he was outdoors in a crowd. I could barely understand him.'

'Did he let you speak with your daughter?'

'No. I asked, I pleaded, but he said I'd get proof of life after I showed "good faith" with the initial payment.'

Superintendent James Bennett from the International Liaison Unit entered. 'Lord Fairchild, did they mention any specific details that only someone who knows Phillipa would know?'

'Not really. Just her name and that she was in Australia.' Fairchild's eyes widened as realisation dawned. 'You think it might be a scam?'

'International virtual kidnapping scams are increasingly common,' Bennett said carefully. 'Especially targeting wealthy families with children travelling abroad.'

'But what if it's real? Phillipa could be in danger while we sit here debating!'

'Where in Australia is she?' Morgan asked.

'Last I heard, Sydney. She's been there two months.' He held her gaze. 'We haven't been on great terms since I remarried. She wanted me to increase her allowance; I refused. That's partly why she took this trip—to prove she could manage on her own.'

Morgan pulled out her phone. 'Can you send me a recent photo?'

Fairchild showed a photo of a young woman with blonde curly hair standing in front of the Sydney Opera House, sunglasses perched on her head.

His phone suddenly buzzed. The same number.

'Answer it,' Bennett said. 'Ask for proof they have Phillipa.'

Fairchild answered, putting it on speaker. 'Hello?'

'Mr Fairchild.' The voice was mechanically distorted. 'Have you arranged the transfer?'

'I need to speak to Phillipa first. How do I know you have her?'

'You don't get to make demands.'

'Just tell me something about her. What was her cat's name?'

A pause. 'You think I need to play games? Transfer the

money or you'll never see her again.'

'Let me talk to her. Now.'

'First payment as good faith. Then you get proof of life.' The line went dead.

'He didn't know about the cat,' Fairchild whispered hopefully. 'Maybe it is a scam.'

A detective entered with information. 'Australian immigration confirms Phillipa Fairchild entered Sydney on June 18. Her credit card was last used at Coolangatta Airport a week ago—a rental car company. Nothing since then.'

Fairchild's phone buzzed with a text. His hands trembled as he checked it.

'It's from her number. Says "Proof of life attached." There's a photo...'

He turned the phone around. The image showed Phillipa, seemingly unharmed but distressed, holding a newspaper with yesterday's date. Her eyes were wide with fear.

'She looks scared,' Fairchild whispered. 'Nothing scares Phillipa. My God, what have I done?'

Bennett took the phone. 'We'll analyse this immediately. We'll contact Australian authorities to locate Phillipa and coordinate with the Federal Police.'

As they escorted Fairchild to discuss next steps, Bennett turned to Morgan. 'What's your read?'

Morgan studied the photo. 'The fear looks genuine, but it could be an act. The voice distortion, the vague demands...'

'Either way, we've got a situation. Let's contact our liaison in Sydney. If she's really in Queensland, that's a big area to search.'

'Unless someone made sure she couldn't leave a trail,'

Bennett replied grimly. 'Let's hope we're dealing with a scam and not something worse.'

Chapter 7

Tuesday, August 16 - 9 a.m.

Pandanus Point Police Station.

Hours after the discovery of the abandoned *Lady Windward*, we had more questions than answers—and now a body to add to the mystery. The blood in the galley was human, substantial in quantity—too much for someone to lose and still be walking around. Type O negative. No fingerprints except where you'd expect them on a regularly used vessel. No signs of struggle beyond the galley. It was as if someone had simply vanished in a spray of blood, leaving no other trace behind. Until a child's fishing line had snagged what was left of them, wrapped in chains and sailcloth beneath the waves.

I poured my third coffee of the morning as the station's air conditioning struggled against the relentless humidity. The preliminary pathology report lay open on my desk; the initial findings from when they pulled her from the water. Female, Caucasian, approximately twenty to twenty-five years old, recovered from waters near Dunk Island. No identification. No obvious match to local missing persons. The pathologist had done a quick assessment at the scene, but the full post-mortem was scheduled for tomorrow afternoon in Cairns. And now, my first major case as Detective Senior Constable Whitfield.

My phone vibrated. I glanced down and answered as soon as I saw Todd's name on the screen. 'Tell me you've got good news,' I answered without a greeting.

'Depends on your definition of good,' Todd replied, his

deep voice instantly familiar and reassuring. 'I'm approaching Mission Beach now. Thought this might be easier face to face.'

Twenty minutes later, Detective Inspector Davenport's imposing frame filled the doorway of our small incident room. Despite the circumstances, seeing him sent a flutter through my chest that I immediately tried to suppress. Professional relationship first, I reminded myself. I had to do something about this; Todd was the first thing that popped into my head when I woke, and the last person I thought about when I went to sleep.

I need to get over it.

'DI Davenport,' I greeted him formally, aware of the interested glances from my new colleagues. 'Thanks for coming down.'

He nodded, reading the room perfectly. 'Detective Senior Constable Whitfield. Let's see what you've got.'

I gestured to the evidence board in the incident room where I'd pinned photos of the recovery scene, the preliminary pathology report summary, and a map marking where the body had been found. Todd studied them intently, his experienced eyes missing nothing.

'No hits on her prints?' he asked, though he surely knew the answer already.

'Nothing. Not in the national database or immigration,' I confirmed. 'Which suggests she's never been arrested, never worked in childcare, healthcare, government positions, or entered the country through official channels after the biometric requirements were introduced.'

He nodded thoughtfully. 'And the DNA?'

'That's why I called you,' I admitted. 'We've got her profile from the initial samples taken at the scene, but with no match in the criminal database, I need to cast a wider net. Fast.

The full autopsy's tomorrow in Cairns—they wanted to get her up there before the weekend.'

Todd pulled up a chair beside me, close enough that I could smell his familiar aftershave—sandalwood with a hint of citrus. 'What did the pathologist say about the cause of death in the preliminary?'

'That's the thing—she couldn't determine it at the scene. Said the water exposure complicated things, made it hard to tell what happened before she went in versus after. That's why they're doing the full post-mortem tomorrow instead of just signing off on drowning.'

'Chains?' Todd asked.

'Hearsay only. None there, so not admissible as evidence. Without the actual chains—Gerry said he saw them, but they slipped off as they pulled the body up.'

'So, there's no tangible evidence. A prosecutor would have to rely heavily on circumstantial evidence and witness testimony. Walk me through what you've looked at so far.'

I tapped my keyboard, bringing up the case notes on my screen. 'Standard upload to NCIDD, of course. No direct hits. No familial matches within the standard parameters. I've submitted requests to expand the search radius and check against Missing Persons DNA Program samples, but you know how long that can take through official channels.'

'Too long when we need answers now,' Todd agreed. He leaned back, studying the ceiling for a moment. 'What about the AFP's international DNA database connections?'

'Requested, but low priority without evidence of a serious crime. The preliminary couldn't rule anything in or out—that's part of why we need the full autopsy results.'

'Right.' Todd drummed his fingers on the desk. 'So, we need to expedite. I might be able to help with that.'

He pulled out his phone, scrolling through contacts. 'Remember Ellie McIntyre from the DNA lab in Brisbane? She owes me a favour after that case last year.'

I raised an eyebrow. 'The one where you found her brother's stolen boat off Bowen?'

'The very same.' Todd's mouth quirked into a half-smile. 'Let me see if she can bump our request up the queue.'

He stepped outside to make the call, and I used the moment to collect myself. It was both comforting and frustrating how easily Todd navigated the system—how many connections he had that could make things happen with a single phone call. Connections I was still building.

When he returned, there was a glint of satisfaction in his eyes. 'Ellie's going to personally oversee our case. She says it will still take at least a week for comprehensive DNA analysis—these things can't be rushed if we want accurate results. But she'll keep us updated on any promising leads earlier if something comes up.'

'That's great.'

'It's just the start,' Todd said, settling back into the chair beside me. 'While we wait for that, we should be exploring other avenues. What about international databases?'

I gestured to a note on my screen. 'I've submitted requests to Interpol and through our channels with New Zealand and the Pacific Islands, but—'

'But bureaucracy moves at its own pace,' Todd finished for me. 'Okay, let's think outside the box. Given where she was found and the sail wrapping, there's a possibility she came off a vessel.'

'I've got Water Police checking the port authority records for all craft in the area over the past two weeks. And of course, there's the *Lady Windward* at Ninney Point.'

Todd's attention sharpened immediately. 'Right, the charter vessel with the bloodstains. Walk me through what you found again.'

'Forty-foot charter boat from Cassowary Charters in Cardwell. Bloodstains on the deck and in the main cabin—enough that I called forensics back, as I told you. They'd not long left to go back to Cairns when the fishing charter called in the body.' I pulled up the photos I'd taken during my examination. 'The company is owned by Graham and Sandra Patterson.'

'And the charter records?'

'Three names on the charter.' Todd studied the yacht photos on my screen, nodding as he reviewed details he'd already heard over the phone. 'The blood evidence?'

'Forensics took samples. They're being processed now, but there was enough to suggest someone on board was seriously injured. No report of an injury at the local medical centres and no body on board, obviously.'

'And you said the timeline fits?'

'Based on where the yacht was found drifting and the patterns, it's been abandoned for roughly the same timeframe as our victim's estimated time of death—somewhere between one to three days. The pathologist estimated she'd only been in the water around thirty-six hours, based on the body condition when they pulled her out.'

Todd nodded approvingly. 'Good work getting out there so quickly. Any other evidence?'

'Nothing on the boat.' I pulled up the photo of the fabric caught on the cleat. 'I wondered if this might be a match to the victim's sarong, but I haven't heard back yet.'

'Have you followed up with the Pattersons about any other details?'

'I spoke to them an hour ago at Cassowary Charters. They're pretty shaken up about the whole thing. I've taken down some details and told them we'd be down this morning. I'm pleased you arrived early.'

'And the forensics from the blood?'

'Will take a few days, but they're rushing it given the connection to our case. If it's our victim's blood, the *Lady Windward* is our primary crime scene.'

I pulled up the evidence photos on my screen. 'Designer swimwear and a sarong—expensive brand.'

Todd studied the photos; his brow furrowed in concentration. 'Any unusual marking or modifications to the body? Tattoos, cosmetic surgery, dental work that might indicate country of origin?'

'Two small tattoos—a butterfly at the base of her back and what looks like a stylised wave and a shell on one ankle. Professional quality. Dental work suggests good healthcare access, but nothing region-specific that could be determined from the initial exam. They'll get proper X-rays done as part of the full post-mortem tomorrow.'

I pulled up another file. 'There's something else. Preliminary tox screen found traces of a European prescription medication in her system.'

'That could be useful. Where is it prescribed?'

'I'm still waiting on comprehensive information from the pharmaceutical database, but preliminary results suggest it's more common in Europe.'

'Good pick-up. Okay.' Todd stood up and paced the small room, thinking. 'So, we have a young woman, possibly from overseas, wearing expensive swimwear that may match fabric you found on the abandoned *Lady Windward* with blood evidence, prescription medication not common in Australia, found in waters near where that charter boat was abandoned. She doesn't match any local missing persons, and her fingerprints aren't in our system. That changes things significantly,' Todd said, his voice taking on a more urgent tone. 'We're looking at homicide. At least one. Maybe more. We need to find the other two off the boat.'

'That's about the size of it,' I agreed.

'Right, here's what we do.' He turned to face me, energised by the challenge. 'While we wait for the DNA results from Ellie and tomorrow's full autopsy, I want to approach this from multiple angles. I can make some calls to international law enforcement contacts—unofficial, to see if anyone matching her description has been reported missing. And now with this yacht evidence, I want to contact maritime security as well.'

I nodded, already typing notes. 'I'll follow up on the medication angle—find out exactly where it's commonly prescribed and reach out to pharmaceutical databases. Some countries track prescriptions more thoroughly than others. And we'll head down to Cardwell shortly?'

'Good.' Todd nodded. 'I'll also reach out to my contact at the Federal Police. They might be able to check immigration records more thoroughly, maybe find a match to her general description among recent arrivals, even without fingerprint matches.'

'The blood evidence from the *Lady Windward* should help prioritise our requests too,' I pointed out.

'Exactly. Once we confirm the blood matches our victim, this becomes a clear homicide investigation, which opens up a lot more resources and international cooperation options.'

'That still leaves us with dozens or hundreds of possibilities,' I pointed out.

'True,' Todd acknowledged, 'but it's a start. We're creating a net. Once we get tomorrow's autopsy results and then the DNA back from Ellie, we can cross-reference against any leads these other approaches generate.'

I nodded, feeling a plan taking shape. 'What about those private DNA databases? The ones people use for ancestry research? I've been reading about some cases in the US where they've had breakthroughs using those.'

Todd's expression grew thoughtful. 'That's an interesting idea. Not standard procedure here in Australia yet.'

'But not impossible either, if we approach it right,' I countered. 'I know Australia has stricter privacy laws than the US, but these companies do have provisions for law enforcement access in certain circumstances.'

'We'd need more than just a court order,' Todd said, shaking his head slightly. 'Under Australian privacy legislation, it's extremely difficult to access those databases. We'd need to prove it's a homicide first—and with the *Lady Windward* blood evidence, we might actually be able to do that. We'd have to establish that conventional methods have been exhausted and demonstrate that the information can't be obtained any other way. Even then, it would require approval from the Federal Privacy Commissioner.'

'So, what you're saying is it's a last resort,' I clarified.

'A very last resort,' Todd confirmed. 'But with the *Lady Windward* evidence, we might have a stronger case for it if needed. Let's focus on conventional methods first, and if those all fail, we can revisit the private database angle with the proper legal framework in place. Plus, tomorrow's autopsy might give us more to work with, especially if they find evidence that correlates with the boat crime scene. But, Bec? Good thinking outside the square.'

I made a note, slightly disappointed but understanding the legal realities.

'Speaking of missing persons,' Todd said. 'Have you seen the Scotland Yard bulletin about the British woman? Phillipa Fairchild?'

I frowned, trying to recall. 'I don't think so. When did it come in?'

Todd pulled out his tablet and opened an email. 'AFP forwarded it to all Queensland stations last week.'

'I was on my way back from Brisbane. I took leave before I started here,' I said. 'It's not up on the noticeboard here, though.'

'The name is Fairchild, Phillipa. Twenty-four. British national from London. Wealthy family. Last known to be travelling in Queensland. Her father reported her missing after he received a ransom demand.'

He turned the screen towards me, showing a photo of an attractive young woman with blonde hair posing in front of the Sydney Opera House, sunglasses perched atop her head.

'More than a coincidence?' I commented.

'The Metropolitan Police has requested our assistance through official channels. They've sent dental records and her

DNA profile for comparison against any unidentified remains,' Todd continued. 'Given the location and timeframe, it might be worth asking them to specifically check our victim's dental records against Phillipa's during tomorrow's post-mortem. Especially now with the *Lady Windward* evidence suggesting foul play.'

'Good thinking. I'll call the pathology department and mention it,' I said, making another note. 'Should I also mention the charter boat connection to Scotland Yard?'

'Definitely. If Phillipa was targeted because of her wealth, chartering an expensive boat fits the pattern.'

'Do we have the Scotland Yard liaison's contact information?'

'Everything's in the bulletin. The Australian Federal Police are coordinating from Canberra, and they've assigned Detective Superintendent Bennett as the point person in Sydney.' He checked his watch. 'We'd better get down to Cardwell before we look at the databases. We can make some calls on speakerphone as we drive. It's only an hour or so down there, isn't it?'

'Less than an hour,' I said. I'd noticed what a pretty town it was on the way up yesterday morning. I hadn't expected to be back down the highway the next day.

Todd frowned. 'It should give me time to get back to Cairns tonight. Since the post-mortem's in Cairns tomorrow anyway, maybe I should attend. Professional courtesy from our end, and I might spot something useful, especially anything that could connect to the *Lady Windward* crime scene.'

'That's a good idea,' I agreed. 'The pathologists always appreciate having detectives who understand what they're looking for. And with the boat evidence, they might find correlating injuries or evidence. What time's the post-mortem?'

'Not sure yet,' Todd said. 'I'll give the pathology department a call now, make sure they're okay with me observing. I'll also update them about *Lady Windward* so they know to look for anything that might connect. And that way I can bring back the preliminary results immediately instead of waiting for the written report.'

I nodded, trying not to let my disappointment show. I'd been hoping he might stay, make use of that spare bedroom sooner rather than later.

As if reading my thoughts, Todd added, 'Unless you think it would make sense for me to stay over tonight. Work late on this, get an early start for Cairns in the morning? You could come with me to the autopsy—might be useful to have both our eyes on it.'

Our eyes met briefly, and I felt that familiar tension—the professional and personal boundaries we'd been careful to maintain.

'Actually, that would be helpful,' I said carefully. 'I've got the spare room set up. And we could use the time to map out a comprehensive search strategy. Plus, I'd like to be there at the autopsy.'

'Not squeamish?'

I shook my head. 'I stood in my fair share of autopsies when I was in Brisbane.'

'Settled then,' Todd said with a nod that was all business, though I caught a flicker of something else in his eyes. 'I'll let Cairns know I'm staying to assist on this case, and I'll call the pathology department to confirm we can both attend tomorrow.'

As he stepped out to make the calls, I turned back to my computer, returning to the methodical work of trying to identify our victim. In this business, patience and thoroughness were just as important as flashes of insight. And tomorrow, the full post-mortem might finally give us the answers we needed, especially whether our victim's injuries matched the blood evidence from the abandoned charter boat.

Chapter 8

Tuesday - 10 a.m.

The sun glinted off the hood of Todd's police-issue SUV an hour later as I slid into the passenger seat, the leather already hot beneath my black trousers. I'd been waiting outside for him, unwilling to spend another minute in the station with Bradley. He'd arrived late, disappeared into his office and shut the door.

The air conditioning was already running, a blessed relief from the tropical heat.

'Ready?' Todd asked, throwing the vehicle into reverse and backing out of the station car park. His hands were steady on the wheel, strong and capable, the kind of hands that inspired confidence.

'As I'll ever be,' I replied, double-checking that I had my notebook and phone. 'I'm curious what we'll find down at the charter company. If they're as slack with ID as some of the businesses I've encountered in the north, we might be wasting our time.'

We headed south, taking the shortcut to the Bruce Highway through South Mission Beach. To our left, the Coral Sea stretched to the horizon, an impossible shade of blue that shifted and shimmered in the morning light like a living thing. To our right, the verdant wall of rainforest rose dramatically, the canopy of the Wet Tropics towering above the road, ancient and watchful. The contrast between the two—the limitless expanse of water and the claustrophobic wall of vegetation—was unsettling in its beauty.

'Congratulations, by the way,' I said after a few minutes of companionable silence. 'I don't think I've properly said it yet. Detective Inspector Todd Davenport. It suits you.'

Todd's grip tightened almost imperceptibly on the steering wheel, his knuckles whitening slightly against the black leather. I found my eyes tracing the contours of his hands, the small scar on his right thumb from a fishing accident on the trip he took after we finished the Delaney case. The tiny white line that marked the spot where he'd been careless with a filleting knife, an uncharacteristic moment of inattention. I forced myself to look away, focusing instead on the passing scenery, mentally cataloguing the subtle changes in vegetation as we descended towards the coast.

'Thanks. It's been a change. I'm still coming to terms with it. But it's good,' he said, his voice dropping to an attractive lower register.

'I'm proud of you,' I continued, meaning every word. 'You deserve it. After everything.'

He glanced at me briefly before returning his eyes to the road, his gaze intense and focused. Something in that quick look—a hint of interest, perhaps, or something deeper—made my breath catch slightly. It reminded me of that night after we'd closed the Delaney case, when we'd shared a red wine on the back porch of the police house I was living in. The way the moonlight had caught Todd's eyes as he'd finally opened up about his wife's death. The raw vulnerability in his voice as he described holding her hand through those final days, the promise he'd made to her that he would find a way to be happy again. I remembered how my heart had ached for him, how I'd reached out and squeezed his hand without thinking. The moment our fingers had touched, something electric had passed between us; something we'd both immediately backed away from, pretending it hadn't happened.

Professional, I reminded myself sternly. Keep it professional. Todd might be a good friend, I told myself firmly, but he is also my superior. The chain of command existed for a reason.

And it's only friendship. That's all it can ever be.

I nodded to myself, watching a cassowary warning sign flash by, the silhouette of the prehistoric-looking bird a reminder of the ancient, dangerous beauty that surrounded us. Once we joined the Bruce Highway, the rainforest crowded close to the edge, massive ferns and tangled vines visible between the towering trunks that lined the road like silent sentinels.

'How are you finding your new role so far? You've been thrown in at the deep end,' Todd asked, changing lanes to pass a slow-moving truck loaded with sugar cane, the sweet, cloying scent briefly drifting through the car's air conditioning. 'How's the station? I hadn't been to Pandanus Point before today. I'm making my way through the LAC. My jurisdiction goes as far south as Cardwell and west to Mareeba.'

'It's challenging, but in a good way. I've finally accepted that I have made it to detective.' I hesitated, then added, not wanting to sound like I was whinging on my first day, 'The station itself is another matter. The mess, the slackness. I've never seen anything like it. The notice about the British girl not being there doesn't surprise me.'

Todd's eyebrows rose. 'That bad?'

'Files piled everywhere, evidence logs incomplete, and the break room...' I shook my head, remembering the unwashed coffee cups and mouldy food in the staff fridge. 'Let's just say health inspectors would have a field day. The whole place reeks of mould. And don't get me started on the patrol boat—' I broke off. I'd said enough.

'Perhaps an intervention is needed,' Todd said, frowning. 'Sounds like I need to spend some more time there.'

'I'm reluctant to push it yet,' I admitted. 'I need to establish myself first. Maybe after our investigation is done.' I stared out the window for a moment, watching a flock of rainbow lorikeets scatter from a flowering tree, then turned back to him. 'You know the Sergeant has nicknamed Trevor Tickle as "Tess"?'

'Tess?' Todd repeated, before understanding dawned on his face. 'Tess Tickle? That's—' he shook his head, his expression hardening—'harassment on a senior level. Clear breach of code. I'll make a note of that.'

'Don't do anything,' I said quickly, not wanting to seem like I couldn't handle my own battles. 'I'll deal with it through the appropriate channels. Once I've got my feet under me.'

Todd nodded, but I watched the way his jaw clenched slightly, the subtle shift in how he held himself. His hands adjusted on the steering wheel, and I found myself noticing how the wedding band he still wore caught the light as he moved. A reminder of boundaries I'd never dream of crossing, yet somehow still made me feel a complicated pang of... something. Loss? Regret? I pushed the feeling away, burying it beneath a layer of professionalism.

Todd interrupted my thoughts. 'Pull up the number of the Federal Police and I'll talk to them on speakerphone.'

After he finished the call, we drove in silence for a while, the only sound the hum of tyres on asphalt and the soft murmur of the radio playing some inane morning talk show. The landscape opened up around us as we passed through Tully, cane fields stretching out on either side, the imposing bulk of Mount

Tyson looming in the background like a sleeping giant.

Finally, Todd cleared his throat. 'There's something else I wanted to talk to you about, actually.'

I turned to look at him, noting the serious set of his jaw, the intensity in his profile as he kept his eyes on the road. Why did I always notice these things about him? It certainly wasn't because I was missing Gray. I'd managed to close off that unfortunate chapter of my life, locked it away like the evidence from a closed case. But Todd? I noticed way too much. The way his dark hair curled slightly at his collar, needing a trim. The tiny lines at the corners of his eyes deepened when he smiled. Details I shouldn't be aware of, but I was.

'What's that?' I asked, keeping my voice neutral, though my heart had picked up in pace.

'I've been—' he began, then sighed '—I've been particularly careful with our friendship lately.'

'What do you mean?' A cold feeling began to spread through my chest.

Todd's eyes remained fixed on the road, his fingers flexing slightly on the wheel. I watched how his shoulders tensed beneath his shirt, the way he seemed to be choosing his words with deliberate care.

'There's been some talk. About favouritism.'

I felt a surge of indignation. 'That's ridiculous.'

'Is it?' Todd asked quietly. 'We've been friends since you came to Bowen River and we worked on the Delaney case together. Now I'm your superior officer. People notice things like that. They make assumptions, whether there's anything to conclude or not.'

The car crested a hill, and suddenly the view opened up

dramatically. Hinchinbrook Island appeared on the horizon, its rugged peaks rising from the sea like the spine of some slumbering prehistoric beast. Todd's profile was silhouetted against the panorama, and for a moment, I was struck by how perfectly he fit into this landscape—strong, steady, and uncompromising against the wild beauty surrounding us.

'I want *you* to get the full acknowledgment you deserve for your work,' Todd continued, his voice low and earnest. 'And if people think you're getting special treatment because of our friendship, well—'

'I see,' I said, my voice carefully neutral even as I felt a twinge of hurt. I understood the logic, but it stung nonetheless. My eyes traced the line of his jaw, the determined set of his mouth, and I quickly looked away, again frustrated by my inability to stop noticing these things about him.

'It doesn't change anything between us,' Todd added quickly, a hint of apology in his tone. 'Not really. I just thought you should know. So you understand if I seem more distant at times. In front of others.'

As far as I knew, there *wasn't* anything between us, apart from friendship and professional respect. Yet as he spoke, I turned to look at him. I had always admired his focus, his dedication to the job. Admiration, respect, friendship—that's all it was. All it could be.

All it should be. I scolded myself for even having to clarify that in my own mind.

The highway curved around the base of a steep hill, and suddenly Cardwell Bay came into view, a perfect crescent of white sand embracing the impossibly clear turquoise water. The early afternoon sun sparkled off the surface of the sea like scattered diamonds, and the distant green bulk of Hinchinbrook

Island provided a dramatic backdrop to the tranquil scene.

'It's beautiful,' I murmured, grateful for the distraction from the sudden heaviness in my chest.

'Hard to imagine anything bad happening in a place like this,' Todd agreed, slowing the car as we entered the small township of Cardwell.

'But we both know appearances can be deceiving,' I said.

The main street was quiet, just a handful of tourists browsing the shops or enjoying lunch at the couple of cafés on the esplanade. Like a lot of rural and coastal towns, many shopfronts were empty, their windows dusty and displaying faded "Closed" or "For Lease" signs that had clearly been there for months, if not years. Some buildings had that particular look of neglect that comes from prolonged vacancy—peeling paint, sagging awnings, and the occasional piece of mail still visible through glass doors. The COVID pandemic had hit these small communities hard, and the cyclones that periodically battered the coast didn't help. Only the most determined businesses survived, hanging on through thin tourist seasons and the wet season when visitors were scarce.

Todd drove through town and pulled into a parking spot directly in front of Cardwell Charter Boats, a tidy building with a cheerful blue and white awning flapping in the sea breeze.

'Let's see what they can tell us about *Lady Windward*,' Todd said, switching off the engine, his professional demeanour firmly back in place, all personal conversation gone.

Chapter 9

Tuesday - 11 a.m.

Cassowary Charter Boats

The office was small but neat, with framed photographs of fishing catches and smiling tourists on chartered yachts covering the walls. A large map of the Great Barrier Reef dominated one wall, with popular routes and fishing spots marked with red and blue pins. The whole place smelled of salt water, sunscreen, and the particular mustiness that comes from proximity to the sea.

A middle-aged woman looked up from behind the counter as we entered, her friendly smile faltering slightly when Todd showed his badge, wariness replacing the welcome in her eyes.

'Detective Inspector Davenport, Queensland Police,' he said, his voice taking on that official tone he used when on duty. 'And this is Detective Senior Constable Whitfield. We're here about the *Lady Windward* charter.'

The woman's hand went to her throat. 'I'm Sandra Patterson. My husband Graham owns the company.' She glanced towards a back room. 'Look, we run a very safe operation here. Whatever happened out there—'

'Mrs. Patterson,' I interrupted, 'we found substantial blood evidence on your vessel. This isn't about your safety record.'

Her face went pale. 'Blood? How much blood? Graham didn't mention that to me.'

'Enough,' Todd said grimly. 'We need to speak with your husband. Now.'

Graham Patterson emerged a moment later, wiping his hands on an oil-stained rag. He was tanned and weathered, with the look of a man who had spent most of his life on the water, his skin creased like well-worn leather. Despite that, he was professionally dressed in navy shorts and a white polo shirt with the charter company logo on the pocket.

'Police?' he said, extending a hand to Todd, and then to me, his grip firm and calloused. 'We've been expecting someone to come by after the call. Shocking business. We're waiting to hear from our underwriters.'

'We understand you chartered the vessel to a group last week,' Todd said, getting straight to the point.

'Yes, on Friday. They were due in today at Clump Point. Our sail guide lives up there, and he meets the boats that do the one-way charter. I haven't been able to get onto him to tell him what's happened. Have the other charterers been found yet?' Graham asked.

'No, we need all of the details that you have, please.'

Sandra nodded, already pulling a file from a cabinet behind the counter. 'That's right. Three people—one man and two women.' She spread the paperwork on the counter, everything neat and in order. 'Here's all the documentation. Charter agreement, photocopies of their ID, credit card details, everything.'

'You're very organised,' I commented, impressed by the thoroughness of the records in a region where many businesses operated on a more casual basis.

Graham shrugged, a motion that spoke of decades spent on the water. 'Standard procedure. Plus, when we heard what happened—' he shook his head, genuine concern in his eyes. 'Blood on the deck, no sign of the passengers? Of course, we pulled all the paperwork right away.'

'Mind if we take these?' Todd asked, gesturing to the documents.

'Not at all,' Sandra said, sliding them towards us. 'These are the copies we made for you. That boat was our pride and joy, but it's the people we're worried about.'

'And our reputation,' her husband muttered. 'Not bloody good for business.'

'Did anything seem unusual about the group?' I asked, studying the forms, my eyes immediately drawn to the names and passport photos: Sally Walker and Victoria Chandler both had dark hair, and Paulo Ramirez was easy to pick as a South American.

The couple exchanged glances, a silent communication that spoke of years together. 'Not really,' Graham said finally, his weathered forehead creasing in concentration. 'They seemed like any other group of friends on holiday. Excited, maybe a bit loud. The guy—Paulo—he knew his way around boats. Asked all the right questions during the briefing.'

'They were well-prepared,' Sandra added, her fingers twisting a gold chain around her neck. 'They ordered all their supplies from the store here and loaded the boat themselves. Food, drinks, and some fishing gear. Most tourists email and get us to do that for them.'

I noted that down, wondering if it could be significant, or just an example of someone organised.

'Cardwell General Store handles most of the provisioning for our charters,' Graham explained, leaning against the counter. 'They've got the manifest if you need it. Might be worth a look, come to think of it. They loaded a fair bit of grog. More than your average holidaymakers. And a lot considering there were only two originally booked on the charter.'

'Describe the process for us.' Todd leaned forwards, his notebook open. 'Walk us through everything from when they first arrived.'

Graham nodded, scratching his greying beard. 'Standard procedure. They arrived around nine on Friday. From what they said, they camped locally on Thursday night. I did the safety briefing first: life jackets, emergency equipment, radio protocols, the lot. We went through the charts, discussed their planned route, weather conditions, and overnight mooring locations.' He traced a finger along an invisible map. 'Then we did a practical—two hours out on the water with me coaching them. It's critical that charterers can handle the vessel before I leave them with it.'

'How did they do?' Todd asked.

'Paulo—the Brazilian bloke—was quite skilled, actually. Said he'd done some sailing in Rio and crewing around the Mediterranean. It showed. He picked up on our local conditions quickly. I was impressed and happy to let them go out.' Graham paused, his expression thoughtful. 'The other two were passengers. Not much interest or knowledge in the sailing side of things.'

'And after the briefing?' Todd prompted.

'It was a four-night charter with the boat to be returned to our representative at Clump Point Marina today. They'd sail up the coast, stopping at anchorages each night, and hand over the vessel there. They were supposed to keep in touch by radio twice a day.'

'And they did?' Todd asked.

'Saturday afternoon was the last time they answered the scheduled radio call. They confirmed they were in Hull River at

Tully Heads where they were supposed to be.'

'Were you concerned when you couldn't reach them again?'

Graham shook his head. 'Not until yesterday morning, when we couldn't reach them again.'

'What did you do then?'

'Well, we have a protocol to follow in these situations,' Graham said, lifting a document off the desk. 'But honestly, I wasn't panicking at first. The weather was dead calm all weekend, perfect sailing conditions. And this guy, the charterer, he knew what he was doing. Had plenty of experience on the water.'

Todd nodded. 'So, what made you hold off on raising the alarm?'

'They were sailing in protected bays north of Hinchinbrook Island, not exactly dangerous waters. And the missed check-in was the late one, around four p.m. Sunday. We put it down to them having too much fun, maybe a few too many drinks, or simply forgetting. Foolishly, I gave them the benefit of the doubt. I didn't follow my own protocols. You know how it is on these charters.'

'No, I don't actually.'

Graham's ruddy colour deepened, and Sandra moved closer to him.

'But Monday morning changed things,' Todd said.

'Yes, when I couldn't raise them, I was concerned. The weather forecast wasn't good. We checked our GPS tracking system first thing.' Graham's expression darkened. 'When it wasn't showing anything no signal at all—that's when we began to worry. There was no tracking record. The boat had plenty of safety equipment for an emergency. Good tender, small motor, all the required gear. But if the GPS wasn't pinging...'

'You were about to notify the authorities?'

'I was just about to pick up the phone to call it in when we got the call from Detective Whitfield.'

I stepped forward. 'Tell me about your representative up there, Graham. What was his take on the situation? Has he heard anything from local boaties up there?'

'I haven't been able to get onto Dave. He's not answering his phone.'

'Do you have an office up there?'

'No. Dave lives up there. Dave Hewson. When we have a one-way charter, he meets the boats at Clump Point Marina, cleans them, takes the rubbish off, refuels, and then brings her back down to Cardwell in time for the next booking. He takes the company van home. The next time we head through, Sandra or I will drive it back. It's an informal relationship we've had for years.' Graham went to the counter and picked up a map with moorings marked on it with times and dates. 'Here's their journey, documented each day. They followed the plan perfectly, until they stopped responding to the radio calls.'

'Excellent, that's a great help.' Todd studied the map with interest. 'And then?'

Graham shook his head in disbelief. 'I was gobsmacked when I got the call. The sea had been like a mill pond for the four days, until the squall that came through yesterday morning. And they hadn't reported in with any motor or sail issues.'

'Thank you,' Todd said. He turned to me. 'Anything else you have, Detective Whitfield?'

I turned to Sandra. 'Can you tell me a little bit more about the dynamics between the group? Any observations? I guess after years of hiring your vessels out, you get a bit of an idea about people.'

Graham smiled at his wife. 'Sandra is an inveterate people watcher.'

'Anything else you can think of? Any other interactions with them?' I asked.

Sandra hesitated, her hand playing with her necklace. 'Well, there was one thing. Probably nothing.'

'We'd like to hear it anyway,' I encouraged, pen poised above my notebook.

'Originally, there was only the couple going. The South American guy had his arm around the girl called Sally most of the time. They seemed pretty cosy, you know? We'd had a cancellation, so I offered them a deal. An extra couple of days for the same charter, or they could take the same length cruise with an extra passenger. When I offered them the deal, only the couple were going. There seemed to be a bit of an argument as they talked about the offer. I got the impression that they weren't a happy group. Paulo seemed happy-go-lucky, teasing the two girls about the small cabins and heads.' Sandra crossed her arms, thinking. 'There was something between the two women; they didn't speak to each other much, and when he said that they'd take up the offer of a third passenger, his girlfriend didn't seem very happy. The other girl didn't say much; she was only in the office for a short time. Once they'd unloaded, she drove off.'

My interest quickened. 'The other girl?'

'Sally and Victoria were the ones going on the charter, and there was another woman who was driving their vehicle. I'm pretty sure they called her Amanda. As it was a one-way charter, I guess she was going to meet them when they arrived up there. She left before Graham took them out for the practical part of the briefing.'

Bec's interest deepened. 'Can you describe her?'

Sandra furrowed her brow in concentration. 'Tall, slender girl with dark hair. Olive skin. Quiet type—seemed a bit aloof. Kept to herself while the others were chatting away.'

'You wouldn't happen to have the number plate for the vehicle, would you?'

She shook her head. 'No, but our security camera would have picked it up. I'll get that for you now.'

'Excellent, thank you.'

As Sandra left to retrieve the security footage, Todd and I exchanged glances. The picture was becoming clearer—a skilled sailor, a tense group dynamic, a carefully followed route until they disappeared, and a fourth person involved with the group.

Sandra came back with the number plate of a Toyota Troop Carrier written on a yellow post-it note.

'Thanks. We'll follow up on that,' Todd said, gathering the documents and sliding them into a folder. 'Could you also email me the rest of the footage from that day? There might be something else we pick up.'

Sandra nodded. 'Of course.'

'Thank you both for your help.' Todd handed his card to her. 'We may have more questions later.'

'Of course, we're happy to come up to Pandanus Point. I'd like to have a look at the vessel when she's in dock.' Graham nodded, his eyes serious beneath sun-bleached brows. 'That boat was our business's pride and joy, but more importantly, I hope those people are okay.'

'I understand how you must be feeling.' Todd leaned forward. 'Have you ever had any other incidents with your boats?'

Graham shook his head again. 'No, we run a tight outfit, and we make it very clear what is acceptable behaviour, and there is a hefty bond if there is damage to the vessel.'

'Thanks for your time. We'll be in touch, and we'll let you know when the boat's cleared for you to go on board. One more thing, can you please give us the contact details for your offsider at the marina?'

I took down Dave Hewson's details, and we headed back to the car.

Chapter 10

Tuesday - noon

Cardwell.

Outside, the sun was high in the sky, beating down on the picturesque esplanade. The beauty of the scene—the tranquil bay, the majestic island offshore, the palm trees swaying in the gentle breeze—stood in stark contrast to the grim purpose of our visit. Somewhere out there, beyond that perfect blue horizon, someone had bled out on the deck of the *Lady Windward*. And someone else had likely put them there.

'Bakery?' Todd suggested, nodding towards a small shop a few doors down, its windows displaying trays of enticing pastries. 'We can grab a coffee and go through these documents. I want to check these IDs ASAP.'

Five minutes later, we were seated at a wooden table on the foreshore with takeaway coffees and two apple slices. The charter paperwork was weighted down against the sea breeze by Todd's keys. The metal glinted in the sunlight, drawing my eye to his wedding ring once more. I wondered if he'd ever take it off.

'So,' I said, taking a sip of my coffee and gazing out at the peaceful waters of the bay, trying to imagine the *Lady Windward* setting sail from here just days ago, its passengers unaware of— or perhaps planning—what was to come. 'What do we have?'

Todd spread out the photocopies of their identification. 'Paulo Ramirez, Brazilian passport. Sally Walker, British passport. And Victoria Chandler, Australian.' He studied the documents carefully. 'Let's run these through the system and see what comes up.'

He pulled out his tablet and opened the RMAL portal—the Register of Movement Alerts List—which tracked international visitors to Australia. 'Advantage of the promotion,' Todd said, noting my surprised look. 'Detective Inspector level gets secure access through encrypted channels. Extra firewalls, VPN tunnels, the whole security suite. Means I can access most databases remotely.' He frowned at the screen. 'Though the connection out here is patchy as hell.'

'Let's start with the guy,' I suggested, leaning over to see the screen, careful not to get too close to Todd. He nodded. We both knew that there was a strong possibility that the body in the morgue in Cairns was one of these two women.

After entering Ramirez's details, the system confirmed his status: Paulo Ramirez, a Brazilian national on a valid tourist visa, entered Australia through Sydney International Airport four months ago.

Todd entered Sally Walker's passport number and details. Within seconds, the system returned a match—a valid British passport issued two years ago to Sally Walker, DOB 14 March 2001, her home address in Gloucestershire. Arrived eleven months ago.

'Two down,' Todd murmured, making a note.

'Both check out so far,' I noted, impressed by the efficiency of the system. I had been aware of it but hadn't had cause to access it until now.

'Now for the Australian woman. I'll switch to the Australian Passport Office Database.'

I watched Todd navigate between systems with ease and entered Victoria Chandler's details into the system.

'That's strange.'

I leaned over and looked at the screen. INVALID/CANCELLED was flashing red. 'What does that mean?'

'Hang on.' Todd clicked through a few screens. 'Okay, this makes sense now. A lost passport number is marked as "cancelled" or "invalid" in the Australian Passport Office database.'

'So, she's reported it lost? But she's still using it for ID. Maybe she found it and didn't report it?'

'That's one scenario. Border control and immigration systems are updated to reflect this status, and the new replacement passport becomes the only valid document. She's possibly got a new passport number. I'll keep digging. We've got her photo, so we can find her by searching for her image in a few other databases.'

Todd's mouth was set in a straight line as he entered the name several times. 'Something's not right,' he said grimly. 'I'll try IABS.'

'What's that?'

'The Identity and Biometric Services system, which can cross-reference facial recognition matches across multiple databases.' He took a photo of the passport image and uploaded it, then drummed his fingers impatiently. 'This will check against multiple databases—immigration, driver's licences, social media, and international watchlists through our INTERPOL connection. Assuming this bloody connection holds up.' He glanced at the signal bars. 'Regional towers aren't built for this kind of data load.'

After a longer wait, the system returned another negative

result: NO CONFIRMED IDENTITY MATCH.

'That's suss,' Todd said. 'It means she hasn't applied for a new passport. She doesn't have a driver's licence, and she doesn't exist on any of the government databases.'

'Suss, but not out of the realms of possibility. How old is she on the original passport?'

Todd flicked back to the photocopy. 'Born 2000.'

'So, at twenty-four, she got a passport, lost it, and doesn't have a driver's licence? Or a Medicare number. Or...'

'A Tax File Number,' Todd said, putting the tablet on the table and reaching for his now-cold coffee. 'No Centrelink history either. No Youth Allowance, nothing. And get this, no bank accounts with any of the major banks.'

'That's impossible for a twenty-four-year-old. What about voter enrolment?'

'Nope. No MyGov account, no superannuation records. It's like she doesn't exist financially or bureaucratically.'

'Wait, there's more,' I said, scrolling through the search results. 'No mobile phone contracts, no rental history, no university enrolment records anywhere in the system.'

'But we have an address on the passport.' Todd stared out over the sea and tapped his fingers on the table. 'Do we call who lives at the address, or do we send the local police to have a chat and find out about her?'

'Run the address through the electoral roll database,' I suggested.

'Good idea.' Todd nodded and reached for the tablet, then waited as the screen buffered. 'Come on,' he muttered at the device. 'Jackpot, she's there. Four people show up registered there: Gordon Chandler, Meredith Chandler, Victoria-Ann Chandler, and Sean Chandler.'

'Name variation? You'd think it would be on her passport though. Okay, we'll give the Chandlers a call when we get to the station.'

Todd closed the tablet. 'We have three missing people and one body. Either way, we need to find out who Victoria or Victoria-Ann Chandler is. Come on, let's get moving, Detective. We've got a lot of work to do.'

I nodded, gazing out at the glittering water of Cardwell Bay, where the *Lady Windward* had set sail just days ago. Three people had boarded that vessel—Paulo Ramirez and Sally Walker, both exactly who they claimed to be, and a woman calling herself Victoria Chandler, who needed some more investigation.

Somewhere between Cardwell and where the blood-stained yacht had been abandoned, something had gone wrong.

The first thing we had to do was identify the body.

'Call Bradley,' Todd said, his jaw set. 'Tell him we need all available units looking for that Amanda woman. And get me a direct line to AFP. This just became a federal case.'

I reached for my phone, adrenaline coursing through my veins. The investigation had just taken a turn none of us had seen coming.

The *Lady Windward* wasn't just a crime scene—it was the starting point of a manhunt.

Chapter 11

Tuesday - mid-afternoon.

Tully.

Ten minutes later, we were back in the car, heading north on the Bruce Highway towards Mission Beach. I drove as Todd trawled more databases. The coastal scenery flashed by—tangled mangroves giving way to sugar cane fields, then back to thick tropical greenery. My mind kept circling back to the charter documents, trying to make sense of the disparate pieces.

I tapped my fingers against the steering wheel, lost in thought. As we approached the turnoff for Tully, my stomach tightened. I'd been debating this detour ever since we'd planned the Cardwell trip, but hadn't mentioned it to Todd yet. I was silent, watching the landscape roll by outside.

'Hey, Todd?' I asked, trying to sound casual. 'Would you mind if we took a quick detour into Tully on the way back? Ten minutes tops.'

Todd glanced at me, eyebrows raised. 'Tully? Sure. Something to do with the case?'

I hesitated, then shook my head. 'No. Personal. My parents moved there after they left Bowen River. I haven't seen them since I arrived. I guess I should do the right thing and call in, just touch base, not stay. As long as that's okay with you?' I glanced across at him, sensing his intent look. 'If you'd prefer not to, especially after you interviewed Dad at Bowen River, I totally understand. Anyway, look, forget about it.' I knew I was rambling. 'I'll come down on the weekend.'

Understanding dawned on Todd's face. He knew enough about my family situation to know this wasn't just a casual visit. He'd also met my father during the Leanne Delaney investigation last year, when Dad was still in Bowen River. That interview had been tense, to say the least.

'Of course. Makes sense to call in,' he said quietly. 'We'll be working late back at the station, so a short detour's not going to make a difference.'

I took the exit towards Tully, my knuckles white against the steering wheel. 'I'll make it quick. It's just—they've called a few times since they found out I was moving to Mission Beach. Mum keeps saying things are different now, that Dad has changed, but—'

'But you're not sure you believe it,' Todd finished.

I nodded, grateful he understood without my having to explain further; he knew me well.

'Do they know you've arrived in town?' he asked.

'No.' I made a left turn onto a residential street lined with small, neat houses. 'Probably better that way. Less time for Dad to prepare a sermon, or worse, turn up at the station.' The bitterness in my voice surprised even myself. Twelve years away, and the resentment still felt fresh. My childhood home, the drafty old manse, had been more like a church than a home—a place of rules and judgment rather than comfort.

'Look for number fifteen,' I said.

Todd peered out his window. 'Another five houses along on the left.'

I slowed the car as we approached a modest weatherboard house painted a cheerful yellow. It had a small, well-tended garden with bright tropical flowers and a picket fence—nothing like the austere manse I'd grown up in. 'We must have the wrong place.'

I parked at the front and sat motionless, staring through the windshield.

'You okay?' Todd asked gently. 'This is number fifteen.'

'Yeah,' I said, not moving. 'Just preparing myself. Maybe this was a bad idea. I'll come another day.'

I turned to look at Todd, and he met and held my gaze. I looked away first.

'Want me to wait in the car?' he asked quietly.

Suddenly grateful for his presence, I shook my head. 'Actually, no. I'd like you to come in with me, if that's okay.'

'Happy to,' Todd said simply.

As we got out of the car, I noticed a figure kneeling in the garden, carefully tending a row of flowering plants. My father. The sight stopped me in my tracks. He wore a faded T-shirt and cargo shorts—casual clothes I had rarely seen him in growing up. No clerical collar, no formal attire that had once signified his position and authority.

'Dad?' I called, my voice sounding strange to my own ears.

He looked up, shading his eyes against the afternoon sun. For a moment, he seemed confused, then his face broke into a wide smile I hardly recognised.

'Rebecca!' He stood quickly, brushing soil from his knees. 'Peggy, come out, Rebecca's here.'

He hurried down the path, pulling off gardening gloves as he approached. Then he hesitated, stopping a few feet away, uncertainty replacing the initial smile.

'Rebecca,' he said again, softer now. 'This is unexpected.'

Before I could respond, the front door opened and my mother appeared, wiping her hands on a tea towel. She froze on the top step, eyes widening.

'Bec? Oh my goodness!' She rushed down, pushing past Dad to pull me into a tight embrace. 'My girl. I can't believe you're here.'

The familiar scent of her perfume—something floral and comforting—brought an unexpected lump to my throat. I stood stiffly at first, then found myself returning her hug.

When I stepped back, I gestured to Todd. 'You remember Detective Davenport?'

'Of course,' Dad said, extending his hand to Todd. 'From the Delaney investigation. Good to see you again under better circumstances, Detective.'

'Likewise, Reverend Whitfield,' Todd replied, shaking his hand.

'Just Jim now, please,' my father corrected with a small smile. 'I'm not leading a congregation these days.'

That simple statement hit me harder than I expected. My entire life, he had been "Reverend Whitfield" first and "Dad" second.

'Will you come inside?' my mother asked hopefully. 'I just made a heavenly tart —still your favourite, I hope.'

The mention of the orange and coconut jelly dessert caught me off guard. I couldn't believe Mum remembered.

'We can't stay long,' I said hesitantly. 'We're heading back to Mission Beach. We just happened to be in Cardwell for work and—'

'Even just for a quick cup of tea,' Mum said hopefully. 'Please?'

I looked at my parents—my mother's pleading eyes, and my father, standing awkwardly with soil on his knees, looking smaller and older than I remembered. Nothing like the imposing figure who had once quoted scripture as punishment.

Todd caught my eye and gave me a small nod.

'Okay,' I agreed. 'A very quick cup of tea. We have to get back to the station.'

The inside of the house was different from the manse at Bowen River—bright and cosy, with comfortable furniture and family photos on the walls. Several framed photos of me sat among them—my police academy graduation, a candid shot from my farewell at Bowen River with Leanne, and even one taken at my Year 12 formal.

As Mum busied herself in the kitchen, Dad gestured for us to sit in the living room. An awkward silence fell.

'So,' he finally said, clearing his throat. 'You're still doing well with the police service. That's good to hear.'

I raised an eyebrow and couldn't help myself. 'Is it? Last I recall, you said it was "no job for a woman of faith".'

Dad flinched, his eyes dropping to his hands. 'I've said a lot of things I regret.'

The simple admission hung in the air between us.

'Your garden looks nice,' I said, changing the subject. 'I didn't know you were interested in gardening.'

A small smile touched his lips. 'Neither did I. After we left Bowen River, I needed something new. The church has kept my pension going, and your mother and I are very happy here. A new start.'

Mum returned with a tray of tea and four slices of tart. 'And we're happy to be closer to you, Bec.'

For the first time, I noticed the relaxed rapport between my parents—nothing like the formal, dominant relationship I remembered where Mum had always deferred to my father's authority.

'How's Mission Beach?' Mum asked, pouring tea. 'Have you found somewhere to live?' She held out a plate with a slice of tart for Todd, and then passed me one.

'Thank you. It looks good.' Todd caught my eye; he had ended up eating both apple slices at Cardwell, so I knew he wouldn't be hungry. He cleared his throat gently. 'Actually, Mr and Mrs Whitfield, Bec has some news she might want to share.' He glanced at me with an encouraging smile. 'About her new position.'

I shot him a look, but his expression was warm and supportive. 'Well, I've been promoted. I'm now working as a detective at Mission Beach. And I've got a great rental house right on the beach.' I hesitated. 'You'll have to come and visit one day when I've got a day off.'

Mum's face lit up immediately. 'Oh, Bec, that would be lovely! And a detective. How good is that, Jim?'

To my shock, Dad reached across and took my hand. His eyes held a glint of tears, and his expression was one of genuine pride—something I'd never seen directed at me before.

'I am proud of you, Rebecca,' he said quietly, his voice thick with emotion. 'Very proud indeed.'

I stared at him, still reluctant to believe he could change so much. 'Really?'

He squeezed my hand gently. 'I guess it was time I woke up to myself, Rebecca. The scripture says, "by their fruits ye shall know them," and your fruits, well, they speak for themselves. You're helping people. That's God's work, no matter what uniform you wear.'

The sincerity in his voice caught me off guard, and for a

moment, I didn't know what to say.

We talked for another ten minutes, a careful conversation that avoided the past but acknowledged its existence. When I finally stood to leave, saying we had to get back to work, my parents walked us to the door. Mum insisted on giving me a Tupperware container filled with the rest of the tart.

'You're welcome anytime,' Mum said, embracing me again. 'Day or night. This is your home too, if you want it to be.'

Dad hesitated, his hands half-raised as though he wanted to reach out but wasn't sure if he should. I surprised myself by stepping forward and giving him a brief, awkward hug.

'I'm glad to see you looking so well, Dad,' I said quietly.

'You too, Rebecca.' His voice was thick with emotion.

'I'll drive,' Todd said as we walked to the car. He gave me space, not commenting on the tears I quickly wiped away. Only when we were back on the highway did he speak.

'They seem different. And your mum's heavenly tart is divine.'

I couldn't help giggling, and it made me feel better. 'It really is called that. It's the name of the recipe. It's the first thing I ever learned to bake.'

'You'll have to bake me one, one day,' Todd said with a grin.

I stared at the road ahead, my emotions still a tangled mess. 'I can't believe the change in Dad. He's lost all that bitterness.'

'People change.'

'Maybe.' I wasn't ready to fully trust the transformation I'd witnessed. 'Or maybe he's just learned to say what people want to hear.'

'What do you think?'

I considered this as the kilometres passed. 'I think... I think he might actually mean it. Which is almost harder to process than if he'd just been the same old judgmental Dad.' I sighed. 'I don't know if I can forgive him yet, but...'

'But it's a start,' Todd finished for me.

I nodded. 'Yeah. It's a start.'

We drove on towards Mission Beach, the rainforest canopy shadowing the road. The case was still sitting in the back of my thoughts, but for now, I allowed myself to dwell on the unexpected developments of the day and the possibility that somehow my family was healing.

Chapter 12

Tuesday - 4.30 p.m.

Pandanus Point Police Station.

The station was quiet when we arrived; Reeves was on the front desk and gave Todd a glowing smile as he followed me down the corridor to my office, our footsteps echoing in the corridor. The other offices, the kitchen, and the incident room were empty.

We stood before the board in the incident room. We had a lot to add from today's visits and conversations. I wrote up the yacht charter information, then added the details about Victoria Chandler's passport being used as ID. Next went the other two charterers: Sally Walker and Paulo Ramirez. And the name Amanda, followed by a question mark.

The initial pathology report went up next, with its preliminary findings about our victim.

Todd pulled out his phone. 'I'll call the Chandlers now.'

He put it on speakerphone as I continued to update the board, and the number rang several times before a gruff voice answered. 'Gordon Chandler speaking.'

'Mr Chandler, this is Detective Inspector Todd Davenport, Queensland Police. I need to ask you a few questions about a Victoria Chandler.'

'Yes, that's our daughter.' A pause. 'Is there a problem?'

'I need to know her current whereabouts. Her passport was recently used as identification to charter a yacht in north Queensland. Is that where she is at the moment?'

'I'll bet she wishes she was on a yacht up there. She's been out doing cattle work with me in a dusty paddock. We've just come in for smoko.'

'May I speak to her, please?'

'Yeah, she's in the kitchen with my wife. Vicki! Police on the phone want a word about your passport.'

A moment later, a voice came on the line, surprisingly deep for a woman. 'This is Vicki Chandler.'

'Vicki, Detective Inspector Todd Davenport, Queensland Police. I need to ask about your passport. You reported it as lost. Is that correct?'

'That's right. I was up in Brisbane. I'd only just picked it up. When I rang up and asked what to do, they gave me a number and I used that to report it online.'

'How long ago was that?'

She hesitated. 'Um, probably about the middle of last month. Hang on, I'll check the calendar on the fridge. Won't be a tic.'

In less than a minute, she was back. 'Twentieth of July. I came home a couple of days later and I've been here ever since.'

'Do you have any idea where you lost it?'

'I can tell you *exactly* where I was. I was in a pub in Hamilton with a few friends, and someone went through my bag. It was on the seat next to me. The pub was really crowded. I lost my wallet, my passport, and a set of keys. It wouldn't do them any good because they were the keys to the house out here.'

'Any suspicions?'

'No. There were heaps of people there. There was a band playing.'

Todd frowned and moved closer to the incident board. 'So, your passport was fairly new.'

'Yeah. I'd only had it for a week. I'm not applying for another one. I don't need it now, and it costs too bloody much to get another one.'

'Could I get you to send me your photo? One that's similar to the one on your passport.'

'I've got a copy of my passport on my phone. Came in handy when I had to report it stolen. Will that do?'

'Yes, please.' Todd gave her his number.

A moment later, his phone pinged, and the photo came through. Todd and I looked at each other. The photo bore no resemblance to the photo on the stolen passport.

'Thanks, Vicki. A couple more questions, just to verify a couple of things. Can you tell me your date of birth and your address?'

'Same as on that copy I just sent you.' She rattled off the details without hesitation.

'One more thing. Do you have other identification under the name Victoria?'

'Nah, everything else is under Victoria-Ann. Driver's licence, bank accounts. What's all this about anyway?'

'Someone's been using your passport as ID, and they've changed the photo.'

'Sneaky bugger.'

'Anyone you were chatting to, or anyone you think might have been hanging around?'

'Not really.'

'If you think of anything else that might be useful, you've got my number. Thanks for your time.'

'Okay, I'll have a think about it.'

After Todd ended the call, we both stared at the incident board.

'So, it's Victoria Chandler's passport, with a different image,' I said.

'So, we have three missing people: the Brazilian and the English girl, who both check out, and an unknown perp. This is getting more interesting.' Todd pointed to the passport photos. 'Someone picked up a brand-new passport. Intentional targeting or just part of the booty of cleaning out bags in a crowded pub?' He stood and stretched his arms overhead. The casual movement drew my attention to the breadth of his shoulders, the way his shirt pulled tight across his chest. I quickly looked away.

'I think we've done all we can today,' he said, moving to the desk and gathering the files into a neat stack. 'I'm going to call the coroner's office to confirm tomorrow's autopsy, then head back to Cairns.' He pulled out his phone and made the call. 'Right, understood. We'll be there by two,' he said, ending the call. 'The autopsy is confirmed for tomorrow afternoon. They need the morning for preliminary work, so I'll meet you at the hospital about one-thirty.'

'What do you want me to focus on here?'

'See if you can track down Dave Hewson from Cassowary Charters. See if he's heard anything locally. Boaties talk. Someone might have seen the *Lady Windward* out around the island where the body was found.' Todd gathered his jacket and case files. 'I'll coordinate with the pathology team in the morning and follow up on those pharmaceutical leads first thing in the morning. I'll call Sandra back and talk to her again about the second woman on the boat.' He paused at the door and held my gaze. 'I'll see you tomorrow.'

The office felt empty after he left. I shook off the feeling and turned back to the board. Something was niggling at me, and

I couldn't place it.

A few minutes later, I heard Trevor's voice out front, and I went out to the foyer. He was at the front desk, and there was no sign of Reeves.

'Trevor, do you know a Dave Hewson from Cassowary Charters?'

'I do. He's a local sailor and runs a charter boat up and down the coast, as well as working for Cassowary Charters. He takes backpackers on as crew sometimes.'

'That's interesting.'

'There's something else, too. I'm not sure if you'll know.'

'What's that?' My pulse quickened slightly.

'The locals are talking. On social media, there's a lot of commenting going on.'

'About the case?'

'Yes, but more about Dave.'

'Why's that?' I pulled my notebook from my pocket.

'Social media is having an absolute field day. Check it out. The local community watch page.' Trevor frowned. 'Someone's dug up an old story about his girlfriend from about ten years back. She was a backpacker, working on his boat. German girl.' He lowered his voice further. 'The story goes that she vanished. Just disappeared one night. Some said murder, but no one was ever charged.'

The hairs on the back of my neck prickled. It was the first I'd heard of anyone else going missing here. 'Do you think there's any truth to it?'

'No.' Trevor's eyes met mine. 'You need to know. I've known Dave for a long time. He's a decent bloke. Keeps to himself mostly, and I understand why.' He hesitated, fingers tapping against the table. 'But you know how small towns are with gossip. They have long memories and love talking up the negatives.'

'Where does Dave live?'

'He's out on a cane farm near the beach about three ks from here.' He glanced at his watch. 'But you'll probably find him at the pub now. He goes there for an hour or so every afternoon if he's in town. Late thirties, long sun-bleached hair in a ponytail, dark tan. Can't miss him.'

'Okay, I'll head over then now. Thanks, Trevor. That's very useful.'

'I'd come with you and point him out if I wasn't manning the desk.'

'That's okay. I'm sure I'll recognise him if he's there.'

As I went to walk down the hall, Trevor called me back. 'Detective Whitfield?'

'Please call me Bec.'

His face flushed. 'Okay, thank you. I hope it's all right, but I was looking at the board in the incident room.'

'Yes, that's not a problem. Any ideas you have are welcome.'

Trevor tipped his head to the side, and he barely looked old enough to be in uniform. 'I want to get into investigation one day. It's really good to have you here at the station. Any help you need, please don't hesitate to ask.'

'It's good to be here.'

'One more thing,' he said, glancing around nervously even though we were alone. 'Don't mention Dave's name in front of Sarge. He's always had it in for Dave.'

I nodded, filing that piece of information away with everything else Trevor had shared. The walls suddenly felt very thin as I went into the incident room. The station was quiet, the fluorescent lights humming their familiar tune above empty desks.

I went back into my office, logged on to the system, opened the Missing Persons Database, and searched for Mission Beach. A case from the local area came up straight away. I read through the notes, sat back and exhaled when I reached the end of the notes.

Case Closed. And there was no further information.

Katja Mueller. Age 22. German citizen. Last seen: Mission Beach area, October 15th, 2015. Status: Missing Person (Cold Case).

The photo showed a vibrant young woman with shoulder-length blonde hair and bright blue eyes. She was laughing at the camera, carefree and alive. Everything our current victim would never be again. I opened the case file, scanning through the sparse details. Katja had been working on a charter boat, last seen at the Clump Point marina. The investigating officer had been Senior Sergeant Tate, now retired. Witness statements were minimal, and the investigation seemingly perfunctory. I pulled up the original witness statements. Three people had been interviewed: the marina harbourmaster, a local café owner, and Dave Hewson himself. His statement was brief—Katja had been working on his boat for a few months, seemed happy, and mentioned wanting to travel to Cairns. He claimed she'd taken her wages and left without notice.

But something didn't add up. According to the harbourmaster's statement, Katja's backpack had been found in the public toilet near the marina after she was reported missing. Her passport was inside. My eyes widened when it was reported that it had been found by Senior Constable Bradley.

I grabbed my keys. It was time to find Dave Hewson.

'I'm heading out now, Trevor. I won't come back tonight.'

'Not a problem, Detective.' His grin was slightly cheeky, and I decided I liked Trevor Tickle.

'One question, Trevor. Did you ever know Senior Sergeant Tate?'

'I did. He lived next door to my parents' place when he was here. He was a really good guy. One of the best. I didn't tell you this, but apparently he used to keep Sarge in line, when he was a constable, that was.'

'Do you know where he is now?'

'Yeah, he lives in Tully in the over-55s village.'

'Great, thanks.'

It didn't take me long to find the number, and it was only minutes before I had Tate on the line.

'Greg Tate. Who's calling, please?' His voice was gravelly but alert.

'This is Detective Senior Constable Rebecca Whitfield from Pandanus Point Station. I'm calling about the Katja Mueller case from 2015.'

A long pause. 'Christ. That name. Been expecting this call for years.'

'Sir?'

'The German girl. Look, Detective, I've got to ask—is this about those missing backpackers everyone's talking about?'

'It might be connected. Can you tell me about your investigation?'

Another pause, longer this time. 'There wasn't much of an investigation, if I'm being honest. Pressure came from above to wrap it up quickly. The tourism board was upset about a missing

German backpacker affecting visitor numbers.'

My grip tightened on the phone. 'What do you mean, pressure from above?'

'The Hewson family carries weight around here. Always have. Dave's uncle was on the council, his father owned half the cane farms. When Dave's lawyer showed up with character references and alibis...' Tate sighed heavily. 'Look, I knew something wasn't right. That girl wouldn't have left without her passport. But I was six months from retirement, and nobody wanted to hear theories.'

'What about other missing persons reports?' I asked. 'Were there any?'

'Unofficially? Yeah. But they were always written off as backpackers moving on. Happens all the time. Young people, no ties, here today and gone tomorrow.' His voice grew bitter. 'Easy to ignore if you want to.'

I thanked him and hung up, my mind racing. I pulled up the regional missing persons database again, this time searching more broadly. The results made my stomach turn.

Emma Rodriguez, 2016. Lisa Thompson, 2017. Manon Laurent, 2019. All young women, all backpackers, all last seen in the Mission Beach area. None officially connected to Dave Hewson, but the pattern was unmistakable.

When I was finished reading, I closed the door firmly and quickly called Todd.

'It's me,' I said when he answered, keeping my voice low. 'Trevor just gave me some interesting information. And I've done some digging. You need to hear this.'

'Go ahead.'

'He told me...' I glanced at the closed door, then continued quietly, filling Todd in on everything Trevor had told me. 'And his final warning was not to mention Dave's name at the station. Says Bradley has always had it in for him.'

There was a pause on the other end. 'That's interesting.'

'I thought so too. I'm going to head to the pub now to see if he's there.'

'Be careful, Bec. If Trevor's right about the station dynamics, you're walking into more than just a case.'

'I know, but I've got more to tell you. I'm not going to write it up yet. I have a feeling we can't trust Bradley.' I quickly filled him in on the Katja Mueller case and mentioned the other three names.

Todd let out a soft whistle. 'Plus, the fact that half the town thinks Dave Hewson is responsible for that German girl's disappearance ten years ago.'

'Katja Mueller,' I said, flipping through my notes, 'worked on Hewson's boat on and off for three months before vanishing. Local police investigated, but there was a note and evidence she boarded a bus to Brisbane.'

Todd was quiet for a moment. 'But no confirmation she ever arrived?'

'Transit cameras were down that week. Maintenance issue.' I stared out at the impossibly blue water glimpsed between the palm trees. 'Tate said the investigation was thorough, although he thought much of what was "found" was due to Hewson family interference. Apparently, they are quite influential around here. But again, that is hearsay and could be gossip. They found nothing.'

'And the rumours persist,' Todd mused.

'Small towns have long memories,' I replied. 'But I'm more interested in what Hewson might know about our current situation.'

'Take care, Bec. Call me after you talk to him.'

I glanced at my watch and looked at a local database. In that time, I found Hewson's current address, a few kilometres out of town in the cane fields. If he wasn't at the pub, I'd head out there.

I jumped when my phone buzzed, and I picked it up as soon as I saw it was Todd.

'Bec, have you looked at the local social media yet?' His voice was tense. 'The MB local community page.'

'Not yet, why?'

'It's going off. Someone's posted photos of cops at Dave Hewson's farm. Problem is, we don't have anyone there.'

I felt ice in my veins. 'I hope we don't. I don't know where Bradley is.'

'Someone's spreading false information. Those photos could be from anywhere, anytime. But someone is putting out that we're about to arrest him.'

I looked back at my computer screen, at the faces of the missing women. 'Todd, do you think I need to bring him in for questioning?'

'Based on what? Social media speculation?'

'Based on a pattern going back ten years. I've found at least four other missing backpackers, all connected to—'

'Bec.' Todd's voice was sharp. 'Whatever you're thinking, don't do anything alone. If Hewson is what people are saying...'

'I won't be alone with him. Do you want me to bring him in?'

I could hear the hesitation in Todd's voice. 'No, not yet,' he finally said. 'We have nothing apart from social media. And we know most of what is there isn't true. Text me if you find him, so I know where you are.'

The social media frenzy was spiralling out of control, but buried beneath the speculation and mob mentality was a disturbing truth. Dave Hewson had been connected to missing women for years, and now we had an unidentified body and three missing people. Four, if you counted the missing English woman, the subject of the ransom demand.

Whether the online vigilantes were right or wrong about the details, they were asking the right question: How many girls had to disappear before someone connected the dots?

I logged on to social media, and I could see what Trevor and Todd were referring to:

@KatjasMum_Germany: Meine Tochter *Katja would be 32 today. Still no real answers about what happened to her in your town. Now another girl is dead. When will this end? #JusticeForKatja #NeverForget*

@AirlieSailor: Saw Hewson's boat at Shute Harbour last month. He was arguing with some backpackers on the dock - young girl looked scared. Wish I'd said something. #Regret #SpeakUp

@MissionBeachLocal: Drive past his farm every day to work. Always boats and strangers coming and going at odd hours. What's he really running out there? #Suspicious #Investigation

@AnonTruth247: Another girl dead, and guess who's conveniently not available for comment? DH. Same pattern as Katja Mueller. Wake up people! #JusticeForKatja #MissionBeachMurders

@MissionBeachMum: My daughter worked at the marina 3 years ago. Dave Hewson asked her to crew on a 'short trip to Cairns.' Thank God her boyfriend talked her out of it. How many parents need to lose their daughters before someone acts? #Enough

@LocalFisherman_Pete: Been working these waters 30 years. That German girl Katja? Her backpack was found at the PUBLIC toilets, not on his boat like he claimed. Why didn't police follow up? Someone's protecting him. #CoverUp

@AnonTruth247: My sister Sally Walker is one of the missing from that yacht. She trusted the wrong people. Dave Hewson's name keeps coming up. Coincidence? I think not. Please share - someone must have seen something. #FindSally #BringThemHome

@ExCrew_Truth: I crewed for Hewson 2019. Guy's got a serious temper when things don't go his way. Asked me to stay

an extra week, got aggressive when I said no. Girls - NEVER sail alone with him. #Warning #StaySafe

There were dozens more posts and comments.

'Who posts about missing persons cases at three a.m.?' I muttered, adding more data points.

@@AnonTruth247 posted at 2:47 a.m. *@MissionBeachMum* posted at 2:52 a.m. *@LocalFisherman_Pete* at 2:55 a.m.

The pattern became clearer with each entry. Clusters of posts appearing within minutes of each other, always in the early morning hours when most people would be asleep. But more telling were the response times— these accounts were liking and sharing each other's content within seconds of posting. I made a note to chase up whether Sally Walker had a sister.

I picked up my phone and called Todd.

'I think I know how they're doing this,' I said when he answered. 'But I need to talk to someone who understands social media manipulation better than I do.'

'What are you thinking?'

'These aren't just fake accounts; this is professional-level astroturfing. The timing, the coordination, the way they're building false credibility by referencing each other... Someone with serious technical skills is behind this.'

'Any idea who?'

I stared at the screen, watching a new post appear from *@ConcernedLocal*; another perfectly timed addition to the narrative. 'Someone who knows enough about Dave's history to make it believable,' I said. 'Someone who knows the area, the people, the local dynamics.'

'That could be anyone in Mission Beach.'

'Not anyone,' I said slowly. 'Someone with a grudge against Dave specifically. And someone smart enough to stay completely anonymous while destroying his reputation.'

I leaned back in my chair, studying the screen. Something about the posting patterns bothered me beyond the obvious coordination. I opened a new spreadsheet and began tracking timestamps.

When I was done, I grabbed my keys and headed for the door. As I drove towards the hotel, my phone continued buzzing with notifications. The virtual lynch mob was growing by the hour, and somewhere in the middle of it all was a man who might be responsible for multiple murders—or an innocent person about to be destroyed by digital vigilantism. Either way, it was time for answers.

Chapter 13

Tuesday - late afternoon.

Salty Dog Hotel.

I slowed as I approached the Salty Dog Hotel. 'Late thirties, blond ponytail,' I murmured to myself, recalling Trevor's description.

The local pub was a weathered wooden structure that looked like it had survived more than a few cyclones. I parked in the gravel lot and killed the engine, taking a moment to steel myself for what could be a difficult conversation.

The pub's dim interior provided blessed relief from the late-afternoon sun outside. Several weathered locals nursed beers at the front table overlooking the footpath, their eyes tracking me with undisguised interest as I entered. A solitary figure sat at the far end—broad-shouldered, weather-beaten, and watching the door as if he'd been expecting me.

'That has to be him,' I thought, studying the man who fitted Trevor's description perfectly.

I crossed to the bar and ordered a lemon squash, then wandered towards the front table. As I approached, Dave looked up, his movements unnaturally still. His eyes—a startling, penetrating blue against his tanned skin—assessed me with immediate wariness. They reminded me of a cornered animal: alert, maybe dangerous.

'These seats free?' I asked.

He nodded. Long sun-bleached hair pulled back in a neat ponytail, skin tanned by years under the harsh Queensland sun.

He wore board shorts and a well-worn T-shirt with a faded sailing logo. Despite the rumours swirling about him, he looked unnervingly at ease, sipping his beer whilst watching the tourists pass by with an intensity that some might consider predatory.

'Mind if I join you?' I asked, maintaining a confident smile.

He gestured to the empty chair without speaking, his gaze never leaving my face. Up close, I could see the network of fine lines around his eyes from years of squinting against the glare off the water. His hands were calloused and powerful-looking, with a jagged rope burn scar across the back of his right hand.

'I'm Detective Whitfield,' I said, extending my hand across the invisible barrier between us. 'I'm investigating a couple of recent incidents here.'

Dave's hand engulfed mine in a firm grip, his expression carefully neutral. 'Dave Hewson. But I expect you already knew that, given all the chatter going around.' His voice was deep and raspy.

I settled into the chair across from him, studying his reaction carefully. Up close, Dave Hewson looked tired—not the exhaustion of physical labour, but the bone-deep weariness of someone under pressure. 'We're investigating some recent incidents in the area,' I began carefully. 'We heard you might have some local knowledge that could help us.' He took a deliberately slow sip of his beer, his eyes never leaving my face. The silence stretched between us for nearly a minute before he spoke.

'I was wondering when you'd show up.'

'Were you?'

'Course I was.' Dave set his glass down, the condensation leaving a ring on the wooden table. 'I was waiting for it.'

'For what?'

'The cops to turn up.'

'Tell me why,' I asked, noticing how his knuckles whitened slightly around the glass.

'Small town like this, something happens and everyone starts looking for someone to blame. And I've got a reputation.'

I kept my expression neutral. 'What kind of reputation?'

'The kind that follows a man around for ten years, no matter what the truth is.' His laugh was bitter. 'You know what's funny? I used to think if I just kept my head down, worked hard, minded my own business, it would all blow over eventually.'

'But it hasn't?'

Dave gestured towards the other patrons in the pub, several of whom were openly staring in our direction. 'Does it look like it has? Half this town thinks I'm some kind of monster, and the other half thinks I'm just bad luck. Either way, most people cross the street when they see me coming.'

The raw honesty in his voice caught me off guard. This wasn't the response of someone trying to deflect suspicion—it was the frustration of someone who'd been fighting rumours for years.

'I'm seeking three persons of interest who hired a yacht that was run aground.'

'Okay, but first let's clear the air about my reputation.' Something in Dave's eyes hardened to steel. 'Her name was Katja. She was from Munich, and she worked on my boat for about three months.' He paused, taking another measured sip. 'Then one day, she packed her stuff and left. Told me she was heading down to Sydney.' His gaze locked with mine. 'I never heard from her or saw her again.'

'That's not why I'm here,' I clarified, keeping my tone deliberately casual. 'What's your take on these recent incidents?'

I couldn't quite read Dave's expression—curiosity or suspicion? Both, perhaps.

'Where were you last week?' I asked.

Dave's shoulders tensed almost imperceptibly. 'At home. I got back here about ten days ago.'

'Where from?'

'I came back from the south. Noosa and Airlie Beach. I had a couple of charters coming up, here on the coast.' His carefully constructed composure seemed to waver slightly.

'Alone? Crew? Witnesses?'

'Yes, to alone and no crew from Airlie north. I dropped my last crew off at Airlie Beach. They crewed with me from Noosa, and then they were meeting up with their friends who did a road trip.'

'Names? Descriptions?' I asked, pen poised over my notepad.

I sat back and observed him, noting every subtle shift of expression. There was something guarded behind those piercing blue eyes; I wondered what he was holding back.

'Two women. I've got their details on my boat. I didn't take much notice of their last names once they were on board.'

My interest quickened.

'What about since you got back? Have you been out on the water again?'

'No, not since I got back from Airlie Beach. I've been working on the interior of my boat and helping my father on the farm.'

'Could I have his name and phone number, please?' I asked.

He nodded, and I noted it down.

'Gerry from *Hookers Fishing* can tell you I haven't had *Seabreeze* out since I got back, if you need more. And I've been here in this seat every afternoon for the past week.'

'Do you often work with backpackers?'

'Only when I'm doing the long haul up the coast. I had *Seabreeze* out of the water at Noosa to have her scrubbed. The rest of the time, I act as a sail guide with a charter company out of Cardwell.'

'So, tell me about the *Lady Windward*,' I said.

Dave shifted in his chair, running a hand over his ponytail, before he spoke slowly. My interest deepened. It was as though he was thinking carefully about what he was saying. 'I was supposed to meet the vessel at the marina this morning. They didn't show. I waited around for a couple of hours, did a bit of work on my boat, and talked to Graham. He'd been trying to call me to tell me she was scuttled on the beach at Ninney Point, and I had my phone off over the weekend.' He paused, his face creasing with concern. 'I drove up there and walked through the rainforest to have a look, and saw some bloke towing her out.'

'What are your thoughts on what happened?' I asked.

'No idea,' he said, shaking his head.

'Do you know anything about the charterers?' I asked, leaning forward slightly.

Dave glanced away briefly, then back at me. 'No. Only that I was meeting them.'

'Do you know who they were?'

He shook his head. 'Standard handover, you know?'

I flipped open my notebook and said the names while watching Dave's reaction carefully. 'Paulo Ramirez, Victoria

Chandler, and Sally Walker.'

His eyes widened, and he sat back in his chair. 'No way.'

'Do you know them, Dave?' I asked, my voice sharp with interest.

'I met them in Noosa.' Dave's voice had changed, become more cautious. 'I told you before about the two girls who crewed for me. They were in that group. Bloody hell. I can't believe it.'

'Tell me about them,' I said.

Dave's expression softened slightly. 'Victoria was confident, but lazy.' He paused, seeming to choose his words carefully. 'Amanda was different. Sweet, really quiet, but she worked hard, and cooked too. Never complained, always willing to learn.' I noticed the way his voice changed when he talked about Amanda, a protective warmth that hadn't been there before. 'She was the one who really got the sailing,' he continued. 'Quick learner, good instincts on the water. Victoria was just along for the ride, I think. Paulo is a Brazilian guy, charming enough, but I got the feeling he was using his looks to get by.'

'You seem fond of Amanda,' I observed.

'She's a good kid...' His expression tightened. 'Look, when you work on boats with people, you get to know them.'

'Anything else you can tell me about them?' I asked.

'Not really.' Dave's brow furrowed. 'They didn't seem to be close friends, and I couldn't figure out why Victora even came with us.'

The silence stretched between us.

But according to the charter documents, the woman calling herself Victoria Chandler had been on the boat, not Amanda. 'Dave,' I said carefully, 'why do you think she would have gone on another charter?'

'No idea. Barely spoke to her the whole trip.'

'Did you hear about the body that *Hookers* found?'

He pulled a face, half grimace, half resignation. 'Yes. I was on my boat at the marina when Gerry came in and all the cops arrived. And of course, if you don't know enough, you can always go to social media.' His tone turned bitter. 'Apparently, I'm responsible for everything that's ever gone wrong in this town.'

'We don't have an ID yet,' I said, watching every micro-expression as he turned back to me. 'That's what we're trying to determine.'

Dave ran both hands through his hair, disturbing his neat ponytail. 'Christ.' He started to say something else, his mouth opening, then stopped abruptly and looked away. When he turned back, there was something different in his expression—more guarded. 'This is fucked up. Really fucked up.'

I noticed the hesitation, the way he'd caught himself mid-thought. There was something he wasn't telling me.

'Are you aware of the social media comments about you?' I asked.

'I never look at that shit,' he said immediately, his voice rough with emotion. 'Social media is poison. People hiding behind screens, spreading lies...' He trailed off, then looked at me with haunted eyes. 'What are they saying?'

I deflected. 'What about the other two?'

'I didn't really get to know them. Sally was pressed to Paulo's side most of the time at Noosa, and I didn't talk to her much. He was very possessive. She was way too classy for him,' Dave said, his tone turning harder. 'He's a dickhead.'

'Why do you say that?' I leaned forward.

Dave's expression darkened. 'Had a run-in with him at the bar one night in Noosa. Guy was all over some other girl while Sally was right there. When I called him out on it, he got aggressive. Started mouthing off, chest-puffing, you know the type.' He shook his head in disgust. 'Sally was embarrassed, trying to calm him down. Amanda was mortified. The whole thing was ugly.'

'What happened?' I asked.

'Paulo got in my face, started pushing. Had to physically remove him from the situation before it got worse. Sally was crying, Amanda was upset... it was a mess.' Dave ran his hand through his hair. 'Felt sorry for Sally, to be honest. Nice enough girl. But she was completely blind to what he was really like.'

'How did it end?'

'Bar staff kicked him out. Sally followed, of course. Amanda stayed back, apologised for his behaviour. That's when I got my first impression of her. We talked a lot that night. Like I said, I liked her.' His voice carried genuine fondness when he spoke about Amanda. 'I told her she deserved better company than that.'

'And after that incident?' I pressed.

'Saw them around town for a few more days. Paulo avoided me, which was fine by me. But Amanda would wave when she saw me. Sally seemed nervous, probably worried about more drama. Can't say I blamed her. Then we hooked up at the bar another night, and I mentioned I was looking for a crew, and Victoria and Amanda decided to sail to Airlie Beach with me.'

We talked for another half hour or so, the conversation flowing more easily. Dave told me about his life on the water, the changes he'd seen at Pandanus Point over the decades, the increasing tourism, the cyclones that had reshaped the coast. He was knowledgeable, articulate, and didn't seem to hold back when we not talking about the investigation.

As I was preparing to leave, I decided on one final question.

'The body we found... female, early twenties, multiple lacerations. Any thoughts?'

The question hung in the air between us. Dave went completely still, his breathing barely perceptible as he considered his response.

'The ocean takes things,' he said finally, his voice low and ominous. 'Sometimes it gives them back, sometimes it doesn't. But it's rarely the only culprit.' He fixed me with those unsettling blue eyes. 'If you're looking for answers, don't get distracted by old stories. Look at what's happening now.'

A chill ran down my spine despite the oppressive heat.

'Anyone specific come to mind?' I asked, keeping my tone light.

Dave's eyes flickered, assessing, considering. Then he shook his head slowly. 'Not my place to point fingers. I've been on the receiving end of that enough to know better.' He stood up abruptly, his chair scraping against the floor. 'Good luck with your investigation. Just try to remember there's a person behind every accusation.'

As I watched him walk away, his movements controlled despite the two empty beer glasses on the table, I found myself re-evaluating everything I thought I knew about this case.

Dave seemed genuine, thoughtful. Not at all the monster whispered about in town. My gut was usually right about these things, and something about Dave appeared authentic. But as I left the pub, stepping into the fading light, I couldn't shake the feeling that Dave Hewson knew more than he was letting on. Not necessarily about Katja's disappearance—I was inclined to believe his version of events there—but about what was happening in Mission Beach now. Something in the way he'd said, "don't get distracted by old stories," made me think he knew more.

What did he know that made those blue eyes look so haunted?

Chapter 14

Wednesday - 8 a.m.

Pandanus Point Police Station.

I arrived early at the station on Wednesday morning, wanting to tackle the paperwork before heading to Cairns for the autopsy. The building was quiet, with only Trevor at the front desk and the familiar hum of fluorescent lights overhead.

I settled into my office with a cup of coffee and pulled up the case files on my computer. The faces of the missing women stared back at me from the screen: Katja Mueller from 2015 and the more recent disappearances I'd uncovered yesterday. The pattern was becoming harder to ignore.

My phone buzzed with a text from Todd: **Autopsy confirmed for 2 pm. See you there.**

I typed back: **On my way up after lunch. Any news on the pharmaceutical leads?**

Nothing concrete yet. Dr Wentworth wants to discuss something with us, though. Wouldn't say what over the phone.

That sent a chill through me. Pathologists, in my experience, didn't like mysteries; if the pathologist was being vague, it meant she'd found something significant.

Back in my office, I opened my laptop and navigated to the Mission Beach community page again. The screen filled with posts about Dave Hewson, dozens of comments speculating about his involvement in everything from the current case to Katja Mueller's disappearance years ago.

But now, knowing what Todd had discovered, I looked at the posts with fresh eyes. I clicked on the profile of *@AnonTruth247*, one of the most vocal accusers. Account created three days ago. Profile picture: generic sunset stock photo. Previous posts: none before the current case began. *@TruthSeeker99* was similar—created five days ago, anonymous avatar, posting history that started exactly when our investigation became public knowledge. I grabbed a notepad and began tracking the patterns. *@ConcernedLocal* had been more active, but when I scrolled back through months of posts, they'd only started posting about Dave Hewson in the past week.

Before that: complaints about council rates and restaurant reviews. 'This is coordinated,' I muttered, screenshot after screenshot building a picture of deliberate manipulation. The most damning posts—the ones citing specific names and dates for the supposed missing women—all came from accounts created within the past week. Someone hadn't just spread rumours; they'd orchestrated an entire social media campaign designed to destroy Dave Hewson's reputation. But who had that level of technical knowledge and access to create so many believable fake accounts? And more importantly—why target Dave specifically?

I grabbed my keys and headed for the door. Time to find some answers before the autopsy revealed even more questions.

Ninety minutes later, my stomach still churned as I parked at the hospital. The Cairns Base Hospital morgue was several degrees colder than the already air-conditioned corridor outside. I suppressed a shiver as I entered, not entirely from the temperature. The familiar scent of disinfectant couldn't fully mask the underlying odour of death. Todd was waiting in the foyer, his usual casual demeanour replaced by a professional stiffness.

'Detective Inspector Davenport,' Dr Lyn Wentworth nodded as we approached. The forensic pathologist was already gowned up, her dark hair tucked neatly under a surgical cap. 'Detective Whitfield. Right on time.'

Todd had worked with Dr Wentworth before, and from his accounts, she was thorough, precise, and didn't waste words. The perfect person to be handling what remained of our victim after days in tropical waters.

'The body was transported from Mission Beach yesterday,' Wentworth said, leading us towards the examination table. 'We prioritised the autopsy given the circumstances.'

A sheet-covered form lay on the stainless-steel table. Even under the bright fluorescent lights, there was something profoundly sad about it. A person reduced to evidence.

'Fair warning,' Wentworth said, pausing before removing the sheet. 'Immersion in seawater for several days has accelerated decomposition. The tropical conditions didn't help.'

I nodded, steeling myself. 'Understood.'

Todd shifted his weight beside me but said nothing. I wondered how many autopsies he'd attended in his career.

Wentworth pulled back the sheet, revealing what had once been a young woman with dark hair. The skin had a bloated, marbled appearance typical of bodies recovered from water. Some areas showed signs of marine life activity. I heard Todd inhale sharply, but to his credit, he didn't look away.

'Female, Caucasian, early to mid-twenties based on dental development and bone structure,' Wentworth began, her voice taking on the detached, clinical tone of a recording. 'Height approximately 165 centimetres. Weight at recovery was sixty-eight kilograms, though that's affected by post-mortem changes.'

I forced myself to look at the victim's face. Features were distorted by decomposition, making visual identification impossible.

'Cause of death?' I asked.

Wentworth pointed to the victim's head. 'There's significant blunt force trauma to the occipital region—back of the head. Depressed skull fracture with radiating fracture lines from the point of impact.' She demonstrated the location on her own head. 'Consistent with being struck by a heavy, blunt object with considerable force.'

'Fatal?' Todd asked, finding his voice.

'Potentially life-threatening, but not the cause of death.' Wentworth moved to the torso. 'This is what killed her.' She indicated a wound on the upper abdomen. 'Single penetrating wound, approximately fifteen centimetres deep, angled upward. The blade tracked through the diaphragm and perforated the left ventricle of the heart. Death would have been rapid due to cardiac tamponade and exsanguination.'

She straightened up. 'Cause of death: penetrating cardiac injury due to stab wound to the chest. The head trauma is a significant contributing injury, but the stab wound was fatal.'

'So, she was hit and then stabbed?' I asked.

'Based on wound healing indicators, yes. The head trauma came first, perhaps minutes before the stabbing. The victim was likely already unconscious or severely disoriented when stabbed.'

'Defensive wounds?' I asked.

'Minimal. Some bruising on the forearms, but nothing suggesting a prolonged struggle. The head injury likely came as a surprise. Or it could have been a fall.'

'But that seems unlikely, followed closely by the knife injury?' I noted that Todd didn't refer to it as a stabbing.

'Time of death?' I asked.

'Given the water immersion and our climate, it's difficult to be precise. We are estimating thirty-six hours of immersion before retrieval, so the time of death would have been some time last Saturday.

'Any identifying features?' Todd asked. 'Scars, tattoos, birthmarks?'

Wentworth nodded and gently turned the body to reveal the lower back. 'Small butterfly tattoo at the base of the spine. Professional work, not recent—at least a year old based on ink settlement.'

I leaned closer. The tattoo was simple but elegant—a purple and blue butterfly no larger than a fifty-cent piece.

'Anything else?' I asked.

'A second tattoo on the right ankle—a sea wave with a small shell at the base. Very recent. Victim was well-nourished, healthy. No signs of chronic disease or recent significant illness.' Wentworth moved to a tray of personal effects. 'No jewellery recovered with the body, but there was this.'

She held up a small evidence bag containing what appeared to be a fragment of a thin gold chain.

'Broken necklace?' Todd suggested.

'Likely. Found caught in her hair. The rest may have come off in the water.'

'Dental records?' I asked.

'Being processed. We've taken full prints as well, though the condition isn't ideal.'

I nodded, making more notes. 'And the DNA sample from the catamaran?'

'Still waiting on the comparison, but I did a preliminary blood type match. The victim is O negative, same as the blood found on the boat.'

That connected our victim to the *Lady Windward* scene. Progress, finally.

'We'll need facial reconstruction for identification purposes,' I said.

'Already in progress,' Wentworth replied. 'Should have something usable by tomorrow.'

As she covered the body again, I felt the familiar mix of determination and sadness that came with these cases. This young woman had been somebody's daughter, maybe somebody's sister or girlfriend. She'd had a life, plans, dreams—all ended violently on what should have been an idyllic sailing trip.

'I'll have the full report sent to you this afternoon,' Wentworth said, stripping off her gloves. 'But my preliminary finding on cause of death is the stab wound to the heart, following incapacitation from the head trauma.'

'Murder, then,' Todd said. 'No question.'

'No question,' Wentworth confirmed. 'And given the precise placement of the stab wound, I'd say your perpetrator either got lucky or knew exactly what they were doing.'

I thanked the doctor and headed for the door, Todd following close behind. In the corridor, he let out a long breath.

'You okay?' I asked him.

He nodded. 'Yeah. Just... puts things in perspective, doesn't it?'

'That's why we do this job,' I replied. 'So someone speaks

for her.'

'Come on. Let's get down there and get to work. I'll meet you at the station.' Todd walked to his SUV, his head bowed.

As I reached the squad car, my phone buzzed with an incoming message. It was from Trevor. **Sarge called from home. He's taking sick leave. Said he got a bad prawn last night.**

I shook my head.

As I stood in the Queensland sunshine, I couldn't shake the image of that small purple butterfly, a delicate mark of individuality on a body otherwise robbed of dignity by death and decomposition. Someone, or maybe more than one person, knew who she was.

And they knew what had happened on that catamaran.

Chapter 15

Wednesday - 5.00 p.m.

Pandanus Point Station.

The drive back from Cairns gave me too much time to think. The autopsy results kept cycling through my mind—our victim had been in the water for approximately three days, the cause of death was stabbing, with a contributing factor of blunt force trauma. There were also defensive wounds on her hands and bruising on her arms where she had been held down. Dr. Wentworth had been thorough; we had a cause of death confirming that this was a homicide, but still no ID.

I detoured home, took a quick shower and washed my hair to get rid of the lingering smell from the autopsy suite at the hospital. When I arrived at the station, all was quiet except for Trevor at the front desk. I found Todd already in the incident room, standing before our makeshift evidence board with his hands on his hips.

'Any luck with those calls?' I asked, joining him.

'Some. Just waiting for the DNA results from the UK.' He turned to me, his expression grim. 'I also called the Queensland Missing Persons Unit. Asked them to run a comprehensive search for missing backpackers in the region over the past ten years.'

'And?'

'That's the interesting part. According to their database, there have been no unresolved missing persons cases involving backpackers in the Mission Beach area since Katja Mueller in 2015. And we know her case has been resolved.'

'Resolved? What happened?'

'I don't know the file is sealed, and it's not listed as a cold case.'

'Strange.'

'I'll be following it up.' He nodded and pulled out his notebook. 'Emma Rodriguez, Lisa Thompson, Manon Laurent—the names you found yesterday? They're all accounted for. Emma Rodriguez returned to Spain in 2017. Lisa Thompson moved to Perth and is working as a nurse. Manon Laurent is back in France, married with a baby.'

I felt my stomach drop. 'So, the social media claims about multiple missing women—'

'Are a complete fabrication.' Todd moved to the whiteboard and began erasing names. 'Someone has been very deliberately spreading false information to make Dave Hewson look like a serial killer.'

'But why?' I sank into a chair, my mind racing. 'Who benefits from destroying Dave's reputation?'

'That's what we need to figure out.' Todd grabbed a marker and started making a new timeline. 'Let's go back to what we actually know. Our victim was found on Monday morning. She'd been in the water approximately thirty-six hours, which puts her death some time Saturday, as Dr Wentworth said.'

'The *Lady Windward* only left Cardwell on Friday, so they must have sailed directly to the area around Dunk Island. That aligns with what Patterson said about not having GPS tracking and not reporting in.'

'So, we need to find out what happened between Cardwell and Dunk Island?'

I pulled out the case files, spreading them across the table.

'Todd, what if our victim wasn't killed for personal reasons? What if she stumbled onto something bigger?'

'Like what?'

'Drug running. People trafficking. The *Lady Windward* could have been used for smuggling, and our victim discovered it.' I traced the boat's supposed route on the map. 'Think about it—a chartered yacht, travelling up the coast, stopping at remote locations. It's the perfect cover for illegal activities.'

Todd's phone rang, interrupting my thoughts. He answered quickly. 'Davenport... Yes, I'll hold.'

He covered the phone and mouthed, 'CIB in Brisbane.'

I watched his face change as he listened to whoever was on the other end.

'Are you certain? Yes, thank you. We appreciate your help.' He hung up and looked at me with a mixture of relief and confusion. 'The Katja Mueller case was solved and the file closed because they wanted to keep the contents away from certain eyes.'

'No mention of who?'

'Not at this point. They're going to talk to me later.'

I leaned back in my chair. 'Dave was telling the truth about her leaving for Sydney?'

'Apparently.'

'Then why was the case opened in the first place?'

Todd's expression darkened. 'That's what I want to know. I'm going to speak with them later and find out who reported her missing and why the investigation was closed so quickly.' He paused, then added, 'And why the file is marked confidential, which is unusual for a simple missing persons case.'

I stood and began pacing. 'This doesn't make sense. Someone has gone to enormous trouble to paint Dave Hewson as a predator. The fake social media accounts, the false information about missing women, even potentially planting evidence to connect him to our current case.'

'But who? And why target Dave specifically?'

Before I could answer, Trevor knocked on the doorframe.

'Can I get you guys a coffee? I'm just going into town for five.'

'Thanks, Trevor. Two flat whites would be great,' I said. 'Any word from Sergeant Bradley?'

'No, ma'am. Still haven't heard from him.' He turned to leave and then hesitated.

'Ma'am?'

'Yes, Trevor?'

His forehead wrinkled in a slight frown. 'I've been thinking about what you asked yesterday, you know, about who might have it in for Dave Hewson.'

'And?'

'Well, there was a business development proposal a couple of years back. Dave opposed the new marina expansion pretty vocally. Said it would destroy the character of the place, bring in too many tourists.'

'Who was pushing for the expansion?'

'A consortium of local business owners. They stood to make a lot of money from increased tourism.' Trevor shifted uncomfortably. 'Dave's opposition helped kill the proposal. Cost some locals some serious cash.'

That familiar tingle of discovering new information hit my fingertips. 'Anyone specific come to mind?'

'Rodney Neville from one of the fishing charter companies was pretty pissed off. Said Dave was holding back progress out of selfishness. But...' Trevor hesitated.

'But what?'

'Sergeant Bradley was pretty involved in supporting the development, too. Had some investment tied up in it, from what I heard.'

The pieces clicked into place. Bradley's convenient absences from the investigation.

'Trevor,' I said carefully, 'what kind of computer skills does Sergeant Bradley have?'

'He's pretty tech-savvy. Runs the station's social media accounts, does all our digital evidence processing.' Trevor's eyes widened as he realised what I was implying. 'You don't think...'

'I think we need to be very careful about what information we share around the station,' I said quietly.

After Trevor left, Todd and I stood looking at our evidence board. Half the information we'd started with had been proven false.

'We're being played,' I said finally. 'Someone wants us focused on Dave Hewson.'

'And for what reason? To set him up as a suspect to draw attention from them? Or is it simply vexatious?'

'It's pointing to vexatious for me at the moment.'

'Keep an open mind, Bec.' Todd circled our victim's photo on the board. 'The question is: who is she, and why did she have to die? We need a motivation for the killer. When we have a positive ID, we'll be one step closer. We're chasing up records for Sally Walker, but the other one being an unknown perp, makes it impossible unless we hit a DNA match somewhere. It won't be long now, hopefully.'

The day had been a whirlwind of revelations that left both

of us feeling unmoored. Katja was alive and well in Germany. Dave Hewson looked more like a victim of rumour than a perpetrator. And now we were back to square one with no clear suspects—except for the growing certainty that someone was orchestrating an elaborate deception.

'You shouldn't drive back to Cairns after a day like this,' I said as we stood in the station car park, the setting sun painting the sky in shades of orange and pink. 'Come back to mine. I can cook us a decent meal, and we can debrief properly. You can crash in the spare room.'

Todd hesitated, keys in hand. 'You sure? I don't want to impose.'

'I'm sure. We need to go through everything we know, and frankly, I could use the company. This case is getting under my skin.'

As we walked back through the empty station to collect our things, Todd glanced at me. 'Happy to keep working while we eat?'

I nodded. 'Yes, it's hard to let go when we're going in circles. We need to figure out who's been pulling our strings, and why they wanted Dave Hewson destroyed so badly that they were willing to frame him for murder.'

'What's for dinner?' Todd smiled—the first genuine smile I'd seen from him all day.

'I'll have to stop at the Minimart on the way. I haven't bought many groceries yet. It's been a huge couple of days. I feel like I've been here for a month.'

The Minimart was one of those small coastal stores that somehow managed to stock everything you needed and nothing you wanted. I grabbed essentials—bread, milk, eggs, salad ingredients. I was standing at the meat cabinet when Todd reached past me and opened the door, picking up two scotch fillet steaks.

'My contribution,' he said when I raised an eyebrow at his additions. 'I'll grab a bottle of wine at the bottle shop too.'

'Thanks, I should warn you, I haven't even looked at the barbeque yet. Hopefully, it has gas.'

'That's the least of our worries,' Todd said.

The bottle shop bags clinked softly as we walked back to our cars.

'Follow me,' I said. 'It's only a couple of streets from here.' He trailed behind my sedan as I navigated the tree-lined streets to the cute beachfront cottage I'd been calling home for only a couple of days.

I unlocked the door and dropped the groceries on the kitchen counter. 'Make yourself comfortable. There's beer in the fridge if you'd prefer.'

'Thanks, I'll stick with a glass of red. It might clear my mind a bit.'

'Or put you to sleep,' I joked.

'Probably. Do you want red or white?' he asked, holding up both bottles of wine.

'Red, please.'

Todd stepped outside to check the barbeque and walked back in, chuckling. 'It's an electric barbeque.'

'I've got a lot to learn about this place,' I replied. 'Would you believe I haven't even stepped on the sand yet?'

'We'll remedy that in the morning. An early walk on the beach might clear our heads before we go back to the station.'

While I scrubbed potatoes and put them in the oven and made a quick salad, Todd started the steaks. The domesticity of it felt strange after the intensity of the day.

As I chopped the tomatoes, he came back into the kitchen, and I seized the moment.

'Todd? I need to run something by you about Dave Hewson. When I interviewed him yesterday, I got a strong impression he was holding something back about Amanda specifically. He started to say something, then caught himself. My gut tells me he's protecting her somehow.'

Todd looked at me with interest. 'What's your instinct telling you about Hewson overall?'

'That he's not our killer. That all this social media hysteria is designed to keep us from looking at the real perpetrator. The way he talked about Amanda—there was genuine fondness there, almost protective.'

He was quiet for a moment, considering. 'I think Dave's being harassed. His story checks out, his alibi seems solid, and from what you've told me about his reaction when you mentioned the names... that wasn't faked. I've put out a BOLO for Paulo's Troop Carrier, but no calls yet from highway patrols.'

'So, if Dave's not our perpetrator, who is? We're back to Paulo, Sally, and identifying our victim. Where is Amanda now? Wouldn't she be looking for her friends?'

'We'll visit Dave unannounced tomorrow and ask him directly. Could be victims, could be perpetrators, could be both.' He rubbed his temples.

We ate dinner on the verandah, the sound of waves providing a peaceful backdrop that contrasted sharply with the urgency of our investigation. The wine was helping us both unwind, and I found myself studying Todd's profile in the soft light from the house as he gazed out at the water.

'This is nice,' he said quietly, breaking the comfortable silence. 'When's the last time you just sat and listened to the ocean?'

I smiled. 'Honestly? I can't remember. I've been so focused on getting settled here, and then I went headfirst into this case within an hour of arriving...' I took another sip of wine. 'What about you? Can you ever just switch off from work?'

'Not often enough.' He turned to look at me, his expression softer than I'd seen it. 'We get so caught up in what we do, sometimes we forget there's still a world out there.'

'So,' I said eventually, settling back in my chair, reluctant to break the spell but knowing we couldn't avoid it forever. 'Where do we even start tomorrow?'

Todd loosened his tie. 'We start over. The post-mortem gave us cause of death and the wave tattoo for identification. The charter company gave us names. Now we match the DNA and figure out which of our missing women is on that slab. It's time we talked to the families back in the UK, but I'm reluctant to do it until we have a positive ID.'

Todd lifted the wine bottle—a good red from the Barossa Valley—and raised his eyebrows. 'Just another half a glass, please.'

As we settled back with our glasses, the conversation flowed more easily.

'You know what's frustrating?' I said, curling my legs under me in the wicker chair. 'We had a theory about Dave. It was wrong, but at least it was something. Now we're starting fresh with a body, missing people, and no clear direction.'

Todd nodded, taking a generous sip of wine. 'Welcome to police work. Two steps forward, three steps back.'

We'd nearly finished the bottle, and I could feel the day's tension finally starting to ease from my shoulders. Todd had shed his professional demeanour along with his jacket, and for the first time since I'd met him, he looked almost relaxed in the soft light from the kitchen.

'Can I ask you something?' I said, emboldened by the wine and the intimacy of the moment.

'Shoot.'

'Do you ever think about leaving? The job, I mean. Starting over somewhere new?'

He was quiet for a long moment, swirling the wine in his glass. 'Every day,' he said finally. 'But then I think about Megan, and how she'd tell me I was being an idiot. She always said running away doesn't solve anything.'

'Tell me about her.'

His face transformed, grief and love mixing in equal measure. 'She was... God, Bec, she was everything I'm not. Warm, spontaneous, messy in the best possible way. She left coffee cups everywhere, sang off-key in the shower, cried at dog videos on the internet.' His voice cracked slightly. 'She made me feel like I was more than just a job.'

'What happened?'

'Breast cancer. Stage four by the time they caught it.' He drained his glass. 'She was only thirty-two. We were trying for kids, had all these plans... and then suddenly we were talking about chemo schedules and prognosis instead of baby names.'

I set down my wine and shifted closer to him. 'Todd—'

'The worst part is how everyone expects you to move on. "She wouldn't want you to be alone forever," they say. "You need to start living again." As if grief has an expiration date.' He looked at me with eyes that held three years of accumulated pain. 'I watched her fight for eighteen months, Bec. Watched her body betray her bit by bit, and I couldn't do anything. All those plans we had—the house we were going to buy, the children we wanted—just... gone.'

The raw honesty in his voice undid something inside me. Without thinking, I reached out and took his hand. His fingers were cold, and I could feel them trembling slightly.

'I'm terrified,' he whispered. 'Not of being alone—I've gotten used to that. But of wanting someone again. Of caring enough that losing them would break me all over again.'

The moment stretched between us, loaded with everything we hadn't said, everything we'd been carefully not acknowledging since the day I'd arrived in Bowen River and worked closely with Todd.

'Todd,' I said quietly, his name a question and an answer all at once. 'It's okay.'

He stood up slowly and moved towards me. I rose to meet him, and suddenly we were inches apart, close enough that I could smell his cologne mixed with the faint scent of wine on his breath.

I reached up and touched his face, feeling the slight stubble along his jaw. 'I know,' I whispered. 'I'm scared too.'

He leaned into my touch, his eyes closing for a moment. When he opened them again, I saw the exact moment he stopped fighting whatever had been building between us.

Without another word, he took my hand and led me inside, the case forgotten, the outside world forgotten, everything forgotten except the simple human need to not be alone anymore.

Later, as we lay together in the darkness, the sound of waves providing a gentle rhythm outside the window, I found myself thinking that sometimes the most important breakthroughs happened when you stopped looking for them.

'Early start tomorrow?' Todd asked softly, his arm tightening around me.

'Early start,' I agreed. 'But first, that walk on the beach. You're right—we need clear heads for this.'

PART 2- the Backpackers

Chapter 16

Friday, August 1 - 9.00 p.m.

Salt Bar - Noosa Heads.

The music at Salt Bar opposite Noosa Beach throbbed through the floorboards as Amanda Priestley nursed her beer, watching her best friend Sally twirl across the dance floor in Paulo's arms. The Brazilian had one hand pressed possessively against Sally's lower back, his smile gleaming with calculated charm under the pulsing lights as he whispered something in her ear that made her throw her head back in laughter.

'They're quite the pair, aren't they?'

Amanda turned to her new companion at the small high-top table, unable to keep the edge from her voice. She pulled a face. 'If you like that sort of guy.'

Victoria Chandler nodded, her eyes tracking the couple with amused interest. Victoria's sensible demeanour was refreshing after four weeks of Sally's constant, breathless chatter about Paulo. Something about her quietness appealed to Amanda.

'How long have you been travelling, Victoria?' she asked, trying to pull her attention away from her friend's increasingly intimate display.

'Not long,' Victoria replied, running her hand over her hair. 'I did Brisbane. My dad wanted me to visit some elderly cousins of his there, but I managed to avoid that. What about you?'

'We've been here eleven months. Sally and I planned this trip for years. Her parents paid for her gap year, and I saved for two years. We both got a working visa because she wanted to work with me and experience "real life", as she calls it. We've done all sorts of jobs while we've been here. And to Sal's credit, she's put everything into it.' Amanda took another sip of her beer, the bitter taste matching her mood.

'Born with a silver spoon?' Victoria's voice had a drawling twang.

'Yep. We met at our local primary school and stayed friends when she went off to boarding school. My mum and dad can't understand how we can be friends. Her family live in this grand country house that goes back centuries, and they mix with all the nobs.'

'And you?' Victoria chuckled.

'Yep, just me from our little village of Northleach, where I shared a bedroom with my sister until she got married.' Amanda grinned. 'The first time Sally came to our place, my mum acted as though Princess Kate was coming to visit.'

'Sounds like your trip's been fun. I should have found a pal to travel with too. It's been a bit lonely by myself.'

'It was great fun to start with. It was supposed to be our grand adventure together, but then we met Paulo in Sydney last month, and well...' She gestured towards the dance floor, where Sally was now pressed against Paulo, her hands running through his thick, dark hair as though they were alone.

Victoria followed her gaze, her expression unreadable. 'That's got to be awkward.'

'You have no idea.' Amanda rolled her eyes dramatically. 'We're sharing this tiny unit at the backpackers' hostel, and the walls might as well be made of tissue paper. Some nights it's like being forced to listen to a wildlife documentary. Have you heard that Bloodhound Gang song?'

'I know the one you mean.' Victoria smiled, but her eyes never left the dancing couple. 'The one that mentions the Discovery Channel.'

'That's the one. The funny thing is,' Amanda continued, warming to her sympathetic audience, 'Sally's parents would be absolutely shocked if they knew. Their perfect daughter moaning like—' She caught herself and blushed. 'Sorry, too much information.'

'No, I get it,' Victoria said, finally turning her full attention to Amanda. 'Third-wheeling isn't exactly what you planned for your trip.'

Amanda sighed; the sound half-lost in the thumping bass surrounding them. 'I love Sally dearly, but I'm counting the days until she wakes up to what he's really like. His type usually moves on pretty quickly. We've met a few like him on our travels.'

'Where are you headed next?' Victoria asked, her eyes drifting back to the dance floor with that same focused intensity.

'Probably up to the Whitsunday Islands. It's not long until we fly home. I'm off to study accountancy, and Sally is going into their family business.'

Victoria's gaze lingered on Paulo as he spun Sally in a circle, his movements fluid.

'What about you?' Amanda pressed. 'Any plans?'

'I was hoping to see the Whitsundays too,' Victoria said, finally turning back to Amanda. 'But I'm running low on cash. I'll probably have to go home early.'

'Where's home?'

'Broken Hill.' Victoria pulled a face. 'Not exactly the global adventure I'd hoped for, but I don't want to go home yet.'

Amanda laughed. 'I can relate to that. Would you believe I'm the first person in my family to own a passport? You know if you want to stay in Queensland longer, you could get a job to get some cash together. There's a lot of work in cafés and on farms. They're desperate for workers here. We never had any problems finding something when our funds ran low.'

Their easy conversation continued as the music thumped around them, swapping travel stories and hometown complaints. Amanda enjoyed Victoria's company—her dry wit and cutting observations were a welcome change from love-struck Sally. 'So, what's his story?' Victoria asked, nodding towards Paulo.

'Paulo? He's a surf instructor from Rio. Claims his family owns half the beachfront there, but I have my doubts. Speaks five languages, if you believe him. Great with a guitar. Absolute charmer.' Amanda shrugged. 'Sally's completely smitten, but I think he's a con artist. He knows she comes from money.'

'I can see why she's smitten,' Victoria murmured, her eyes tracking Paulo's movements. 'Good body.'

'Oh, God. Don't you fall for him too!'

'No chance of that.' As Victoria turned back to Amanda, the song changed to something slower, more intimate, and Amanda groaned as Paulo pulled Sally close, his hands sliding possessively down to her hips. Her best friend looked happier than she'd ever seen her, face flushed and eyes bright. She shook her head. 'Sally is going to come down to earth big-time when he drops her. I tried to warn her, but—'

'But you can't tell someone in *lurve*,' Victoria said with even more elongated Aussie drawl. 'You want me to help?'

'Help?' Amanda frowned.

'Get his interest away from your friend?'

'I wish.'

Victoria smiled. 'I'm happy to give it a go.'

'Go for it.' Amanda slid off the stool. 'I'll grab another round. Same for you?'

Victoria nodded. 'Thanks. I'll settle up with you later.'

As Amanda made her way to the bar, she glanced back. Sally was heading towards the restrooms, and Paulo was making his way back to their table, straight towards Victoria. By the time Amanda returned with the drinks, Paulo had taken the seat next to the newcomer, and the charm was being rolled out.

Victoria was a striking woman—short black hair cut in a feathery pixie cut that emphasised her sharp cheekbones and intense dark eyes. She was slim and lithe, with the kind of super-fit, muscled physique that spoke of serious dedication to training. Even seated, Amanda could tell she carried herself with an athlete's confidence.

Paulo's intent was clear—the slight lean in his posture, the deliberate way his knee pressed against Victoria's thigh. It was the same routine she'd watched him perform with Sally in Byron Bay. But Victoria wasn't Sally. Where Sally had blushed and giggled at Paulo's attention, Victoria sat perfectly still, her expression unreadable as she listened to whatever line he was spinning.

He'd never shown one scrap of interest in Amanda; then again, maybe she hadn't given him the same come-hither look that Sally had given most guys they'd met over the past few months.

'There you are!' Paulo exclaimed as Amanda approached, though his eyes lingered on Victoria with unmistakable interest. 'Amanda, my favourite English rose.'

'I thought that was Sally,' Amanda corrected sarcastically,

setting down the drinks with more force than necessary. 'Where is she, anyway?'

'Freshening up,' Paulo replied with a dismissive wave of his hand. 'Women, always with the makeup, no?'

Amanda noticed how Victoria didn't move her leg away from Paulo's. Instead, she lifted her chin slightly as Paulo's gaze travelled over her face. Her fair skin was flawless, her eyebrows naturally arched and her dark eyelashes long and lush.

'So, Victoria,' Paulo said, turning his full attention to the newcomer, his voice dropping to that practised, intimate register Amanda had heard him use on Sally. 'You travel alone? Very brave.'

'Not brave,' Victoria replied, her voice quieter than before, a vulnerability in it that hadn't been there moments ago. 'Just independent.'

Paulo's smile widened, showing too many teeth. 'I like independent women. They know what they want.'

Amanda cleared her throat loudly, but neither of them seemed to notice.

'And what about you, Paulo?' Victoria asked, leaning forward slightly, her fingers tracing the rim of the glass holding the shot of tequila before she lifted her hand and licked the salt from her finger. 'What do you want?'

'Me?' Paulo leaned closer to Victoria. 'I want to experience everything life offers. All the beauty, all the adventure.'

Their eyes locked, and Amanda watched as something unspoken passed between them. Victoria's lips curved into a small smile, encouraging without words, a spider inviting a fly. She was good, if she was doing what she'd said. Then again, maybe he'd sucked her in too.

For the first time since they'd started their travels, Amanda was over the backpacker life. Homesickness and the call of the familiar tugged at her. 'I'm going to look for Sally,' she said coldly.

Paulo didn't take his eyes off Victoria. 'She knows where to find us.'

'I'd love to hear more about Brazil,' Victoria said, her fingers continuing to trace the rim of the glass. 'I've never been overseas.'

'It is paradise,' Paulo replied, his voice dropping lower, more intimate. 'The beaches of Rio make Noosa look like nothing. The parties go all night, the people are beautiful, the music...' He made a chef's kiss gesture. 'If you come, I show you places tourists never see.'

'Is that so?' Victoria's eyebrow arched playfully, and her hand dropped to cover his.

'Yes,' Paulo said, his confidence growing visibly. 'In fact, when I finish this trip, I go back to manage my family's hotel. Very exclusive, on Ipanema Beach. You could stay—as my special guest, of course.'

What a total prick. Amanda's disbelief grew as Paulo used the same line—word for word—he'd used on Sally.

Victoria reeled him in—her body language open, inviting, her eyes never leaving his face. It was like watching a scene from a movie, both parties playing roles. Maybe Victoria was an actress.

For the first time, Amanda worried that Sally would come back and see them at it. As much as she hated Sally being in Paulo's thrall, she didn't want to see her best friend hurt.

'That sounds amazing,' Victoria said breathlessly, a slight

flush appearing on her cheeks. She caught Amanda's eye and winked as Paulo gestured to the barman for another round of tequila shots. 'But what about your girlfriend?'

Paulo waved dismissively as he looked at her. 'Sally is sweet girl, but we are just having fun. Nothing serious.'

Amanda's mouth fell open. 'That's not what—'

'There you are!' Sally's voice cut through as she appeared beside them, her lipstick freshly applied, oblivious to the tension crackling in the air. She slid her arm around Paulo's shoulders and kissed his cheek. 'I thought I'd lost you to the dance floor.'

Paulo smoothly shifted his attention, pulling Sally onto his lap. 'Never, *linda.* I was just telling the girls about Brazil. Maybe one day you visit me there, yes?'

Sally beamed, completely unaware of the undercurrents swirling around her. 'I'd love that. Maybe I'll go to Brazil with you instead of home.'

Amanda caught Victoria's eye across the table and was taken aback by the cool assessment in her gaze as Victoria watched Paulo whisper something in Sally's ear that made her giggle.

'Hey,' Paulo said. 'We're heading north tomorrow. Victoria, why don't you come with us? We've got room in the car, and it would be fun to have another person along.'

Sally clapped her hands together. 'Oh, that's a brilliant idea! Please say yes, Victoria. Chip in for a bit of fuel; it'll be cheaper than getting a Greyhound. As long as you're sure, Paulo, it's your car.'

Paulo's eyes flickered between the women, his expression calculating before settling into his usual easy smile. 'Yes, another beautiful woman on the trip. How can I complain?'

Victoria hesitated. 'Where do you all sleep? Would there

be room?'

'We stay in backpacker hostels, and a couple of times when the weather's been warmer, we've slept on the beach,' Sally said.

Victoria's eyes lit up. 'You know what? That sounds like fun. I'd love to come with you if you're all happy for me to join you.'

Sally giggled. 'There's one condition.'

Victoria raised her eyebrows. 'And that would be?'

Amanda smiled as she and Sally each lifted their right leg and pointed to their matching tattoos. 'You'll have to get a tat.'

Victoria's grin was wide. 'I'm up for that.'

As Sally told her of the places they'd camped, Amanda watched how Victoria's eyes continued to track Paulo, and the brief secret glance they shared when Sally wasn't looking. A sense of foreboding settled in her stomach along with the tequila. Maybe her suggestion hadn't been that wise; their trip was about to get a lot more complicated.

The crowd at the bar shifted, and a tall figure approached their table. Amanda looked up and immediately recognised the tanned face of the guy with the blonde stubble.

'Hey, Dave, over here,' she called out, sliding over to make room beside her. 'Remember me? We had a dance here the other night.'

The man nodded, a smile crinkling the corners of his eyes. 'Of course I do, Amanda. Mind if I join you?'

'Please.' Amanda patted the space on the cushioned bench beside her, grateful for his presence.

Dave had the rugged look of someone who'd spent his life in the sun. His sun-bleached hair was pulled into a no-nonsense ponytail tonight. When he smiled, laughter lines fanned out from the corners of his eyes—sexy crinkles that lent him charm rather than age, making him unexpectedly handsome. A flicker of interest ran through Amanda.

Maybe?

Paulo straightened immediately, his arm tightening possessively around Sally's waist. 'Friend of yours?' he asked Amanda, his tone territorial.

'Dave's a skipper,' Amanda explained. 'He has a charter business.'

'Dave Hewson.' He held his hand out to Paulo, who shook it briefly.

'My family has a charter business too. How many boats for you?' Paulo asked.

'Just the one, but twenty years on the water,' Dave confirmed in that laconic Australian way, raising his beer in a casual toast. 'Seen pretty much every inch of the Queensland coast more times than I can count.'

Paulo's chin lifted slightly. 'We plan a boat trip north ourselves. I'm taking these three lovely ladies to Airlie Beach next week. The Whitsundays. Best sailing in Australia.'

Dave took a slow sip of his beer, his expression neutral, but something in his eyes suggested he'd sized up Paulo in seconds. 'Airlie's alright if you don't mind sharing paradise with a thousand other tourists and every grey nomad with a caravan.'

Paulo's smile tightened, a flash of irritation breaking through his carefully maintained charm. 'You have better suggestion?'

'Mission Beach,' Dave said without hesitation, no trace of the boastfulness that characterised Paulo's every utterance.

'Never heard of it,' Paulo said, shaking his head.

'A couple of hours north of Townsville. Paradise and

practically deserted compared to the Whitsundays. Better reefs, great fishing, no crowds, and the rainforest comes right down to the shore.' Dave glanced around the table. 'I'm sailing north tomorrow. Got a few charters booked for the season. My boat's been on the hard getting scrubbed.'

'We have our transportation,' Paulo said dismissively. 'A four-wheel drive.'

'That old Troopie I saw you pull up in before?' Dave chuckled, his tone light but his eyes watchful. 'Hope you've got good breakdown cover for the coastal route. The Bruce Highway is pretty rugged.'

Paulo flushed, his carefully cultivated image cracking slightly. 'My car is a classic, a vintage Troop Carrier.'

'That's one word for it,' Dave replied, a glint of amusement in his eyes.

Sally chimed in, stroking Paulo's arm soothingly. 'Your car has character.'

'Can't argue with that,' Dave conceded. 'But if any of you fancy seeing the Queensland coast the way it's meant to be seen—from the water—I've got room on my boat. Leaving tomorrow, first stop, the Whitsundays.'

'On a yacht?' Amanda asked, suddenly interested. She hated the Troop Carrier, with its hard seats and perpetual smell of diesel. She'd been peeved when Sally had decided to hand in their Juicy van without asking her first, even if travelling with Paulo had meant saving money.

'Forty-foot catamaran,' Dave confirmed. 'Plenty of space. Three cabins, two heads and a separate bathroom. Beats driving for days on end on that highway.'

Paulo scoffed, his accent suddenly thicker. 'We have our

plan already. Very good plan.'

'Just putting it out there,' Dave said with a shrug. 'No pressure.'

Amanda exchanged a glance with Victoria and raised her eyebrows questioningly. Victoria's lips curved into a small, interested smile.

'Sounds interesting,' Amanda said.

'It does,' Victoria added, with a nod and a side glance at Paulo. 'How long would it take to sail up there?'

'About a week, nice and easy,' Dave replied. 'Nothing too fancy onboard, but she's a great boat.'

Paulo's jaw tightened. 'Sounds very expensive, this private yacht trip.'

'I need crew, not paying passengers,' Dave said calmly. 'Help with the sailing, cooking, that sort of thing. Fair exchange.'

'I can cook,' Victoria offered quickly.

'I've done some sailing at home,' Amanda added, suddenly eager to escape the claustrophobic atmosphere of Paulo and Sally's romance. They could take the road north, and she and Victoria could go by sea. Excitement churned in her stomach; meeting Victoria tonight had been fortuitous because she wouldn't have gone on the boat by herself with Dave.

Sally looked torn, glancing between Paulo's increasingly thunderous expression and the look on Amanda's face. For the first time, Amanda realised how agreeable she'd been to Sally's organising everything since they'd started out.

Now it was her turn to have fun.

'But our road trip...' Sally began hesitantly.

'I'll meet you up there,' Amanda finished. 'How often will I get a chance to sail up the Queensland coast? And besides, it will leave you and Paulo alone to get to know each other even better.'

Paulo stood abruptly, pulling Sally up with him. 'We need to discuss this. In private.' He shot a cold look at Dave before leading Sally towards the bar.

As soon as they were out of earshot, Amanda turned to Dave. 'Were you serious about taking us?'

'Wouldn't have offered otherwise,' he replied with typically Australian directness. 'I often sail with a backpacker crew. More fun that way.'

'Even if it's just two of us?' Victoria asked, nodding towards herself and Amanda.

Dave took another sip of his beer. 'I've sailed solo plenty of times. Any help is better than none.'

'What about Paulo and Sally?' Amanda asked, watching the couple engaged in intense conversation by the bar, Paulo's gestures becoming increasingly excitable.

Dave shrugged. 'They're welcome too, but...' He trailed off, his eyes on Paulo's animated gestures, a hint of wariness in his expression.

'But you don't think they'll come,' Victoria finished for him.

'Let's just say your friend seems to have her hands full with that one,' Dave said diplomatically. 'And he strikes me as the type who doesn't like sharing the spotlight.'

Amanda couldn't help but smile. It was the most accurate assessment of Paulo she'd heard yet.

'Well, *I'll* think about it,' she declared, feeling more excited than she had in weeks. 'Victoria?'

Victoria's eyes drifted towards Paulo and Sally for a

moment, something unreadable in her expression before returning to meet Amanda's gaze. 'When do you need to know by?'

Dave lifted his glass. 'Noon tomorrow. I'll be at the marina. She's called *Seabreeze*.'

Victoria grinned at Amanda. 'That'll give me time to get my tattoo in the morning.'

Chapter 17

Saturday, August 2 - noon.

Noosa Marina, Tewantin.

The Noosa Marina stretched alongside the Noosa River at Tewantin, a collection of weathered wooden jetties extending from the shore like fingers reaching into the calm water. Palm trees swayed gently along the boardwalk, providing dappled shade over the marina's small collection of shops and cafés. Tourists and locals mingled on the decks of the riverside restaurants, enjoying breakfast with views of the moored vessels bobbing in their berths. The marina wasn't large or fancy— nothing like the glitzy Gold Coast harbours they'd seen further south—but it had a relaxed charm that matched the laid-back vibe of Noosa itself.

The early morning sun glinted off the water as Amanda and Victoria made their way down the marina walkway. Amanda wheeled her backpack, and Victoria had hers on her back. Weekend fishermen prepared their boats for a day on the water, and a few charter vessels were already loading passengers for river cruises.

'I still can't believe what a jerk Paulo was last night,' Amanda said, shaking her head.

'Yeah, he wasn't very nice,' Victoria admitted, adjusting her sunglasses. 'Though I'm not entirely surprised.'

Amanda glanced at her. 'Where did you two disappear to? Sally got a bit upset when you disappeared for so long.'

'He tried to talk me out of going with Dave.'

'For almost an hour?'

'And he wanted to vent about Sally,' Victoria said with a shrug. 'Besides, I thought that's what you wanted.'

Amanda shook her head. 'Not really. I'd had a few too many tequilas.'

'Not a problem. I don't want to sleep with him. He and Sally can get all lovey-dovey again on their road trip,' Victoria replied. 'Look, there's the wharf where Dave said to meet him.'

Amanda let it drop, but she couldn't shake the feeling that maybe more had happened between Victoria and Paulo. But it was none of her business. They were all grown-ups. 'I still can't believe Dave offered to take us to Airlie Beach,' she said, unable to keep the smile from her face. 'Talk about perfect timing.'

'You seem pretty excited about seeing him again,' Victoria observed with a knowing smile. 'You mentioned you met him at the bar a few nights before I did?'

'Mm.' Amanda nodded. 'I danced with him a couple of times.'

'Paulo didn't like him.'

'Paulo doesn't like any man who isn't intimidated by him,' Amanda replied. 'Dave saw right through him in about five seconds flat.'

'So, you do like him?' Victoria teased.

Amanda felt herself blushing slightly. 'I don't know. Maybe? There's something about him—not just that he's attractive, but he seems... like a decent guy.'

They approached the white catamaran at the end of the finger wharf. It was clean and well-maintained, but not the luxury vessel of Amanda's imagination. The white paint had a weathered look, and there were a few scratches along the hull.

Dave was on deck, coiling rope. He spotted them and

waved. 'G'day, ladies! Welcome aboard *Seabreeze*!'

He hopped onto the dock and reached for their backpacks. 'Let me help you with those.'

Amanda studied him in the bright morning light. The flicker of interest she'd felt at the bar returned, stronger now even without a skinful of tequila.

'This is yours?' Amanda asked, taking in the vessel.

'She is,' Dave said with obvious pride. 'Not the fanciest girl on the water, but she's reliable and she's all mine.'

'You own it outright?' Victoria asked, clearly impressed.

'Took me ten years of payments, but yeah,' he replied. 'Come aboard, I'll show you around.'

As Dave guided them onto the boat, Amanda couldn't help but appreciate his easy confidence. There was nothing showy about him—just someone completely comfortable in his own skin. You couldn't get someone more different than Paulo.

'Been running charters long?' Victoria asked as they stepped onto the deck.

'About ten years,' Dave replied. 'And loved every minute of it.'

The interior was compact but functional. The main cabin served as a galley, dining area, and lounge all in one. The small galley occupied one side, with a fold-down table and bench seats that could convert to additional sleeping space.

'It's cosy,' Amanda observed, trying to sound positive.

Dave laughed, the sound warm and genuine. 'That's the polite way of saying it's small. But it's perfect for coastal cruising.'

He showed them to the sleeping quarters—two small cabins in each bow.

'A head in each,' Dave said, pointing to a door at the end of the bed cabins. 'That's boat-speak for toilet—and a small shower. Water's limited, so navy showers are the rule.'

'Navy showers?' Amanda asked.

'Get wet, turn water off, soap up, rinse off. Two minutes max.'

'I've done that before,' Amanda said. 'I actually sailed one summer when I was at school.'

Dave's interest visibly piqued. 'Really? Whereabouts?'

'In the Scilly Isles, off Cornwall. There was a sailing program at my secondary school when I was sixteen.' Amanda smiled at the memory. 'Nothing fancy—mostly small dinghies, but we did an overnight trip on a yacht at the end. I loved it.'

'Well, that's brilliant.' Dave nodded, their eyes meeting again. 'You'll pick everything up quick smart then.'

There was something in his gaze that brought warmth to Amanda's cheeks. She was reminded of why she'd so readily agreed to his offer at the bar after the argument with Sally. There had been an instant connection between them when they had first danced together, and now she was keen to see where it would go. If anywhere.

Back in the main cabin, Dave explained the basics of living aboard. 'Storage is tight, so try to keep your gear organised. The fridge is small, but it works. I've stocked some basics, but we'll need to pick up fresh supplies along the way.'

A honk from the parking lot interrupted his explanation. They moved to the deck just as Paulo's white Troop Carrier pulled up to the marina.

Sally jumped out first, her face puffy as if she'd been crying. Paulo followed, looking irritable until he spotted them.

'Final goodbyes?' Dave asked quietly.

'Apparently,' Amanda sighed.

Sally approached first, climbing awkwardly onto the deck. 'So, this is the boat,' she said, her tone flat.

'This is it,' Dave replied. 'I'll just check on something below.'

As he disappeared into the cabin, Paulo joined them, eyeing the catamaran with a critical gaze.

'Not luxury, is it?' he commented.

'It's perfectly fine,' Amanda said. 'And it beats being crammed in that car of yours for days.'

Sally frowned. 'We should get going if we want to make it to Airlie Beach today.'

'You could still change your mind,' Amanda told Sally quietly. 'Come with us instead.'

Sally's expression hardened. 'We've been through this. I'm going with Paulo.'

'Sally—'

'Don't start again, Amanda,' Sally snapped. 'You made your feelings perfectly clear last night when you called Paulo a con artist and said I was being naive.'

'I didn't say that,' Amanda corrected. 'I said you deserved better than someone who treats you the way he does.'

'And I told you to mind your own business,' Sally retorted. 'Paulo and I love each other. We have plans. Just because you can't see that—'

'Plans?' Amanda couldn't help herself. 'Like what? Following the surf up the coast until his money runs out and he needs another girl to pay his way?'

Paulo stepped forward. 'That's enough.'

'No, it's not,' Amanda said, turning to him. 'You've been

mooching off Sally for weeks. And when she's not enough, you try to shake down her friends for cash.'

'The fuel money was fair,' Paulo argued. 'You're going the same way I am.'

'Were,' Amanda corrected. 'I'm going by sea now.'

Paulo's eyes darted to Victoria again. 'Yeah, I can see that worked out well for you both.'

Victoria lifted her chin and shrugged.

'Come on.' Sally tugged at Paulo's arm. 'Let's just go. They've made their choice.'

Paulo's mood seemed to shift suddenly. He smiled, all charm again. 'You're right, babe. We don't need them anyway.' He turned to Amanda. 'Forget about the fuel money. Consider it my gift to you.'

'How generous,' Amanda said dryly.

As they prepared to leave, Victoria stepped forward and gave Sally a quick hug. 'Take care of yourself, okay?'

'You too,' Sally replied, her anger seemingly fading. 'Did you get your tattoo?'

'I did.' Victoria lifted her right ankle, and Sally smiled at the wave and shell tattoo. 'Good, you've joined the gang now.' She turned to Amanda with a conflicted expression. 'I'll see you in Airlie Beach, will I?'

'We'll be there,' Amanda promised, feeling their friendship strain but not yet break.

After they left, Dave emerged from below deck. 'Everything okay?'

'Just peachy,' Amanda said with a sigh.

Dave's eyes searched her face, his expression sympathetic. 'Travelling with friends can be tricky. Sometimes the best friendships can crack under the pressure.'

'Speaking from experience?' Amanda asked.

A rueful smile tugged at his lips. 'Let's just say you're not the first group I've seen fall out on the road. Or should I say on the water?'

There was an understanding in his gaze that Amanda found surprisingly comforting. It wasn't just his physical attractiveness, though that was undeniable, but something in his manner, a quiet perceptiveness that suggested depths beneath the easy-going exterior.

'Well,' Dave said, clapping his hands together, 'how about we get this show on the road? Or on the water, rather?'

He began explaining the departure procedure, pointing out various lines and cleats around the boat.

'Victoria, if you could cast off the bow line when I give the signal,' he instructed. 'Amanda, you're on the stern line. Once you've cast off, hop aboard quickly—don't worry, I'll keep her steady against the dock until you're on.'

'What about the middle line?' Amanda asked, noticing a third rope securing the boat.

Dave smiled approvingly, his eyes crinkling at the corners in that way that made her heart beat a little faster. 'Good eye. I'll handle that one myself. Once we're clear of the marina, I'll show you both how to handle the sails.'

As they prepared to depart, Dave cleared his throat. 'One more thing—I was hoping we could work out a bit of a deal. I handle the sailing, and in return, you two take care of the cooking? I'm not exactly a chef, and it would be nice to have decent meals for a change.'

'I'm happy to cook,' Amanda agreed quickly. She enjoyed cooking and was quite good at it.

'Sure, no problem,' Victoria added, though with noticeably less enthusiasm.

'Great!' Dave beamed. 'Galley's fully stocked, and we can pick up anything else we need along the way.'

Twenty minutes later, they were motoring slowly through the no-wake zone of the marina, the morning sun warm on their faces. Dave stood confidently at the helm, occasionally calling out instructions.

'Amanda, can you check that all the hatches below are secured? Victoria, there's a chart in the cabin—can you bring it up?'

Amanda headed below while Victoria hesitated, then slowly moved towards the cabin entrance.

'It should be right on the table,' Dave called after her.

As Amanda finished checking the hatches, she passed Victoria, who was rummaging half-heartedly through some papers on the table.

'Need help?' Amanda offered.

'I don't even know what a chart looks like,' Victoria admitted with a shrug. 'You find it.'

Amanda located the nautical chart immediately—it was unfolded prominently on the table—and handed it to Victoria. 'Here.'

'Thanks,' Victoria said, taking it and heading back up to the deck without offering to help check the remaining hatches.

Amanda frowned slightly as she completed the task alone. It wasn't a big deal, but she couldn't help noticing that Victoria seemed disinclined to pull her weight. Was she planning to coast through the entire trip while Amanda did all the work?

When Amanda returned to the deck, Dave had already guided them out of the marina and into the more open waters of the Noosa River. The houses and shops of Noosaville slid past on their port side, the morning sun casting them in a golden glow.

'Ready to raise the sails?' Dave asked, eyes bright with excitement.

Amanda nodded eagerly, while Victoria lounged on one of the seats, seemingly more interested in applying sunscreen than helping with the boat.

'Absolutely,' Amanda replied, meeting Dave's gaze.

He held her eyes for a moment longer than necessary, and the attraction she'd felt since their first meeting at the bar intensified. There was something incredibly appealing about his capable hands on the wheel, the easy confidence with which he handled his vessel, the way the sun brought out the blonde in his tousled hair. When he smiled at her—a genuine smile that reached his clear, alert eyes and deepened the lines around them—Amanda felt a warmth spread through her that had nothing to do with the Queensland sun.

'Come take the helm for a minute,' he said, gesturing her over.

Amanda moved beside him, their shoulders almost touching as he guided her hands to the wheel. His skin was warm, his touch gentle but sure.

'Just keep her steady while I raise the mainsail,' he instructed, his voice close to her ear. 'Remember how to read the wind?'

'I think so,' Amanda said, surprised by how natural it felt to stand there beside him, how right.

As Dave moved away to work the lines, she found herself hoping that Victoria's apparent laziness would continue. It would give her more opportunities to work closely with Dave, to learn from him, to spend time in his company.

As the engine quieted and the sails filled with wind, catching the morning breeze, the *Seabreeze* picked up speed. They glided past the sandbanks of the river mouth and into the open sea, leaving Noosa—and all its complications—behind them.

Amanda stood at the helm, the wind in her hair and a smile on her face. She glanced at Dave, who was adjusting a line nearby, and found him watching her with unmistakable appreciation. This journey, she decided, was going to be even more interesting than she had anticipated.

Chapter 18

Sailing on Seabreeze.

The *Seabreeze* cut through the glassy morning waters as they left the Noosa River behind, the coastline stretching before them like a painting coming to life. Amanda stood beside Dave at the helm, feeling the gentle rock of the catamaran beneath her feet. A peculiar sense of freedom washed over her as the shoreline receded—a mixture of excitement and tranquillity she hadn't experienced in years.

'We'll head north past Double Island Point and hook into Hervey Bay,' Dave explained, pointing to the nautical chart spread on the console. 'We'll spend the first night at Urangan Harbour—it's about fifteen hours from here if we make good time.'

Amanda nodded, absorbing every word. 'And after that?'

'Day two takes us to Lady Musgrave Island,' Dave replied, tracing the route with his finger. 'It's part of the southern Great Barrier Reef—has one of the few navigable lagoons among the reef cays. We'll spend a full day there for snorkelling and exploring.'

Victoria emerged from below deck, her hair perfectly styled despite the sea breeze, phone clutched in her hand. 'Any reception out here?' she asked, frowning at her screen.

'You'll get patchy service along the coast,' Dave said. 'But once we're further out, it'll be spotty at best. There's a satellite phone for emergencies.'

Victoria's face fell. 'Great,' she muttered, retreating to a cushioned seat at the bow.

As the morning progressed, Dave taught Amanda the basics of sailing the catamaran—how to read the wind indicators, the difference between points of sail, when to tack versus jibe. She was a quick study, her earlier experience with dinghies providing a solid foundation.

'You're a natural,' Dave commented as she successfully adjusted the jib sheet during a tack. 'Most people take days to get comfortable with the lines.'

Amanda felt a flush of pride warm her cheeks. 'It's coming back to me. Though this is quite different from the tiny boats I sailed in England.'

By midday, they had settled into a comfortable rhythm. Dave managed the boat with Amanda's increasingly confident assistance, while Victoria remained firmly ensconced at the bow, alternating between sunbathing and staring at her phone. When Amanda called her for lunch—simple sandwiches she had prepared in the galley—Victoria took hers back to her spot without a word.

'Is she always like this?' Dave asked quietly as they ate together in the cockpit.

Amanda shrugged. 'We only met her last night.' She glanced towards her travelling companion with concern. 'We cooked up something together that I regret now. Too much tequila and now Sally's got the shits with me. With Paulo.'

'Ah,' Dave nodded knowingly. 'I saw him talking to Victoria outside. Didn't look like a casual conversation.'

'She said they were talking about Sally. It's my fault. She offered to make a move on him to stop his interest in Sally. I guess I wasn't thinking of Sally's feelings.'

'You're a good person, Amanda.' The warmth in his voice sent a pleasant shiver down her spine.

The afternoon brought stronger winds and choppier seas as they passed Double Island Point. The catamaran handled the conditions beautifully, but the rolling motion began to take its toll on Amanda. A creeping nausea settled in her stomach as they pitched over the swells.

'You're looking a bit green,' Dave observed with gentle concern. 'Why don't you go up to the bow? Keep your eyes on the horizon.'

Amanda nodded weakly and made her way forward, gripping the handrails. Victoria barely glanced up as Amanda settled beside her.

'Seasick?' Victoria asked sympathetically.

'A little,' Amanda admitted. 'Dave says it should pass.'

'Hmm,' Victoria replied, her attention already back on her phone.

'Are you okay, Victoria? You seem preoccupied.'

'I'm looking to see what jobs are going up at Airlie. There's a cattle property looking for a station hand with free accommodation, but that's the last thing I want to do.'

'Is that what you do at home?'

'Yes.' Victoria sighed dramatically. 'But don't worry about me. I'm fine. Just not as enthusiastic about playing sailor as you are.'

Before Amanda could ask her about leaving Paulo alone, a particularly large wave sent the bow dipping sharply. Her stomach lurched, and she barely made it to the railing before emptying its contents into the sea. Cool hands suddenly gathered her hair back from her face, and she was surprised to find Dave beside her, not Victoria.

'Deep breaths,' he instructed kindly. 'In through the nose,

out through the mouth. It helps to look at the horizon, not the water near the boat.'

His steadying presence beside her and the practical advice helped. Within an hour, her nausea had subsided to a manageable level, and by sunset, she felt almost normal again.

The first day set a gruelling pace. They sailed through the afternoon and into the night, Amanda taking turns at the helm while Dave caught brief periods of rest. As darkness fell, he taught her to read the navigation lights of other vessels and the illuminated markers along the coast. Victoria retreated below deck, emerging only briefly to grab a sandwich before disappearing again.

They reached Urangan Harbour in Hervey Bay just after dawn, exhausted but exhilarated. Amanda had never experienced overnight sailing before, and the magic of watching the stars wheel overhead while the phosphorescent wake trailed behind them had been worth every moment of fatigue.

After a few hours of much-needed sleep, they set off again the next morning for the long stretch to Lady Musgrave Island.

'This is about another fifteen-hour run,' Dave explained as they cleared the harbour. 'We'll time it to arrive tomorrow morning when the light's good for navigating the lagoon entrance.'

Each morning after that, Amanda woke early, joining Dave for coffee as they planned the day's sailing. She absorbed his knowledge like a sponge, learning to read nautical charts, monitor the weather, and predict the wind shifts based on cloud patterns. Victoria, meanwhile, emerged later and later each day, contributing little beyond occasional, half-hearted assistance when directly asked.

'You need to pull your weight a bit more, Victoria,'

Amanda told her as they approached Lady Musgrave Island on the morning of the third day, preparing breakfast for the three of them. 'It's fun out there.'

Victoria looked up from her phone. 'You seem to have it covered, but do you really think you're the first backpacker he's brought out here?'

'I'm just trying to pull my weight,' Amanda protested, heat rising to her face.

'Whatever you say,' Victoria replied with a knowing grin. 'I've seen how you look at him.'

Amanda couldn't deny the attraction, which grew stronger with each passing day. There was something about Dave's quiet competence, his patience as he taught her, the way his eyes crinkled when he smiled—a smile that seemed increasingly directed at her.

As they approached Lady Musgrave Island, Amanda stood transfixed. The atoll appeared like a mirage on the horizon—a perfect ring of coral surrounding a lagoon of such vibrant turquoise it seemed artificially coloured. Dave guided the *Seabreeze* carefully through the narrow entrance channel, the water beneath them so clear she could see fish darting among the coral heads below.

'It's like sailing through liquid crystal,' she breathed.

Dave's eyes were on her face, not the view. 'Wait until you see it underwater.'

They anchored in the protected lagoon, surrounded by a near-perfect ring of coral. The island itself was small—a pristine coral cay crowned with a dense Pisonia forest that served as a nesting site for thousands of seabirds.

'We can go ashore later,' Dave explained as they had

breakfast. 'The island's a national park, so we'll need to be careful not to disturb anything. But later this morning, we should snorkel the lagoon while the tide's still high.'

Amanda could barely contain her excitement. She'd never seen a coral reef before, and the prospect of exploring one with Dave made the anticipation even sweeter. She was so pleased they'd taken up his offer. The trips that she and Sally had looked at had been too expensive for Amanda to justify. Sally had offered to pay, but Amanda had her pride.

The conditions were perfect—calm water, clear skies, and gentle sunshine; Dave brought out snorkelling gear for them all.

'You coming, Victoria?' Amanda asked as she adjusted her mask.

Victoria didn't look up from her phone. 'I'll leave the mermaid act to you and Dave. Looks like you're doing fine without me.'

'Come on.'

'No, but thanks. I'll mind the boat.'

Amanda exchanged a puzzled glance with Dave, who shrugged subtly.

'Her loss,' he said quietly as they slipped into the water.

The underwater world took Amanda's breath away. Fields of coral spread in all directions—branching staghorns, massive brain corals, delicate fans waving in the gentle current. Fish in impossible colours darted among them—electric blue damsels, striped angelfish, curious butterflyfish that approached to investigate the strange visitors to their realm.

Dave stayed close, pointing out creatures she might have missed—a well-camouflaged stonefish, a tiny nudibranch creeping along a coral branch, a massive giant clam with iridescent blue mantle tissue pulsing within its scalloped shell.

Occasionally, his hand would brush against hers, sending a thrill through her body that had nothing to do with the marine life surrounding them.

When they finally surfaced, Amanda was giddy with joy. 'That was incredible! Did you see that green turtle? It came so close to me!'

Dave was beaming at her enthusiasm. 'You're a good snorkeler. Most first-timers splash around and scare everything away.'

'I didn't want to miss anything,' she said, treading water easily beside him. 'Thank you for bringing me here.'

Their eyes met, and for a moment, Amanda thought he might kiss her right there in the crystal-clear lagoon. But instead, he simply smiled and said, 'We should head back. Check on Victoria. Hopefully, she might have lunch ready.'

Amanda climbed the narrow ladder at the back of the boat, her heart still thudding from the snorkel. Water streamed from her limbs, trickling in rivulets over the backs of her knees. The reef had been more dazzling than she'd imagined: walls of coral in impossible colours, fish like painted glass flickering in and out of the shadows. When she pulled off her mask, the sun seemed almost too bright, the water's surface glittering in the stiff breeze that had sprung up.

Victoria was exactly where they'd left her, though she'd moved to the shaded part of the deck. She didn't look up from her phone.

'All done playing mermaid?' she murmured. Amanda forced a smile, towelled her face and sat cross-legged on the warm timber deck. Dave stood at the back of the boat, taking his flippers off.

Her gaze lingered a second too long. The way he moved—efficient, easy—set something fluttering in her stomach. He hadn't just shown her fish; he'd pointed out tiny creatures tucked in the coral, motioned for her to slow down, to float and look more carefully. He made her feel like the reef was alive just for her.

But now, with Victoria's words echoing, 'YOU REALLY THINK YOU'RE THE FIRST BACKPACKER HE'S BROUGHT OUT HERE,' a prickle of doubt crept in. Had she been reading too much into his attention?

The sea stretched wide around the boat, a silky expanse of cobalt melting into turquoise. In the distance, the low line of an island shimmered in the heat haze, fringed with coconut palms and golden sand. Amanda watched a pair of seabirds wheel overhead, their cries thin and sharp. It felt like paradise. It *was* paradise.

So why did her chest feel tight?

She hugged her knees, suddenly unsure. Maybe she'd only glimpsed what she wanted to see.

'Is she always this antisocial?' Dave asked a while later as they prepared a light lunch together in the galley.

Amanda sighed. 'I don't know her that well. If I'd known she was going to be so lazy, I would never have suggested that she join our group.'

They spent the afternoon exploring the island, following the designated walking track through the Pisonia forest. The ground was covered with leaf litter and fallen branches, the trees forming a dense canopy overhead. Thousands of black noddies and wedge-tailed shearwaters nested among the branches, creating a constant chorus of calls.

'The birds have been nesting here for so long that their

droppings have formed a phosphate-rich soil,' Dave explained as they walked. 'That's why the vegetation is so lush.'

Amanda absorbed every detail, asking questions that Dave answered with obvious pleasure. By the time they returned to the boat, the sun was setting, turning the sky and sea into a canvas of orange and gold.

Victoria was on deck, still engrossed in her phone.

'You missed an amazing walk,' Amanda told her. 'The bird colony is incredible.'

'And he's not bad either, right?' Victoria said drily. 'I'm going to skip dinner tonight. Not hungry.'

They spent a second full day at Lady Musgrave, with Amanda taking full advantage of the pristine environment—snorkelling multiple times, paddleboarding around the calm lagoon, and even spotting a small reef shark that Dave assured her was harmless. Victoria remained aboard the entire time, her only acknowledgment of the paradise surrounding them an occasional glance up from her phone.

'Gosh, she's a strange one,' Amanda commented to Dave when they were in the water.

On the fourth day, they set sail for Great Keppel Island. The winds were favourable, and Dave showed Amanda how to trim the sails for maximum efficiency.

'We're making great time,' he commented as the afternoon wore on. 'Should reach Great Keppel by evening.'

The island appeared on the horizon just as the sun began to set—a mountainous silhouette against the darkening sky. They anchored in a sheltered bay, the waters calm and clear around them.

'There's a nice little beach bar ashore,' Dave mentioned as

they secured the boat. 'Thought we might grab dinner there for a change.'

'Sounds perfect,' Amanda agreed enthusiastically.

Victoria, predictably, declined. As they continued north, her behaviour became increasingly withdrawn. She spent most of her time in her cabin, emerging only to grab snacks that she took back to her solitary confinement.

'I wonder if she's depressed,' Amada ventured as they sat at the bar that night. 'She's never off her phone.'

'Could be,' Dave said with a nod. 'Not like any other backpacker I've come across. Most of them pull their weight.'

'You've met a few, then?' Amanda asked with a playful smile.

'I've been doing this for ten years.'

An unexpected pang of disappointment hit Amanda. Maybe she'd been reading too much into what she thought was a developing relationship. A seed of doubt lodged itself. How many times had Dave done this before—with others like her, eager to learn, eager to please?

Their fifth day took them to Pearl Bay, a remote and stunningly beautiful anchorage flanked by steep, forested hills.

'The military sometimes conducts exercises in this area,' Dave explained as they dropped anchor. 'We're lucky it's open today. This is one of my favourite spots along the coast.'

They explored the deserted beach together, collecting shells and watching eagles soar overhead. That evening, they caught fresh fish, which Amanda prepared with herbs in the galley.

'Should we be worried?' Amanda asked Dave as they prepared dinner together in the galley. 'She's barely said ten words today.'

Dave considered this as he filleted the fish. 'Has she seemed depressed before?'

'She was pretty vibrant that first night, but I can't really say,' Amanda said, chopping vegetables. 'Takes all kinds, I suppose.'

'Some people need more time to adjust to boat life,' Dave suggested. 'Could be that.'

'Maybe,' Amanda conceded, though she suspected there was more to it. 'But she was so enthusiastic about coming.'

But the next day brought no change in Victoria's mood as they sailed to their next destination—Middle Percy Island. The island was famous among sailors for its A-frame hut where visitors left mementos of their passage.

'It's tradition to add something to the collection,' Dave explained as they walked up from the beach. Inside the A-frame, every surface was covered with carved plaques, flags, T-shirts, and sailing memorabilia from boats that had passed this way over the decades.

Amanda traced her fingers over the names. 'It's like a physical guestbook.'

'Want to leave something?' Dave asked.

She nodded, and together they found a small piece of driftwood. Using Dave's knife, Amanda carved "*Seabreeze 2024 - Amanda & Dave*" into the wood. She hesitated, then added "*& Victoria*" as an afterthought.

As they approached the Whitsunday Passage on their final day, Victoria remained quiet, appearing briefly and speaking rarely. Her mood was a little snappish when Amanda tried to ask what was wrong.

After a few moments of sitting beside her, Victoria sighed.

'I'm sorry, Amanda. I know I've been a pain, but an awful lot is going on in my life.'

'At home?' Amanda asked.

'Yes, Dad wants me to come home to help with the big muster coming up, but you know what?'

Amanda shook her head, pleased that Victoria had finally opened up to her. 'No, what?'

'I don't want to go home. Ever.'

'I know what you mean. After seeing all this, I want to stay forever.'

Victoria grinned. 'Are you sure it's not the Dave attraction?'

Amanda nudged her. 'Are you sure yours isn't the Paulo attraction?'

Victoria's eyes widened. 'God, no. I was just trying to ease him away from Sally for you. He's a looker and he's buff, but he's a right royal pain in the butt.'

She wondered if Victoria would go her own way when they reached Airlie and met up with Sally and Paulo. Amanda wouldn't mind if she took off by herself. Maybe that was why she was travelling alone; she found it hard to get on with others.

But Amanda decided not to let Victoria's issues worry her; she was having the time of her life; it was going to be hard to say goodbye to Dave at the end of the trip. Amanda's relationship with Dave deepened daily. Their conversations flowed easily, covering everything from marine biology to favourite books to childhood memories. She learned that he'd grown up at Mission Beach, the son of a cane farmer, and had been drawn to the sea from an early age. He'd worked on commercial vessels and charter boats before saving enough to buy the *Seabreeze*.

'She's not much to look at,' he admitted one evening as

they sat in the cockpit, watching the sunset, 'but she's solid and dependable.'

'I think she's beautiful,' Amanda said sincerely. 'She feels like a home.'

Dave's expression softened. 'That's exactly what she is to me.'

On their final night before reaching Airlie Beach, they anchored in a sheltered bay off Shaw Island. The Whitsunday Islands surrounded them—lush, mountainous forms silhouetted against the darkening sky. After another dinner that Victoria declined, Amanda found herself sitting on the foredeck, watching as the first stars appeared.

To her surprise, Victoria emerged from below and settled on a cushion nearby, her ever-present phone finally absent.

'Beautiful evening,' Amanda offered cautiously.

Victoria nodded. 'I've been a terrible travelling companion, haven't I?'

The frank admission caught Amanda off guard. 'You've been quiet.'

They sat in companionable silence for several minutes before Dave joined them, carrying a thermos. 'Thought you might like some tea,' he said, pouring three cups and passing them around.

'You've been teaching Amanda to sail,' Victoria observed, accepting the tea with a slight smile—the first Amanda had seen in days.

Dave nodded. 'She's a quick study. Almost ready to captain her own vessel.'

'Hardly,' Amanda laughed, warmed by the compliment.

'You could,' Dave insisted. 'A few more weeks of practice,

and you'd be set.'

They fell into comfortable conversation, the most normal interaction they'd had as a trio since leaving Noosa. As night fully descended, the stars emerged in breathtaking profusion, the Milky Way arching overhead in a brilliant band of light.

'I've never seen so many stars,' Amanda marvelled, leaning back to take in the celestial panorama.

'No light pollution out here,' Dave explained. 'Just wait until I turn off all the boat lights.'

When he did, the darkness became absolute, the starlight reflecting on the still water surrounding them, creating the illusion that they were floating in space, stars above and below.

'Before GPS, sailors navigated by these stars,' Dave said, pointing upward. 'See that bright one? That's Canopus, the second brightest star in the sky. And there's the Southern Cross.'

He guided her gaze across the heavens, naming constellations and sharing the techniques of celestial navigation. Victoria listened for a while before quietly excusing herself, leaving them alone under the vast canopy of stars.

'To navigate by the stars, you need a sextant, an accurate chronometer, and nautical almanac tables,' Dave continued. 'You measure the angle between the horizon and celestial bodies like the sun or stars at precise times.'

'How does that tell you where you are?' Amanda asked, genuinely fascinated.

'Each celestial body is directly overhead at a specific point on Earth at a specific time. By measuring the angle to a star, you're essentially measuring your distance from that point. With measurements from multiple stars, you can triangulate your position.'

'That's incredible,' Amanda said softly. 'To find your way

across oceans using just the stars.'

The gentle breeze pushed them along, the boat rocking almost imperceptibly. In the distance, a flying fish broke the surface, skimming across the water before disappearing with a tiny splash.

'I think I could do this for the rest of my life,' Amanda whispered, the words escaping before she could consider them.

Dave laughed softly; the sound warm in the darkness. 'What, listen to me ramble about navigation?'

'No,' she said, emboldened by the cover of night. 'This. Sailing. The sea. All of it.'

A comfortable silence stretched between them before Dave asked, 'What are your plans when you get home? After Airlie Beach?'

Amanda sighed, looking up at the stars. 'We've got about three weeks left of our gap year trip before we fly home to England. I'm supposed to be starting university at the beginning of the semester. Accounting degree.' She pulled a face.

'Accounting, eh?' Dave's voice held a note of interest. 'That's a good field.'

'I've always loved numbers,' Amanda said with a small smile. 'But after this trip, I think I'll be focusing on an environmental degree. This year has been such an eye-opener for me. Maybe I'll even come back to Australia.'

'You'd be good at it,' Dave observed. 'You've got a natural affinity for the water.'

Amanda's smile faded slightly. 'This trip was supposed to be a great adventure with Sally. A last hurrah before we all went our separate ways, but Sally hooking up with Paulo ruined everything.'

'People surprise you,' Dave said softly. 'Sometimes in good ways, sometimes not.'

'You surprised me,' Amanda admitted. 'In a good way.'

In the starlight, she could just make out his smile. 'You surprised me too.'

His hand found hers on the cushion between them, warm and calloused. The simple touch sent electricity coursing through her veins. Slowly, giving her every opportunity to pull away, he interlaced their fingers.

'Amanda,' he said, her name like a caress on his lips.

She turned towards him, heart pounding. 'Yes?'

'I've wanted to do this since you first stepped aboard,' he murmured, leaning closer.

Their lips met in a gentle, tentative kiss that quickly deepened as Amanda responded with unexpected fervour. His hand came up to cup her face, thumb stroking her cheek with exquisite tenderness. She melted into him, all the attraction that had been building over the past week culminating in this perfect moment under the stars.

When they finally pulled apart, both slightly breathless, Dave rested his forehead against hers. 'I don't usually do this with crew,' he said softly.

'I don't usually kiss boat captains,' she replied with a smile he could hear in her voice.

His thumb traced her lower lip. 'This week with you has been—'

'I know,' she whispered. 'For me too.'

The night wrapped around them like a velvet cloak as they kissed again, more urgently this time. His arms encircled her, drawing her closer until she was practically in his lap, her hands exploring the firm muscles of his shoulders and back.

'Amanda,' he murmured against her lips. 'Would you like to come to my cabin?'

She hesitated only briefly, considering what she was about to do. She'd never been impulsive in this way before, had always been the cautious one, the planner. But something about Dave, about this entire journey, had awakened a part of her she hadn't known existed—a part that craved adventure, that wanted to seize this perfect moment rather than analyse it to death.

'Yes,' she whispered, the single word carrying the weight of a decision she knew she wouldn't regret.

He stood, offering his hand to help her up. Their fingers remained intertwined as he led her across the deck, the boat gently rocking beneath them.

Chapter 19

Saturday, August 10 - 11. a.m.

Coral Sea Marina, Airlie Beach.

The Coral Sea Marina at Airlie Beach gleamed in the late morning sun, but Amanda barely noticed the rows of sleek yachts or the hum of tourists. After a week on the water, the humidity hit her like a wall—so did the realisation that it was over. She stood at the bow, watching as Dave expertly manoeuvred the Seabreeze into its assigned slip. Her stomach was a knot of emotions—the exhilaration of their final morning together mingled with the hollow ache of imminent separation.

They had said their real goodbyes at dawn, wrapped in each other's arms on the deck as the first light painted the eastern sky in watercolour hues of pink and gold. His lips had been gentle against hers, his hands memorising the curve of her face as if committing it to memory.

'I'll be at Mission Beach,' he had whispered against her hair. 'If you ever come back. No pressure, but I'm going to miss you.'

She had nodded, not trusting her voice, knowing that real life—remaining weeks of travel, home and university—stood between them like an invisible barrier. They had exchanged phone numbers and promises to stay in touch, but Amanda had been around enough to know how these holiday romances typically ended. Still, something about Dave felt different, substantial in a way that made her heart clench painfully at the thought of walking away.

'We're here,' Victoria announced unnecessarily, emerging

from below deck with her backpack already packed, looking more animated than she had in days.

Amanda blinked in surprise. That was fast. Victoria had barely spoken for days—what had changed? Gone was the sullen, withdrawn figure who had haunted the boat like a ghost. In her place stood the old Victoria—eyes bright, hair freshly styled, lips curved in a smile.

'I see them,' Victoria added, pointing towards the marina office.

Amanda followed her gaze and spotted Paulo's distinctive Troop Carrier parked in the lot. Sally stood beside it, waving enthusiastically, while Paulo leaned against the driver's door, sunglasses hiding his eyes but not the easy smile on his face.

They looked... happy. The observation hit Amanda with unexpected force. After the bitter arguments and tearful separation in Noosa, she had imagined them miserable—or at least tense with each other. Instead, they appeared relaxed, Sally's body language open and excited as she bounced on her toes. She really hoped that Victoria would go her own way. If she was totally honest, she wished Paulo would go too, so she and Sally could enjoy the last month of their trip together.

'Ready?' Dave asked quietly from behind her, the single word carrying layers of meaning.

Amanda turned to face him, memorising the sunlines around his eyes, the way his hair fell across his forehead, the steady warmth of his gaze. 'No,' she admitted with a sad smile. 'But I guess I have to be.'

His hand found hers, hidden from Victoria's view, and squeezed gently. 'Sometimes the journey matters more than the destination.'

The marina staff helped secure the final lines, and then it was time. Dave insisted on carrying their bags to the parking lot, a small kindness that stretched their time together by precious minutes.

'Dave!' Sally exclaimed as they approached, her voice warm with genuine pleasure. 'You took good care of our girls!'

'They took good care of themselves,' he replied diplomatically, though his eyes flickered briefly to Amanda.

That brief glance was enough. Sally's gaze darted between them, her expression shifting subtly as understanding dawned. Amanda could almost see the questions forming behind her friend's eyes—they had known each other far too long to hide things from each other.

Paulo stepped forwards, hand extended. 'How was the trip, man?'

Dave shook his hand, his expression neutral but not unfriendly. 'No problem. How was your drive up?'

'Long,' Paulo admitted with a grin that seemed more sincere than Amanda remembered. 'But beautiful. This country has some incredible coastline.'

As the men chatted, Sally sidled up to Amanda. 'So?' she whispered, nudging her gently.

'Later,' Amanda replied under her breath, but couldn't stop the colour rising to her cheeks.

'Oh my God,' Sally gasped quietly. 'You totally did!'

'Sally!'

'I want every detail,' her friend insisted, eyes dancing with delight.

Meanwhile, Victoria had transformed entirely into her social self, laughing at something Paulo said, touching his arm briefly as she spoke.

The moment of departure arrived too quickly. Bags were loaded into the Toyota, hugs exchanged, and suddenly Amanda found herself standing before Dave for the last time.

'Safe travels,' he said formally, aware of the others watching.

'Thank you for everything,' she replied, the words utterly inadequate for what she wanted to express.

His eyes said what his lips couldn't, and then he stepped back, hands in his pockets.

Amanda climbed into the vehicle, taking the window seat that would let her watch him until the last possible moment.

Paulo started the engine. Dave raised his hand in a final wave. He looked smaller somehow, standing alone in the parking lot, the sea at his back. Amanda pressed her palm against the window glass, her throat tight with unspoken words.

They pulled away, Paulo navigating through the marina complex towards the main road. In the side mirror, Amanda watched Dave's figure recede, then disappear around a corner, and just like that, the most extraordinary week of her life slipped into memory.

She pressed her hand to the glass, remembering the warmth of his fingers just that morning, now replaced by cold windowpane and emptiness.

'Well,' Sally announced brightly from the front seat, twisting to face the back where Amanda and Victoria sat. 'You two look fantastic! A week on a boat clearly agrees with you.'

Amanda forced a smile, not yet ready to process the hollow feeling in her chest. 'How was the road trip?'

'Dreadful roads,' Sally groaned dramatically. 'Free camping most nights because we're running low on funds. No toilet facilities sometimes—I had to squat behind bushes!'

'Oh my God, that sounds awful,' Victoria said. 'More the sort of thing I have to resort to out in the paddocks. Not on holidays.'

'I thought you were going to drive up in one day?' Sally asked.

'Paulo miscalculated the distance, but it was an adventure,' Sally said with a shrug, though her tone suggested it had been more endurance than enjoyment. 'But enough about us—how was sailing? Did you see whales? Dolphins?'

'We saw both,' Amanda replied, finding comfort in the neutral topic. 'And turtles at Lady Musgrave Island. The snorkelling was incredible.'

'Amazing reef,' Paulo added. 'I've dived it a few times.'

Of course he had, Amanda thought. *Ask him. He's done everything.*

'Victoria didn't snorkel,' she couldn't help adding. 'She stayed on the boat most of the trip.'

Sally's eyebrows rose. 'Really? You missed the Great Barrier Reef?'

Victoria shrugged, suddenly very interested in her nail polish. 'I needed time to chill.'

'We're staying at the Beachcomber Backpackers,' Paulo announced as they turned onto the main street of Airlie Beach. 'Six-bed dorm room, but we lucked out—no one else booked the other two beds, so it's just us.'

The hostel was typical backpacker fare—slightly worn but clean, with a pool area and communal kitchen. As they checked in and carried their bags to the room, Sally fell into step beside Amanda.

'You didn't tell me what happened with Dave,' she

whispered.

'And you didn't tell me why you and Paulo are suddenly all lovey-dovey again,' Amanda countered.

Sally's expression turned serious. 'We had some good talks on the drive. And he's going to take me on a romantic cruise while we're here.'

A laugh rang out. Amanda followed Sally's gaze to where Victoria was laughing at something Paulo had said.

'How was she?' Sally asked, her tone showing that she wished Victoria was still on the boat.

Amanda pulled a face. 'She barely spoke the entire week. Just stayed on her phone whenever she had service. And now she's suddenly back to normal? It's weird.'

Once in the room, they claimed their bunks—Sally and Paulo taking the double bed on one side, Amanda and Victoria the single beds opposite. They left the two vacant beds between them. As they unpacked, the conversation flowed more easily, catching each other up on their respective journeys.

'So, when did you two make up?' Amanda finally asked, nodding towards Paulo.

Sally exchanged a glance with him before answering. 'About two days in. We had a big fight our first night on the road, then got everything out in the open.'

'She called me a selfish twat,' Paulo admitted with surprising cheerfulness. 'I didn't know that word, but her expression showed me what she meant.'

Something had shifted between them. The Paulo that Amanda remembered from Noosa had been defensive and manipulative; this Paulo seemed more self-aware, almost thoughtful.

'What about you, Amanda?' Sally pushed, eyes twinkling.

Amanda felt the heat rise to her face. 'Dave's a good guy.'

'Oh please,' Victoria suddenly interjected. 'They've been all over each other since day one. It was like watching a romance novel unfold.'

'That's not true,' Amanda protested, though her blush betrayed her.

'It's fine,' Victoria said, waving a dismissive hand. 'You two were perfect together. The sailing enthusiasts, cooking meals, watching sunsets.'

'I'm going to check out the kitchen to make some lunch.' Amanda needed to be alone.

The hostel kitchen buzzed with a mix of laughter, clattering dishes, and the faint scent of overcooked pasta, while the pool area was alive with sunburnt backpackers sprawled on plastic loungers, their loud conversations cutting through the humid air. Beer bottles clinked, and laughter filled the air. The others were ready to slip effortlessly into the social backpacker world, but Amanda suddenly missed the quiet rhythm of life aboard *Seabreeze*—the soft creak of the mast, the movement of the waves beneath them. She knew in that moment that she was done with travel, yet uncertain what awaited her at home. All she knew was that Dave lingered in her thoughts, and she couldn't let go.

She jumped as Sally appeared behind her and grabbed her arm.

'Let's go out for lunch! There's a great place on the esplanade. Best cocktails in town.'

As they headed back out into the humid Airlie Beach afternoon, confusion filled Amanda. Nothing made sense anymore—Paulo's transformation, Sally's contentment,

Victoria's mood swings—all contributed to the odd tension she sensed in the group.

But one thing was certain: she knew with absolute certainty that Dave Hewson was not someone she would easily forget—or perhaps ever want to.

Chapter 20

Friday, August 15 - 8.30 a.m.

Cardwell.

Amanda could feel the tension building in the van as they drove towards Cassowary Charters in Cardwell. The coastal town was picture-perfect—brilliant blue sea stretching east, verdant mountains rising west, palm trees swaying in the salt-scented breeze. But Paulo had been insufferable again as she and Victoria talked about their charter with Dave, rolling his eyes dramatically at every mention of sailing or making snippy comments about "regular people having to pay for luxury."

'You know,' he said for what felt like the hundredth time, turning around from the passenger seat to face Victoria and Amanda in the back, 'where I come from, my family has connections with all the best charter companies. We never pay full price.'

Amanda caught Victoria's eye, and they shared a discreet eye-roll. Paulo's claims about his wealthy background had grown more elaborate with each passing day, but something about them rang hollow to Amanda. The way he'd scrutinise the bill at cafés, his reluctance to replace his worn-out sandals, and now this desperate need to one-up their free charter experience all painted a different picture than the affluent lifestyle he kept talking about.

'Well, you're about to experience the wonders of paying customers,' Amanda said, keeping her voice sweet. 'I'm sure it will be absolutely magical.'

Sally, driving with a dreamy look on her face, seemed

oblivious to the undercurrents. 'I can't wait for our romantic cruise,' she said, reaching over to squeeze Paulo's hand. 'Three whole days, just us and the sea.'

Amanda bit her tongue. She'd noticed the way Paulo's gaze lingered on Victoria whenever Sally wasn't looking—the way he'd find excuses to touch her arm or stand close to her. Sally was her friend, and Amanda hated seeing her so thoroughly charmed by someone she increasingly distrusted.

'Here we are,' Victoria announced as the small building with the Cassowary Charters sign came into view.

The office was small but neat, with large windows overlooking the marina where several gleaming boats bobbed in the gentle waves. The water lapped softly against the wooden jetty, catching the midday sun in thousands of sparkling reflections. Seabirds wheeled lazily overhead, occasionally diving for fish in the crystal-clear shallows.

A woman with tanned skin and salt-streaked blonde hair looked up from her computer as they entered.

'G'day,' she said cheerfully. 'You must be the Ramirez party? I'm Sandra, one of the owners.'

Paulo stepped forward, chest puffed out slightly. 'Yes, that's us. My girlfriend and I are very much looking forward to our three-day cruise.' He emphasised "girlfriend" while giving Victoria a quick sideways glance that made Amanda's skin crawl.

Sandra typed something into her computer, then looked up with a smile. 'Actually, we've had a bit of a change in the bookings. We've had a cancellation for one of our premium packages, and I can offer you an upgrade.'

Paulo's expression brightened immediately. 'An upgrade?

But for how much cost?'

'Yes, instead of the three-day charter you booked, we can offer you a five-day charter for the same price,' Sandra explained, then added with a glance towards Victoria and Amanda, 'or, if you'd prefer, you could bring your two friends and be out four nights for no extra charge.'

She leaned forward on her elbows, her smile widening. 'And as for timing, we're quite flexible. We can get you out on the water today once we see your ID and sort the payment, or if you'd prefer to prepare another day, you could head out tomorrow. The weather forecast is great for both days.'

The silence that followed was thick enough to cut with a knife. Amanda watched Paulo's face cycle through a series of emotions—excitement, calculation, and then barely concealed happiness when Victoria spoke up.

'That sounds amazing!' Victoria exclaimed. 'I'd love to join if Sally and Paulo are okay with it.'

The look on Sally's face made Amanda's heart sink. Her earlier dreamy expression had vanished, replaced by something between confusion and hurt as she looked between Paulo and Victoria. What the hell was Victoria playing at? She'd hated the trip on Dave's boat.

'I thought...' Sally began quietly, 'I thought this was supposed to be our romantic getaway.'

Paulo recovered quickly, slipping an arm around Sally's waist. 'Of course it is, darling. But wouldn't it be more fun with friends? Four days with Victoria sounds perfect.'

'I'd rather do the five days with just us,' Sally persisted.

'We'll take the offer to bring friends,' Paulo said, ignoring Sally's words, 'and we'd like to head out today.'

Amanda stepped forward. 'Actually, I won't be going. I'll

drive the car up to Mission Beach like we planned.' She avoided mentioning Dave explicitly, but she knew Victoria would understand her eagerness to see him again.

'Are you sure?' Sandra asked. 'It's quite a deal.'

'Positive,' Amanda replied firmly. 'Someone needs to drive up. Isn't this a one-way trip?'

'Yes.' Sandra nodded. 'A set route from Cardwell to Clump Point marina at Pandanus Point.'

Amanda frowned. 'I thought it was Mission Beach.'

'It is. Pandanus Point is a small hamlet a couple of kilometres to the north of the township.' Sandra nodded. 'Alright then. While we process your paperwork, why don't you all head down to take a look at the boat? It's the *Lady Windward,*' the third one along the main dock. My husband Graham is down there doing some maintenance.'

As they walked along the marina, Amanda marvelled at the scenery. The foreshore was lined with towering palms, their fronds rustling in the gentle breeze. Beyond the harbour, the dark shapes of tropical islands dotted the horizon, mysterious and inviting. The water in the bay was so clear she could see colourful fish darting between the moorings.

The *Lady Windward* was a sleek sailing catamaran, its white hulls gleaming in the sunlight. A tall man with a deep tan and cropped beard was checking something on the deck.

'Graham?' Paulo called out, waving. 'We're your charter for today.'

Graham straightened up and grinned, waving them aboard. 'Come on up and have a look around!'

Amanda followed Victoria up the gangplank, taking in the polished teak decking and well-maintained equipment. It was certainly a fine vessel—spacious and luxurious, with a large cockpit area and comfortable-looking seating. Still, as she ran her hand along the smooth wooden railing, she couldn't help comparing it to Dave's boat. This one was newer, fancier even, but somehow lacked the character and warmth she'd felt aboard Dave's vessel. Or maybe it was just that Dave wasn't here.

While Victoria excitedly explored the cabins and galley six steps down, Amanda remained on deck, watching the gentle lapping of the water against the hull and enjoying the sun on her face.

'You'll need some provisions,' Graham was saying. 'There's a grocery store just two blocks away that caters to charters.'

'I'll take care of the shopping,' Amanda offered, seeing an opportunity. 'Sally, want to come with me and tell me what you want? I've got a bit of an idea after being on Dave's boat, although there's probably a much bigger fridge on this one.'

Sally nodded, looking relieved to have something to focus on.

Graham turned to Paulo and Victoria. 'While they're doing that, I'll give you two a proper briefing on how to sail her. Safety equipment, navigation, the works.'

'No need to worry about the basics,' Paulo said with a dismissive wave of his hand. 'I've got plenty of sailing experience. My family owns a yacht in the Mediterranean.'

Amanda caught this as she was stepping off the boat and exchanged a quick glance with Graham, who didn't look entirely convinced. She bit back a comment and instead guided Sally towards the Troop Carrier.

As they walked, Amanda could sense Sally's disappointment.

'I thought it would just be Paulo and me,' Sally said finally, once they were out of earshot. 'I don't understand why Victoria had to invite herself along.'

Amanda chose her words carefully. 'Victoria's excited about sailing again, I guess.' She tried to reassure Sally, but she couldn't understand why Victoria wanted to tag along. Maybe she *was* attracted to Paulo. 'And maybe... maybe it's good to have someone else around.' She hesitated, then added, 'Sally, I just want you to be careful. I'm not sure Paulo is always... honest.'

Sally stopped walking. 'What are you trying to say?'

'Well, I thought his family had yachts in Brazil? Now the Mediterranean?'

'He exaggerates,' Sally said. 'He might look like he has a lot of self-confidence, but he really doesn't.'

'All these stories about his wealthy family—they don't quite add up. And,' Amanda hesitated and then forged on. It was Sally's happiness that was at stake here. 'I've noticed the way he looks at Victoria sometimes.'

'So? What, you think he's lying to me? That he's after Victoria?' Sally's voice rose with emotion. 'You're supposed to be my friend, Amanda!'

'I am your friend,' Amanda insisted. 'That's why I'm concerned. Just... try to see Paulo for what he is, not what he says he is.'

Sally's face flushed. 'You're just jealous because I've found someone who cares about me. Paulo loves me. He tells me all the time.'

Amanda sighed, recognising the defensive anger in her friend's eyes. She'd made things worse, not better. 'I'm sorry.

You're right, it's not my place. Let's just get the groceries, alright?'

They shopped in strained silence, filling a box with meat, fresh fruit, vegetables, bread, and other essentials. By the time they paid, called into the bottle shop, and headed back towards the marina, the tension between them had eased slightly, but Amanda knew she'd touched a nerve.

When they returned to the *Lady Windward*, Amanda's heart sank. Graham had disappeared, presumably having completed the briefing. Paulo and Victoria were lounging on the foredeck, looking all too comfortable together. Victoria had already changed into a brief bikini that showed off her athletic figure, and Paulo sat suspiciously close to her, pointing out something on the horizon.

As they watched, Victoria laughed at something Paulo said and casually placed her hand on his back, letting it linger there for a moment too long.

The look on Sally's face as she saw this made Amanda wince. Her friend clutched the box of groceries tighter, knuckles whitening.

'If she touches him again, I'll kill her,' Sally muttered under her breath, just loud enough for Amanda to hear.

Amanda glanced at her friend in alarm. Sally's usually gentle features had hardened into something almost unrecognisable—a mixture of hurt, jealousy, and raw anger that Amanda had never seen before.

'Sally—' Amanda began, but was cut off.

'Here's our food and wine,' Sally called out, her voice overly bright as she climbed aboard, the sudden shift in her demeanour almost more unsettling than the anger. Paulo jumped up, suddenly attentive, helping her with the box.

Paulo came over and looked at the box holding the wine. 'Oh, Sally. That's not enough for four nights. Come on, we'll go and get some more.'

Sally looked triumphantly at Victoria, who waved a lazy hand.

'Get a couple of bottles of vodka too. I'll fix you up when you come back.'

Amanda remained on the dock, deeply conflicted. The situation was clearly volatile, but she wasn't sure whether her presence would improve things or make them worse. In the end, she decided that Sally was smart enough to handle the situation. She'd made her choice to go along, and Amanda had to trust her friend's judgement.

'Well, I guess this is goodbye for now,' Amanda said, forcing a cheerful tone.

Sally set down the groceries and came back to give Amanda a quick hug. The gesture surprised and relieved her—perhaps her flash of anger had subsided.

'Try to have fun,' Amanda whispered, hugging her back. 'I'll see you at Pandanus Point.'

As she walked back towards the van, Amanda couldn't shake her uneasiness about the situation she was leaving behind. But ahead lay Mission Beach, a hundred kilometres of tropical scenery, and at the end of that road, Dave. The thought lightened her mood considerably as she started the engine and pulled away from Cassowary Charters, watching the *Lady Windward* grow smaller in her rear vision mirror.

Part 3: The Finale

Shadows on the Shore

Chapter 21

Friday, August 15 - 2.00 p.m.

Mission Beach.

Amanda rolled down the windows of the Troop Carrier, letting the warm coastal air rush through her hair as she drove towards Mission Beach. The one-and-a-half-hour journey from Cardwell had given her time to think, to breathe, to feel the stress of the past few weeks disappearing.

Four days away from them—four whole days without having to pretend everything was fine or avoid Sally's searching looks. She'd become an expert at pushing thoughts of Sally into a box labelled "deal with later." Not now. Not during these precious days of freedom with Dave.

The realisation hit her as she drove through the cane fields—she was chasing after a man whose last name she didn't even know. It should have felt reckless, but something about Dave had gotten under her skin in a way no one ever had before.

As Mission Beach came into view, with its endless stretches of sand and glittering water beyond, excitement fluttered in her chest.

She followed the signs to the marina at Clump Point, her eyes scanning the rows of boats until they landed on the familiar shape of *Seabreeze*. Seeing it again made her smile, memories of laughter and love washing over her.

But the boat sat silent, with no sign of Dave anywhere. She pulled out her phone and dialled the number he'd given her.

Her heart sank as a robotic voice told her that the number was unable to be connected.

'Brilliant, Amanda,' she muttered to herself, turning the van around and heading into town, disappointment settling over her like a heavy blanket. Maybe this whole trip was a mistake.

She parked near the main street and decided to walk around before looking for accommodation. The township was small but vibrant, with cafés and shops lining the oceanfront road. Maybe she'd bump into Dave, though, considering how many houses dotted the hills around Mission Beach and Pandanus Point, finding him would be like looking for a needle in a haystack. Still, he'd mentioned living in a small house beside a cane farm, and she'd passed plenty of those on the way in.

Mission Beach's main street unfolded before her like a postcard come to life. Palm trees swayed gently in the sea breeze, their fronds casting dappled shadows across the sun-warmed pavement. The storefronts were painted in cheerful colours—aquamarine blues, coral pinks, and sunny yellows—many with hand-painted signs that gave the whole place a distinctly laid-back, artisan feel.

Amanda paused outside a boutique with sarongs hanging in the window, a riot of tropical patterns and colours that seemed to capture the essence of this coastal paradise. On impulse, she pushed open the door and went inside, a small bell tinkling to announce her arrival. The air inside was scented with coconut and something citrusy—maybe lime. A wave of regret washed over her. She would miss Australia so much when she and Sally headed home next month. Especially North Queensland.

Especially Dave. The thought surprised her with its intensity. When had this man become so important to her?

'Need a hand, love?'

'Just browsing, thanks.'

The woman behind the counter nodded and returned to arranging a display of shell jewellery.

Amanda ran her fingers over the silky fabrics of the sarongs on another rack, admiring the intricate patterns—sea turtles swimming through azure waters, hibiscus blooms exploding in pinks and reds, abstract swirls in ocean hues. She selected one in shades of turquoise and emerald green that reminded her of the water in the cove where she and Dave had spent that magical evening on *Seabreeze*.

As the shopkeeper wrapped her purchase in tissue paper, Amanda cleared her throat.

'I'm actually looking for someone,' she began. 'A sailor named Dave? He has a boat at the marina.'

The woman's hands stilled for a moment, then continued wrapping with deliberate care. 'Lots of Daves around here, love. Any last name?'

Amanda felt her cheeks flush. 'Actually, no. I know that sounds ridiculous. Tall guy, late thirties? Long blonde hair in a ponytail, deeply tanned? He runs charter boats and sometimes takes on backpacker crew.'

The woman's expression changed instantly. Her friendly demeanour evaporated, replaced by something that looked like genuine alarm. She glanced towards the shop entrance, then leaned closer to Amanda.

'Dave Hewson?' Her voice dropped to barely above a whisper. 'Love, you need to stay well away from that one.'

Amanda's stomach clenched. 'Why? What's wrong with him?'

The shopkeeper's eyes darted around the empty shop again before she spoke. 'Listen to me carefully. That man... he's not what he seems. About ten years ago, a German girl was working on his boat. One night, she just disappeared. Never found.'

Amanda felt the blood drain from her face. 'What do you mean, disappeared?'

'I mean, gone. No trace. Her passport, her backpack, everything left behind on his boat. Police questioned him for days, but...' The woman shook her head grimly. 'Money talks in small towns, if you know what I mean. Dave's family owns half the cane farms around here. The investigation just faded away.'

'But surely if there was evidence—' Amanda started.

'Evidence has a way of disappearing too,' the woman cut her off, her voice gaining urgency. 'And it's not just the German girl. There've been whispers over the years. Other girls. Backpackers who worked for him and then just... disappeared. Moved on, that's what he says.'

Amanda gripped the counter, her knuckles white. The Dave she thought she knew—charming, attentive, funny—suddenly felt like a stranger. Had she been completely blind? 'Why hasn't anyone—'

'Because he's clever about it,' the woman said quietly. 'Always picks girls who are travelling alone, no real ties here. Backpackers drift in and out all the time—who's to say they didn't just catch the next bus to Brisbane or Darwin?' She fixed Amanda with an intense stare. 'But I've been here a long time, love. I see the patterns.'

The shop suddenly felt suffocating. Amanda's mind reeled, thinking of all the times she'd been alone with Dave on his boat, how isolated they'd been. How trusting she'd been.

The woman grabbed Amanda's wrist gently but firmly. 'Promise me you won't go looking for him. Whatever you think you know about him, whatever he told you—it's all lies.'

Amanda nodded numbly, unable to find her voice.

'Good girl.' The woman released her wrist and handed over the wrapped package, her hands shaking slightly. 'Now you go straight back to wherever you came from, and you forget all about Dave Hewson.'

Amanda stumbled towards the door, her legs feeling unsteady. At the threshold, she turned back.

'The German girl,' she managed. 'What was her name?'

The shopkeeper's face crumpled with old grief. 'Katja. Her name was Katja Mueller. She was only twenty-two. Sweetest thing you ever met.' A tear rolled down her cheek. 'She reminded me of my own daughter. Used to come in here all the time, always buying little gifts to send home.' She pointed to some photos pinned up behind the counter. One at the top had curled edges. 'That's Katja, wasn't she beautiful?'

Amanda nodded and got out of the shop as fast as she could, the woman's words echoing in her mind. Outside, the cheerful tropical setting felt surreal, almost mocking. How could such dark secrets exist in paradise?

She continued down the main street, but her earlier enthusiasm had evaporated. Between buildings, she caught glimpses of the Coral Sea, impossibly blue and stretching to the horizon, but even its beauty couldn't lift the weight of what she'd learnt.

A small juice bar caught her eye, its front counter adorned with pyramids of fresh tropical fruits. The rich, sweet scent of ripe fruit drew her in, and she ordered their specialty—mango, passion fruit, and lime—hoping the familiar ritual of eating might steady her nerves.

The sun was dipping lower in the sky, casting long shadows and painting the clouds in soft pinks and oranges. She needed to find somewhere to stay, and if nothing else was available, she could sleep in the back of the Troop Carrier. People were beginning to fill the outdoor tables of restaurants and cafés, the atmosphere shifting from lazy afternoon to the more vibrant energy of evening in a tourist town.

Her stomach growled, reminding her that the fruit juice, delicious as it was, hadn't been much sustenance. She noticed a pub at the end of the street, its weathered wooden façade suggesting it had been there for decades. A hand-painted sign swung gently in the breeze: "The Salty Dog".

The building was rustic, with exposed wooden beams darkened by years of sea air, and walls decorated with fishing nets, old buoys, and black-and-white photographs showing the town's history. The front area featured a high deck overlooking the street and, beyond it, the ocean. The evening was too beautiful to be inside.

Amanda climbed the steps to the deck, looking for an empty table where she could watch the sunset and try to process everything she'd learnt. The mingled aromas of beer, grilled steak, and hot chips filled the air, along with the sound of conversations and distant waves.

She was scanning for a vacant spot when her breath caught. There, at a bench near the front of the deck, she spotted a set of broad, tanned shoulders and a familiar blonde ponytail.

Dave was nursing a beer and watching the crowds walk by. Even from a distance, she could see the tension in his posture, the way he kept glancing around as if expecting trouble.

When their eyes met, his face lit up with genuine surprise and pleasure. 'Amanda!' He stood and waved her over. 'My God! I can't believe you're here.'

She approached slowly, every instinct warring within her. The shopkeeper's warnings screamed in her mind, but the man in front of her was still the Dave she remembered—warm, welcoming, real.

Dave noticed her hesitation immediately. His smile faded, replaced by something that looked like weary recognition.

'You've already heard the local gossip about me, haven't you?' His voice was quiet, resigned.

Amanda's eyes widened. 'You know about it?'

'Hard to miss when people cross the street to avoid you and anonymous accounts blast you on social media.' His laugh was bitter. He gestured to a more secluded table tucked away from the main thoroughfare. 'Come on, let's sit somewhere we can talk properly.'

Once they were seated, Dave leaned forward, his expression serious. 'Where did you hear it? What did they tell you?'

A server approached, her arms inked with colourful sea creatures that seemed to dance as she moved. 'Can I get you anything?' she asked Amanda.

'Whatever he's having,' Amanda replied, nodding towards Dave's glass.

The server returned quickly with Amanda's beer, condensation already beading on the cold glass. Amanda took a grateful sip, the crisp, hoppy flavour refreshing, but she couldn't avoid the conversation any longer.

'The woman at the gift shop,' she began reluctantly. 'She said there was a German girl who disappeared from your boat ten years ago. Katja Mueller. And that there have been others. She told me to stay away from you.'

Dave's face went very still. For a long moment, he stared

at his beer, and Amanda felt her heart hammering against her ribs. Was this where he would reveal his true nature? Make excuses? Become angry?

Instead, when he looked up, his eyes were filled with a pain so deep it took her breath away.

'Amanda,' he said quietly, 'Katja Mueller is alive and well in Germany. She's a government economist now, married, living in Munich with her husband and two children.'

Her eyes went wide. 'What?'

'The German girl everyone thinks I murdered. She's alive.' Dave's voice was steady but weighted with years of exhaustion. 'She left Mission Beach suddenly because someone was stalking her—following her home from work, leaving notes on her car, calling her at all hours. She was terrified. She asked me not to tell anyone where she was going because she was afraid he'd follow her.'

Amanda stared at him, trying to process this information. 'But... if she's alive, why don't you prove it? Why don't you clear your name?'

Dave gave her a look that was equal parts sad and cynical. 'I tried, at first. But who was I supposed to tell? The anonymous accounts spreading rumours on social media hide behind fake profiles, Amanda. You can't reason with them. It just inflames it more. So, I just stay off it.'

'But the police—'

'The police investigated thoroughly at the time. My family's lawyers got involved, yes, but the investigation was legitimate. They found no evidence of foul play because there wasn't any. The case was closed, but the details were never made public—privacy laws, you know. The truth doesn't make for good gossip.' He pulled out his phone and scrolled through it before showing her the screen. 'I still get Christmas cards from Katja. She sends photos of her kids.'

Amanda looked at the phone screen. There was a cheerful holiday message in German and photos of a smiling blonde woman with two young children, standing in front of what looked like a Christmas market. The woman looked older than twenty-two now, but Amanda could see it was the same person from the old photos she'd glimpsed in the shop.

'She knows about the rumours,' Dave continued. 'I asked her once if she'd be willing to make a public statement, but she's built a new life. She doesn't want to be dragged back into all this. And I can't blame her.'

Amanda felt something shift inside her chest. The evidence was right there—concrete, undeniable. But more than that, she could see the toll this had taken on Dave, his shoulders now bowed like a man who'd been fighting a losing battle for years.

'There's more,' Dave said, his voice dropping lower. He glanced around to make sure no one was listening. 'The police did have a suspect at the time. Someone who was known to have been bothering several young women in town, including Katja. But he... let's just say he has connections. Influence. The investigation was shut down quietly, and his name was never made public.'

'Who was it?'

Dave shook his head. 'I can't say. Legal reasons. But he's still here, still... well. Let's just say I'm not the only one who knows the truth, but I'm the one who it's safe to blame. I try to rise above it, and when I'm home, I come here and sit watching the world go by every afternoon. A few of the locals have come around, but every time, it seems to get better, the social media accusations flare up again.'

Amanda reached across the table and touched his hand. The gesture was instinctive, and she felt him start with surprise before his fingers intertwined with hers.

'I'm sorry,' she said. 'I'm so sorry I doubted you.'

'You spoke to me despite what they told you,' Dave replied, his thumb brushing across her knuckles. 'Quite a few locals won't even do that anymore. That means everything, Amanda.'

They sat in silence for a moment, hands clasped across the table. The sun was setting now, painting the sand in gold and highlighting Dunk Island across the water. Amanda studied Dave's face—really looking at him. She saw the weariness there, the way his eyes carried a sadness that hadn't been there during their carefree days on the boat. But she also saw integrity, kindness, and a quiet strength that came from enduring years of undeserved suspicion.

'I need to ask you something,' she said finally. 'And I need you to be completely honest with me.'

Dave nodded, his expression serious.

'Is there anything else? Any other reason why people might have turned against you? Any other secrets I should know about?'

Dave was quiet for a long moment, considering his words carefully. 'There was a period, after the rumours started spreading, when I became pretty bitter. I drank too much, got into a few fights with people who were spreading lies about me. I'm not proud of that. It only made things worse, made me look more guilty.' He met her eyes directly. 'But I've never hurt anyone, Amanda. I've never hurt a woman. The thought of it makes me sick.'

Something in his voice, in the way he looked at her, convinced Amanda completely. This wasn't the voice of a manipulator or a killer. This was a man who'd been wrongly accused and had spent years paying the price.

'Listen,' Dave said eventually, his voice soft. 'I know this is a lot to process. If you want to leave, to go back to your life, I understand. This isn't exactly what you signed up for when you decided to visit.'

Amanda looked into his eyes, searching for any trace of deception and finding none. What she found instead was something that made her heart race—a depth of feeling that matched her own growing attachment to this man.

'Actually,' she said, surprising herself with her certainty, 'I'd like to stay. If you'll have me. I'd like to hear the whole story, and I'd like to spend these few days getting to know the real you, not the version everyone else thinks they know.'

Dave's face transformed, relief and joy replacing his guarded expression. 'Are you sure? Because once you're seen with me around town, some of that suspicion is going to splash onto you too. People talk.'

Amanda squeezed his hand. 'Let them talk. I'm a big girl, Dave. I can make my own decisions about who to trust.'

'In that case,' he said, his smile returning—the one she remembered from their time on the boat, 'how about we get some dinner here? I know the food's good, and...' He glanced around at the other patrons. 'Well, if we're going to face the gossip mill, might as well do it head-on.'

Amanda admired his courage. 'You're sure? Won't it make things harder for you?'

'Probably,' Dave admitted. 'But I'm tired of hiding. And

you're worth it.'

They ordered fish and chips—the pub's speciality—and found themselves talking easily. Dave told her about his charter business, how bookings had dried up over the years as the rumours spread. Amanda shared stories about her travels with Sally, carefully avoiding the complicated parts of that relationship.

As the evening wore on, she found herself watching Dave's interactions with the staff and other patrons. Some people did avoid eye contact or whisper when they thought he wasn't looking, but others—particularly the younger staff—treated him normally, even warmly. It wasn't the unanimous condemnation the shopkeeper had suggested.

'The girl who served us,' Amanda observed quietly. 'She likes you.'

Dave glanced over at the tattooed server, who was laughing at something one of the kitchen staff had said. 'Jess? Yeah, she's a good person. Her mum knows the truth about what happened with Katja, but...' He shrugged. 'One voice against many doesn't count for much.'

After dinner, they walked along the beach as the stars emerged. The sand was cool beneath their feet, and the sound of waves provided a gentle backdrop to their conversation. Amanda looked up at Dave, his face shadowed, this man who had somehow become so important to her in such a short time.

'Can I ask you something?' she said, stopping to face him.

'Anything.'

'Why did you want to see me again? After everything you've been through, wouldn't it be easier to keep people at arm's length?'

Dave was quiet for a long moment, his hands in his pockets as he looked out at the dark ocean. 'Because when I'm with you, I remember who I used to be. Before all this started. You see me, Amanda. The real me. Not the monster they've made me out to be.' He turned to her, his eyes serious in the starlight. 'I know this is complicated, and I know you're leaving Australia soon. But these few days with you... they might be the only normal I get for a long time.'

The honesty in his voice made her chest tighten. She reached up and touched his face, feeling the slight roughness of stubble beneath her palm.

'Dave,' she said softly.

And then he was kissing her, gentle at first, then deeper as she responded. When they broke apart, both were breathing hard.

'I should probably find somewhere to stay,' Amanda said, though she made no move to step away from him.

'There's a decent motel just up the road,' Dave replied. 'But Amanda... would you consider staying at my place? I know how that sounds, given everything we've talked about, but I have a spare room. I just... I don't want this evening to end yet.'

She looked into his eyes, seeing the vulnerability there alongside the desire. The old Amanda might have been cautious, might have chosen the safer option. But standing here on this beach, with this man who had shown her such honesty and courage, she realised she was changing.

'Yes,' she said simply. 'I'd like that.'

As they walked back towards his truck, Dave's hand found hers again. The realisation hit her with startling clarity: she was falling in love with Dave Hewson. Not the mysterious sailor she'd romanticised during those first carefree days on the boat, but the real man—damaged and hurt by what had happened to him—but a good man. And for the first time in longer than she could remember, she was happy. Really happy.

It felt like coming home.

Despite everything—the gossip, the warnings, the doubt that had almost made her turn away when she saw him in the pub—Amanda knew she was making the right choice. Not only because of the evidence he'd shown her, but because of what she saw in his eyes when he looked at her. Whatever was growing between them was real, and it was worth fighting for.

Chapter 22

Sunday, August 17 - 11.45 p.m.

Lady Windward.

The sound of voices above deck stirred Sally from her restless sleep. She'd been having trouble sleeping since they'd left Cardwell; the confined space of the cabin made her feel claustrophobic. The small berth that had seemed cosy in the daylight now felt like a coffin.

Disoriented, she checked her watch—surprised to see it was almost midnight. After a few wines in the sun, she'd come down to their cabin in her bathers for a quick rest.

Paulo and Victoria were still up on the deck; their voices carried down through the open hatch. Sally stretched, trying to work the kink out of her neck, wrapped her sarong around her, and then padded barefoot towards the companionway steps. She was going to make a cup of tea, and she'd go up and sit with them. The way Victoria was monopolising Paulo was getting under her skin.

As she climbed the narrow stairs to the deck, something in their tone made her pause just below deck level, her head still concealed by the cabin structure. There was an urgency to their conversation, a tension that hadn't been there during dinner. She widened her eyes as the words drifted down to the galley.

'...the final payment should clear tomorrow. Once Daddy transfers the remaining money to the Swiss account, we disappear forever,' Victoria was saying. Her voice sounded different. The Aussie twang was gone, and she sounded as English as Sally.

What the hell? Sally frowned, pressing herself against the side of the companionway. *Swiss account? What money?*

'You're sure your father will pay the rest?' Paulo's voice, but without the warmth she'd grown to love. This was all business.

'Daddy will pay anything to get his precious daughter back,' Victoria replied with a cold laugh. 'Ten million pounds is pocket change to him. The beauty is, he'll never report it to the police—not with the family reputation to protect.'

'Why has he been so slow then? Are you sure he wouldn't involve the police?'

Sally's blood turned to ice. Ransom. They were talking about ransom. But Victoria wasn't kidnapped—she was right here, orchestrating it.

'Because all he cares about is his money and his reputation, Lord bloody Fairchild.'

Sally put her hand over her mouth, holding in a gasp.

'He could keep his money and let you be killed?' Paulo said.

Victoria sighed.

'He cared about me once, before bloody Glenys and her bastard kids turned up.'

Confusion had Sally backing away as they kept talking.

'And the calls?' Paulo asked.

'Perfect. I sounded terrified enough, didn't I? All those drama lessons at boarding school are finally paying off.' Victoria's laugh was brittle, calculating. 'The distress in my voice when I begged him not to contact the authorities—Oscar-worthy. And those stupid girls fell for my Aussie accent.'

'What about when we get back? Won't he realise—'

'That's what the psychiatric hospital story is for, darling. Poor me, traumatised by my ordeal, needs extensive private treatment in Switzerland. I'll be conveniently unavailable for months while I "recover" on Daddy's money. By the time I surface, the heat will have died down. That'll teach that bitch of a stepmother. A lot less money for her to get her greedy hands on. My next project is to get rid of her. Want to help me with that?'

Sally pressed her hand over her mouth to stifle another gasp. The Paulo she'd fallen in love with—gentle, romantic, and passionate —didn't exist. It had all been an act.

She had to get off this boat. Moving as quietly as possible, Sally began to back down the stairs, but her foot caught on the bottom step and she stumbled, grabbing the handrail to steady herself. The movement caused a slight creak in the boat's structure.

The voices above stopped

Sally froze, hardly daring to breathe. After what felt like an eternity, she heard Paulo murmur something she couldn't make out, followed by Victoria's low, throaty laugh.

Heart pounding, Sally crept back to her small cabin and fumbled for her phone in the darkness. She had to call Amanda, had to—

Movement on deck made her look up. Through the small porthole above her berth, she could see the reflection of light from the main cabin. On tiptoes, she moved to where she could see through the galley windows that looked up to the cockpit area.

What she saw made her stomach lurch.

Paulo's back was to her, and Victoria was straddling him, her bikini top undone, kissing him with hungry passion. His hands roamed over her body, gripping the sides of her bikini bottoms as she ground against him. This wasn't just physical attraction—it was raw, desperate lust between two people who already knew each other intimately.

How long had this been going on? How long had she been the fool, the third wheel, the convenient cover story? She pulled her phone from her pocket, and her fingers flew over the keys as she texted Amanda, her best friend, who had tried to warn her about Paulo, but she'd been too stupid to see it.

As if sensing she was being watched, Victoria turned her head without breaking the kiss. Her eyes met Sally's through the open hatch, and a slow, cruel smile spread across her lips.

'Want to come and join in, darling?' Victoria called out, her voice dripping with mock sweetness.

Something inside Sally snapped. All the humiliation, the betrayal, the realisation that her entire relationship with Paulo had been a lie—it all erupted in a surge of fury she'd never experienced before.

She bounded up the companionway stairs, erupting onto the deck like a force of nature.

'You fucking bitch!' she screamed, her voice carrying across the dark water. 'How long has this been going on?'

Victoria slid off Paulo, making no attempt to cover herself, while Paulo fumbled to pull his shirt back on.

'Sally, this isn't—' Paulo started, his accent thicker with panic.

'Isn't what? Isn't you fucking her while I'm sleeping ten feet below you?' Sally's voice was shrill, breaking with emotion. 'How long, Paulo? How long have you been using me?'

'Nobody's using anybody,' Paulo said, but his eyes

wouldn't meet hers. 'This just… it just happened.'

'Bullshit!' Sally rounded on him, her fists clenched. 'You planned this whole thing, didn't you? Was any of it real? Any of it?'

'Sally, calm down,' Victoria said, her voice maddeningly controlled as she retied her bikini. 'You're hysterical.'

'Hysterical?' Sally whirled on her. 'I'm being hysterical? You're conning your father out of millions, and I'm hysterical?'

Paulo went very still. 'What did you say?'

Sally realised her mistake too late, but the fury driving her forward wouldn't let her stop. 'I heard you, both of you. The ransom calls, the Swiss account, all of it. You're both criminals.'

'Sally—' Paulo stepped towards her, his expression shifting from guilty to dangerous.

'No!' Sally backed away from him. 'I'm done. I'm calling Amanda right now, and then I'm getting off this boat at the next port. I'm out of here, and I'm taking Amanda with me. You both disgust me.'

She turned to go back below, but Victoria was faster, darting past her to block the companionway.

'I don't think so,' Victoria said coolly.

Sally tried to push past her, but Victoria grabbed her arm. In the struggle, Sally's foot slipped on the wet deck, and she fell hard, her elbow cracking against the cockpit seating.

Pain shot up her arm as she looked up to find Victoria standing over her, silhouetted against the star-filled sky.

'You were listening to us, weren't you?' Victoria's voice was ice-cold, all pretence of friendship gone. 'How much did you hear?'

Sally scrambled to her feet, cradling her injured elbow. 'Everything. I heard everything.'

She made a desperate lunge for the companionway and ran down the steps, but Victoria was ahead of her, blocking the way to the cabin. Sally turned to run back up the stairs, but stopped dead.

Victoria had moved to the galley and pulled something from the knife block—a long, sharp blade that gleamed in the moonlight.

'Victoria,' Sally breathed, backing away as her heart hammered against her ribs. 'What are you doing?'

'What I have to do,' Victoria replied, advancing slowly, the knife held steady in her hand. 'You always were too curious for your own good, Sally.'

As Sally stepped back to get away from the crazy bitch, her foot slipped on the bottom step. She fell backwards and her head hit the corner of the step.

Chapter 23

Monday, August 18 - 4.00 p.m.

Dave's house.

Dave's weathered timber cabin was perched on the top of Pandanus Point, surrounded by towering sugar cane that formed dense green walls that almost reached the sand. The modest structure sat in a small clearing; tin-roofed with a wooden veranda wrapped around three sides. The floorboards were weathered to a silvery-grey by countless wet seasons.

Amanda sat on the steps, nursing a cold beer, watching as Dave wrestled with the ancient ride-on mower he'd been trying to start for the better part of an hour. His white T-shirt was darkened with sweat, clinging to the lean muscles of his back as he cursed and cajoled the reluctant machine.

'I think it's a lost cause,' she called, amusement colouring her voice.

Dave straightened, wiping his brow with the back of his arm, leaving a streak of grease. 'Never say die,' he replied with a lopsided grin that did strange things to her insides. 'She's temperamental, but we have an understanding.'

'Is that what you call this relationship?' Amanda laughed, taking another sip of her beer. The cold glass felt heavenly against her hands in the oppressive heat. 'Looks more like mechanical domestic abuse to me.'

Dave chuckled, the sound warm and genuine, like everything else about him was. He abandoned the mower and climbed the steps to join her, accepting the beer she offered from the small cooler on the steps.

'Thanks. I'll try again later when she's had time to think about her behaviour.'

Amanda smiled, studying his profile as he drank deeply from the bottle. Her life had changed so much in the four days since she'd left Sally, Paulo, and Victoria in Cardwell.

'Penny for your thoughts,' Dave said, breaking into her reverie.

Amanda shrugged, aiming for casual. 'Just thinking how strange life is. And how good this is.'

'Regrets?' Dave asked, his expression suddenly serious beneath the easy-going exterior.

'None,' she replied truthfully. These days with Dave had been a gift—simple, honest, healing in a way she hadn't expected. 'Best impulse decision I've made in a very long time.'

Dave's smile returned, crinkling the corners of his eyes in the way she loved. 'Glad to hear it. Now, since this mechanical beast won't cooperate, what do you say we head down to the boat instead? If we're going to meet your friends when they get back tomorrow, I'd like to have her looking shipshape.'

Dave had told her about his project: a thirty-foot former fishing vessel he'd been slowly converting into a private charter boat. Amanda's stomach tightened at the mention of tomorrow—reality intruding on the bubble they'd created. But she nodded, grateful for the distraction. 'Lead the way, Captain.'

The small boatshed at Clump Point Marina was littered with tools and marine equipment. Dave's project sat gleaming in the afternoon light.

'Hand me that sander, would you?' Dave called from the scaffold alongside the hull.

Amanda passed up the tool, admiring his confident

movements as he worked. There was something attractive about watching someone who knew exactly what they were doing.

'So how does a local boy end up restoring boats instead of cutting cane?' she asked.

Dave switched off the sander, considering his words. 'Followed a girl, if you want the embarrassing truth. Swedish backpacker. Three months later, she was headed home, and I was choosing between the family farm and the sea.'

'But you chose the water.'

'I chose the water.' He gestured around the shed. 'Ten years later, here I am. The family thinks I'm mad, but they support me anyway. Almost have enough saved to buy out the Pattersons and run my own operation.'

Amanda ran her hand along the boat's freshly varnished gunwale. 'She's beautiful.'

'Thanks. I've put everything into her.' Dave climbed down from the scaffold. 'Speaking of which, I'm starving. What do you say we pack it in and grab dinner?'

As they put away the tools, Amanda found herself imagining what it would be like to do this every day—to build something real with someone real, instead of just drifting.

Chapter 24

Tuesday, August 19 - 5 a.m.

Dunk Island.

The sandflies were relentless in the pre-dawn darkness, swarming around Paulo's face as he huddled beneath the thin boat blanket. Two nights sleeping rough on Dunk Island had left him hollow-eyed and jumpy, starting at every sound from the dense rainforest behind their makeshift camp. The second blanket lay crumpled beside Victoria, who seemed untroubled by either the insects or their predicament.

'We can't stay here much longer,' Paulo whispered, his voice hoarse from the salt air and stress. 'What if there are crocodiles? This is their territory.'

Victoria didn't open her eyes. 'Crocodiles are the least of our problems.'

They'd made camp in a small clearing just above the high tide mark, hidden from view by a screen of pandanus palms. The tender was pulled deep into the mangroves fifty metres away, branches carefully arranged to camouflage its white hull. Paulo had done that part—he was good with his hands, meticulous. It was one of the reasons Victoria had chosen him.

'I keep thinking about Sally,' Paulo said. 'All that blood...'

Victoria's eyes snapped open, cold and assessing. 'It was an accident.'

'But how—'

'She fell. Hit her head on the galley steps. You couldn't have cared that much about her anyway, considering the way you came onto me the moment we were alone.'

'That's not true. I did care about her. She was a lovely girl. Sweet. Innocent.'

'Innocent?' Victoria's laugh was harsh. 'She would have ruined everything.'

'We should have stayed on the boat. Called for help.' Paulo's hands shook as he reached for the water bottle they'd salvaged from the *Lady Windward*. 'Said she fell. Now we look guilty.'

'We *are* guilty, Paulo. Just not of what they'll think.'

Paulo took a shaky sip of water, his dark eyes haunted. 'But all that blood... where did all the blood come from? It was everywhere.'

Victoria sat up, her movements sharp and controlled. 'Head wounds bleed. You know that.' Her voice was ice-cold, matter-of-fact. 'Lots of blood vessels in the scalp.'

'Her sarong was wet with blood. The way it splattered—'

'Are you questioning me?' Victoria's voice carried a warning that made Paulo shrink back. 'Because if you are, we have bigger problems than crocodiles.'

Paulo shook his head quickly. 'No.'

Victoria pulled a packet of crackers from the bag of food they'd grabbed hastily from the boat's galley before abandoning it. The rest had gone overboard with everything else. 'Eat something. You need to keep your strength up. We have calls to make once you're calm enough to handle it. Can't have you break down in the middle of a conversation.'

Paulo's head snapped up. 'You still want to go through with it? After what happened?'

'Especially after what happened.' Victoria's smile was predatory. 'Think about it, Paulo.'

'Jesus, Victoria. Sally's *dead*.'

'Yes, she is. And she will stay at the bottom of the ocean. Your idea with the chains was brilliant.' Victoria leaned forward. 'Finishing what we started will make her death mean something. We invested too much to walk away now.'

Paulo stared at her, seeing something in her expression that made his stomach turn. 'You're not... you weren't bothered, were you? When it happened.'

'Upset?' Victoria considered this. 'I was annoyed. She was complicating things. She went for me and then she ran up the steps, slipped and fell. As simple as that.' She shrugged. 'Problems have solutions, Paulo. Always. She would have told the authorities. Can you imagine? After everything we'd planned, everything we'd put in place. All those months of preparation.' Victoria's voice hardened. 'She would have destroyed it.'

Paulo wrapped his arms around his knees, rocking slightly. 'I never signed up for murder.'

'No one *signed up* for it. But here we are.' Victoria stood, brushing sand from her clothes. 'And we can either fall apart, or we can finish what we started and disappear with enough money to start over somewhere far from here.'

'The family will be expecting contact soon.'

'I know.' Victoria checked her watch. 'Another hour or two, then we make another call. Let them stew a bit longer. Desperation increases compliance.'

Paulo looked up at her, his face pale in the growing dawn light. 'What if they've already called the police?'

'I know my father. He won't. Not yet. He'll want to handle it quietly, keep it out of the press. Rich families always do.'

Victoria's smile was cold. 'Trust me, he'll pay.'

'And after? When it's over?'

'After, we disappear. New identities, new lives. The money we discussed will be more than enough.' Victoria paused, studying Paulo's haggard face. 'Unless you're having second thoughts?'

The threat in her voice was unmistakable. Paulo shook his head quickly. 'No. No second thoughts.'

Victoria's expression suddenly sharpened. 'There is one thing that concerns me. What if Sally texted Amanda before... before it happened? If she did, we're in trouble.'

'But you checked her phone?'

'I couldn't get in. Even her face recognition wouldn't work.'

Paulo stared at her in horror. 'Fuck. She was dead, and you tried to get the phone to open with her face? What are you, Victoria?'

Victoria's smile was cold. 'I'm not as soft as you, clearly. The phone is now at the bottom of the sea, so we'll never know for certain. We just need to suss out Amanda when she picks us up.'

'What will we tell her about Sally? They're best friends.'

'We tell her that Sally had a fight with us because she saw us together. She stormed off and got off the boat at Tully Heads.' Victoria's smile turned sly. 'Sally was always dramatic. Amanda will believe it.'

'Alright,' he said slowly.

'Good.' Victoria settled back down, pulling the blanket around her shoulders. 'Get some rest. After sunrise, we'll head out to sea, find somewhere with better phone reception. Then we make our calls.'

Paulo lay back down, but his eyes remained open, staring at the lightening sky through the palm fronds. Somewhere in the distance, a fish jumped, the splash echoing across the still water. It sounded almost like a body hitting the surface.

Chapter 25

Tuesday, August 19 - 7 a.m.

Dave's house.

Morning light filtered through the faded curtains of Dave's bedroom, painting golden stripes across the rumpled sheets. Amanda lay on her side, watching Dave sleep, studying his face relaxed in slumber. His arm was draped protectively across her waist, warm and solid, anchoring her against him.

She'd slept better these past four nights than she had in months. Just peaceful, dreamless sleep followed by slow, sun-drenched mornings like this one.

Dave stirred, his eyes blinking open to find her watching him. A sleepy smile spread across his face. 'Morning,' he murmured, his voice husky with sleep.

'Morning,' she replied, reaching out to brush a strand of hair from his forehead.

'What time is it?' he asked, making no move to check himself, seemingly content to remain exactly where he was.

Amanda glanced at the vintage alarm clock on the bedside table. 'Just after eight.'

'Mmm, plenty of time,' Dave murmured, pulling her closer. 'I don't have to go to the marina for a while. They're due at noon. What time are you expecting Sally and the others to call you?'

'She said they'd give me a call when I had to pick them up.'

'Are you going to tell them where you've been?'

The mention of Sally sent a jolt of reality through

Amanda's peaceful bubble. Today was the day. The others would return to Mission Beach, and reality would hit.

Dave must have felt the change in her because he pulled back slightly, concern in his eyes. 'Hey, what's wrong?'

Amanda stretched beside him, trying to recapture the easy intimacy of moments before. 'Nothing's wrong,' she said. 'I just... I don't want to leave. I don't want today to happen.'

Dave stroked her hair, his expression soft. 'Who says you have to leave? Meet them, give Paulo his car back, do whatever you need to do, then come back. The cabin isn't going anywhere.'

'It's not that simple,' Amanda sighed, wishing more than anything that it could be.

'Why not?' Dave asked, his directness one of the things she'd grown to cherish about him. 'Look, I know we've only known each other a few days, but... there's something here, Amanda. Something real. I don't find that very often.'

'I never have before either,' she admitted, the words catching in her throat. 'There's Sally. I committed to travelling with her. And I have to go home.'

'She seemed happy to dump you when she met Paulo.'

They lay in silence for a moment, the ceiling fan spinning lazily above them, stirring the humid air.

'There's something I need to tell you,' Dave said suddenly, an uncharacteristic nervousness in his voice. 'About today. About meeting your friends.'

Amanda tensed. 'What about it?'

Dave sat up, running a hand through his tousled hair. 'I haven't been entirely honest with you. I'm supposed to meet them too—I'm meeting the *Lady Windward* at the marina.'

'What?' Amanda sat up too, clutching the sheet to her chest, confusion and alarm battling for dominance in her mind. 'How? Why?'

'It's my job,' Dave admitted, looking slightly ashamed. 'I work for Cassowary Charters as well. I'm their Mission Beach representative—I meet their boats when they come in, check them over before they head back to Cardwell.'

Relief flooded through Amanda, but confusion remained. 'Is that all? Why didn't you tell me?'

Dave's expression was sheepish. 'I wanted to impress you. When we met and you mentioned your friends were on a charter, I implied I had my own business. It was stupid, I know. But you were so beautiful, and I was just—'

'Just trying to make yourself sound more important,' Amanda finished for him, a surprised laugh escaping her.

'Yeah,' Dave nodded, looking relieved at her reaction. 'Pathetic, right? I should have just told you from the start.'

Amanda shook her head. 'It's not pathetic. It's human.' She took his hand, entwining her fingers with his. 'We all present versions of ourselves we think others want to see.'

'So, you're not mad?' Dave asked cautiously.

'No,' Amanda replied truthfully. 'I understand better than you know.'

Dave smiled, that warm, genuine smile that had drawn her to him from the first day. 'Do you want to come with me?'

Amanda hesitated only a moment. 'I will. I'll give them the Troop Carrier back. I'll talk to Sally and tell her I'm not going to go home with her. I'm going to stay here for a while.' She looked up at him. 'If you'll have me?'

'If I'll have you?' Dave pulled her into his arms and covered her face with kisses. 'If I have my way, I'll never let you go.'

Today would be hard. Sally and the other two would arrive eventually, and she knew she had decided what she was going to do. She wanted to stay with Dave while the others continued north to Cairns—and maybe even stay here. The thought of leaving this simple, honest life they'd begun to build together felt almost impossible now.

Morning sunlight filtered through the kitchen window as Amanda sipped her coffee, watching Dave move around the small space, preparing breakfast. She'd grown accustomed to the domestic rhythm they'd developed over just a few days—his early rising, the careful way he measured coffee grounds, how he hummed tunelessly while he worked.

'What time are you supposed to be at the marina?' she asked, savouring the warmth of the mug between her hands.

Dave glanced at the clock on the wall. 'I should head over by eleven, I guess. Graham likes me to be there well before the charter boats are due in.' He placed a plate of toast in front of her. 'You said Sally was going to call when they're coming in?'

Amanda nodded, the knot in her stomach tightening at the mention of Sally. 'Yeah, that's the plan.'

Her phone had been buzzing intermittently with texts, but she'd ignored them, revelling in her blissful cocoon with Dave. Now, as Paulo's name flashed on the screen with an incoming call, she felt Dave's eyes on her as she answered.

'Change of plans, *querida*,' his smooth voice came through the line, the familiar accent wrapping around the endearment in a way that made her skin crawl. 'We've had to dock at Dunk Island, and we're getting the water taxi across. Drive down to

South Mission Beach and collect us.'

'South Mission? Why?' Amanda asked.

'A change in the charter,' Paulo replied, his tone clipped in a way that brooked no argument. 'There's a small access path at the far southern end, near the mangroves. Park by the picnic area and walk down.'

Amanda frowned. 'That doesn't make sense, Paulo. Why aren't you coming to the marina as planned?'

Dave looked at her curiously.

'Just meet us there, Amanda. One hour.' The line went dead.

Amanda disconnected and shook her head. 'I can't stand Paulo, and I don't want to travel with them again.'

'What was that about?' Dave asked, his brow furrowed.

'He says they've docked at Dunk Island instead of the marina. They're getting the water taxi across, and he said to meet them near the picnic area at South Mission in an hour.' Amanda shook her head. 'That's what he said.'

Dave's frown deepened. 'That doesn't make sense. There's no proper docking at Dunk Island—certainly nothing suitable for the *Lady Windward*. She draws too much water for those shallows. And I don't think the water taxi is in operation anymore.' He stood up, reaching for his phone. 'Something's not right here.'

'What do you mean?' Amanda asked.

'Look, you go to South Mission Beach and pick them up; they'll have some explaining to do. I'll go to the marina as planned. I'll call Graham on the way and find out what's going on. *The Lady Windward* should be at Clump Point, not over at Dunk Island.'

'It does seem strange, but you know what Paulo's like.'

'I do. Who knows what he's done to the boat?' Dave stood and grabbed his keys. 'Give me a ring when you meet them. I'll see you back here. If I get held up, I'll call you.'

The sound of Dave's ute faded into the distance as Amanda snatched her bag from the kitchen counter. The Troopie's keys felt cold in her palm as she hurried across the yard to the shed, wondering what was going on with the boat. Hopefully, Dave would find out and give her a call.

She yanked open the driver's door and threw her bag onto the passenger seat. The phone buzzed again, and she noticed a text from Sally with a timestamp from Saturday night.

Amanda's breath caught in her throat as she read the preview, then unlocked the phone to read the full message:

Amanda, she is an utter bitch. Paulo has dumped me. I just saw them on the deck. He had his hands all over her. She looked at me over his shoulder and she SMILED. I hate her, I hate him, I want to get off this boat. I heard them talking about something bad too, and I don't trust either of them. I'll tell you when you meet us. Love you, girlfriend. I'm sorry.

She typed back quickly: **I'm so sorry, Sal. I missed your text. Are you okay? Just ignore them. I'm on the way to get you. Hang in there xx**

Her hands shook as she fumbled for the keys. The engine roared to life, and she reversed out of the shed with a spray of gravel, already planning the fastest route to South Mission Beach. Whatever was happening on that boat, Sally was in trouble, and Amanda was the only one who could help her.

Victoria and Paulo? She could picture Sally's devastation, alone on that boat with the two people who had clearly betrayed her. The urge to call Sally immediately warred with her own complicated feelings about their relationship. Part of her wanted to comfort Sally, but another part—a part she wasn't proud of—felt a guilty sense of relief that Sally was finally seeing Victoria's true colours.

Sally's text echoed in her mind. The timing was cruel—just when Amanda had discovered something wonderful with Dave, Sally's world was falling apart.

Guilt gnawed at her as she turned onto the road.

She couldn't abandon her best friend now.

Chapter 26

Tuesday - late morning.

South Mission Beach.

The drive to South Mission Beach took Amanda through the now-familiar main street of Mission Beach. Dave's words haunted her as she drove.

There's no proper docking at Dunk Island, and the water taxi isn't at South Mission. His words had planted unease that grew with every kilometre.

She parked near the picnic area as Paulo had instructed, the Troop Carrier's engine ticking as it cooled in the oppressive morning heat. The mangroves stretched before her, a tangle of roots and murky water that seemed to swallow sound. Even the usual chorus of birds was muted here, as if nature itself sensed something wrong.

Amanda followed the narrow path through the mangroves, her footsteps squelching in the muddy ground. Mosquitoes buzzed around her face, and she swatted them away irritably, her nerves already frayed. Where were they?

She heard voices before she saw them—Paulo's distinctive accent carrying across the water, followed by Victoria's low voice. Amanda pushed through a curtain of mangrove branches and emerged into a small clearing where a tender was pulled up onto the muddy bank.

Paulo lifted their bags from the rubber boat while Victoria stood nearby, her designer sarong incongruous against the wild backdrop. Both looked up as Amanda appeared, and she noticed immediately that their usual easy confidence seemed forced.

'Amanda!' Paulo called out, his smile as dazzling as ever, though it didn't quite reach his eyes. 'You found us.'

'Where's Sally?' Amanda asked without preamble, her gaze sweeping the clearing. The tender was small—designed for short trips to shore from a larger vessel. 'And where's the *Lady Windward*?'

Victoria and Paulo exchanged a glance. Paulo stepped forward, his hands spread in a gesture that tried to be reassuring, but only increased Amanda's alarm.

'Ah, *querida*, that's what we need to talk to you about.' Paulo's voice was smooth, practised. 'Sally... she became very upset yesterday. The situation with us, it was too much for her.'

'What situation?' Amanda's voice was sharp.

'She asked us to put her ashore at Tully Heads,' Victoria interjected. 'She said she couldn't bear to be on the boat any longer with Paulo and me.'

Amanda stared at them both, her mind racing. 'She just... left?'

'She was very emotional, Amanda,' Paulo said quickly. 'Very hurt. She said...' He paused, as if the words pained him. 'She said she didn't want to see you either.'

The words hit Amanda like a physical blow. 'She said what?'

'She blamed you for inviting me to join you all,' Victoria added, her voice gentler now but with a confident undertone.

Paulo nodded. 'She said if you hadn't invited Victoria to come with us, none of this would have happened. She was very nasty about you.'

Amanda felt the ground shift beneath her feet. Sally could be vindictive when hurt; that much was true. But to leave without a word? Without telling her she was going?

When I didn't reply to her text, she must have thought I'd abandoned her too.

Tears filled Amanda's eyes. 'I feel so bad.'

Paulo's smile faltered slightly. 'I understand this is hard for you to hear, but—'

'Where did she go?' Amanda's voice rose.

'We dropped her at Tully Heads and she was going to get the bus to Cairns,' Victoria said. 'She's probably there by now, booking her flight home.'

'Come on,' Paulo said, moving towards Amanda with his usual easy manner. 'Let's get out of this swamp. We talk properly in the car, yes? Victoria and I, we're heading north to Cairns. You can come with us, and we can sort all this out.'

'No. I'm not going anywhere with you. I was travelling with Sally.'

Paulo's expression shifted, just for a moment, and Amanda caught a glimpse of something cold behind his warm brown eyes. 'Amanda, be reasonable—'

'I am not travelling with you.'

Victoria stepped forward, but Paulo cut her off with a sharp look.

'If that is your choice, Amanda,' he said.

'Hurry up,' Victoria interrupted, her impatience taking over. 'We need to get going. We've got a long drive ahead.'

Paulo nodded slowly, his gaze never leaving Amanda's face. 'Of course. But, Amanda, you should know—Sally made it very clear she doesn't want any contact with you. She was quite... determined about that. At least let us drive you back to where you're staying.' Paulo's tone shifted to something more conciliatory.

Amanda hesitated, then nodded. 'I'm staying at Dave's.' She needed to get back, and it was too far to walk.

The drive in the Troop Carrier was tense and mostly silent. Amanda sat in the back while Paulo and Victoria occupied the front seats. Victoria seemed nervous, fidgeting with her phone and avoiding eye contact in the rear-view mirror.

When she had directed Paulo to the gate of Dave's property, he pulled over and turned to face her.

'Are you very sure about this?' Paulo asked one last time as Amanda climbed out. 'Once we leave, it will be difficult to find us again.'

'I am,' Amanda replied, though her voice sounded steadier than she felt. 'And I don't really care if I never see you again. Between the pair of you, you've broken my friendship with my best friend.'

Paulo nodded, a forced smile pulling at the corners of his mouth. 'Whatever.'

The tyres spun as the vehicle pulled away, heading north towards the highway. Amanda watched until it disappeared around a bend, then stood beside Dave's gate for several more minutes, trying to process what had just happened.

Something was wrong. Paulo's smooth talking and Victoria's fidgeting bothered her. And Sally? Her friend might be impulsive and dramatic, but Sally wouldn't take off by herself like that; she would have called or at least messaged again.

Amanda walked up the driveway towards Dave's cabin, her mind churning as she tried to process what had just happened. She needed to make sense of what Paulo and Victoria had said about Sally.

She needed to talk to Sally. Pulling out her phone, she tried to call, but Sally's phone went straight to voicemail. She kept trying, but the same cheery message greeted her each time:

Amanda and I are having too much fun to take your call right now. Leave a message, and I might get back to you.

Amanda's eyes filled with tears as she remembered Sally recording that message a few nights before they'd met Paulo in Byron Bay.

***

Tuesday-early evening.

Dave's house.

Amanda was sitting on the veranda, staring out at the walls of sugar cane that surrounded the property, when Dave's ute came up the drive. The sound of gravel crunching under tyres had never been so welcome.

He emerged from the truck looking grim, his usual easy smile nowhere to be seen. Amanda stood up, dread settling in her stomach like a lead weight.

'Dave? What's wrong? Where have you been?'

'Sorry I was so long. I stopped in at the pub on the way back.' He climbed the steps slowly, his expression troubled. 'Amanda, we need to talk.'

'What is it?' She could hear the panic in her own voice. 'What's wrong?'

Dave sat down heavily beside her, running a hand through his hair. 'Graham had left me a few messages to call him. There's been a problem with the *Lady Windward*.'

Amanda's heart began to race. 'What kind of problem?'

'They found her yesterday. Scuttled at Ninney Point, about five kilometres north of here.' Dave's voice was quiet. 'The local police and forensics have been there investigating, and they've been down to interview Graham and Sandra at Cardwell too.'

The world seemed to tilt around Amanda. 'Scuttled? What does that mean? Does that mean it sank?'

'Someone tried to sink her. Damaged one hull, but she washed up not far from here on Ninney Beach. The tender had been taken from the vessel.' Dave reached for her hand. 'Amanda, when I rang Graham, he asked me to go and look at her on the beach to make sure it was her. I walked through the rainforest from the road. There's no doubt—she was being retrieved this morning.'

Amanda stared at him, trying to process what he was saying. 'But that's impossible. Paulo and Victoria just told me that they put Sally ashore at Tully Heads yesterday. They said she was upset and didn't want to see me.'

Dave's expression darkened. 'They told you what?'

Amanda repeated the conversation, watching Dave's face grow increasingly troubled. When she finished, they sat in silence for a long moment.

'To wash up on Ninney Point, *Lady Windward* must have been scuttled and set adrift out around Dunk Island a couple of days ago, with the tides and the way the wind was blowing.'

'Dave,' Amanda said quietly. 'Paulo and Victoria weren't in a water taxi; they came in on the boat that was behind the yacht.'

'The tender,' Dave said. 'Where is it now?'

'They left it in the mangroves near where I picked them up. If the boat was scuttled, and they got in the tender, where's Sally? They couldn't have dropped her off yesterday.'

'I don't know,' Dave replied, but his expression was closed. 'Amanda, we need to think about this carefully. Why would they lie to you? They have no reason to.'

'We have to call the police,' Amanda said immediately. 'She sent me a text the other night. I found it as I headed out after you left.'

Dave hesitated, and Amanda saw the conflict in his eyes. She knew what he was thinking—his reputation, the rumours that still followed him, the suspicion that would inevitably fall on him if another young woman had gone missing in his vicinity.

'Dave, I know what you're worried about, but we can't just do nothing. Sally could be in danger.'

'I know,' Dave said quietly. 'I know you're right. It's just...'

'I understand,' Amanda said, squeezing his hand. 'But we have to do the right thing.'

Dave nodded slowly. 'You're right. Of course you're right.' He looked at her, his eyes reflecting her own fear. 'Amanda, try calling Sally again. Maybe Paulo was telling the truth; maybe she's just upset and screening her calls.'

Amanda pulled out her phone with trembling fingers and dialled Sally's number. It went straight to voicemail again, just as it had every time she'd tried since receiving Sally's distressed text this morning.

'Nothing,' she whispered.

Dave stood up, pacing to the edge of the veranda. 'When did you last actually speak to her? Not text—speak?'

Amanda thought back, her heart sinking. 'Days ago. When I left them at Cardwell.' She paused. 'Dave, she texted me.' She pulled out her phone. 'I only saw it this morning, but it was sent Saturday night.'

Dave read it, his expression grim.

'I'm going to call her parents,' Amanda said. 'If she's gone home, she would have called them by now. She's dramatic, but she's not that thoughtless.'

Amanda scrolled through her contacts until she found the number Sally had given her for emergencies. Her hands were shaking as she dialled the international number.

The phone rang several times before a woman's voice answered, cautious and formal. 'Hello?'

'Mrs Walker? This is Amanda Priestley.'

'Oh, Amanda!' The woman's voice warmed immediately. 'How lovely to hear from you, dear. How are you both getting on?'

Amanda's heart sank. 'Mrs Walker, I'm calling because... well, I was wondering if you'd heard from Sally recently?'

'Not for several days, no. But that's not unusual. She tends to go quiet for stretches and then call with all her news at once.' There was a pause. 'Is everything alright, dear? You sound worried.'

Amanda closed her eyes, trying to keep her voice steady. 'I'm sure everything's fine. It's just that we got separated, and I wanted to make sure she was okay.'

'Separated? Oh my. Well, I'm sure she'll turn up. Sally's very resourceful, you know. Always lands on her feet.' But Amanda could hear the note of concern creeping into the older woman's voice. 'If you do hear from her, will you have her call us?'

'Of course,' Amanda managed. 'I'll have her call as soon as I see her.'

She ended the call and looked at Dave, who was watching her, his eyes full of concern.

'They haven't heard from her,' she said unnecessarily.

Dave put his arms around her, but she could feel the tension in his body, the way he held himself too carefully. When she pulled back to look at his face, she saw something there that made her stomach clench. 'It's going to be okay,' he said, but his voice shook.

'What's wrong?'

He stepped back, and the look on his face sent a chill down her spine.

'Dave?' Her voice trembled. 'Tell me.'

'Graham told me. There was blood on the boat… and…' Dave stopped and took a deep breath.

'And what?'

'As well as the boat being washed up on Monday, a body was found near Dunk Island.'

Dave's words hung in the air. Amanda stared at him, her mind refusing to process what he'd just said. The world seemed to tilt sideways.

'No,' she whispered, shaking her head. 'No, that's not... it can't be...'

Her legs gave out beneath her. Dave caught her as she crumpled, her body going limp against his chest. A ragged sound escaped her throat: raw, barely human. It started as a gasp and became something else entirely, a keening wail that seemed to come from somewhere outside of her.

'No, no, no,' she sobbed against his shirt, her fists clutching at the fabric. 'It's not Sally. No one would hurt Sally.'

Dave held her tightly, his voice breaking as he whispered, 'I'm sorry. God, so sorry. But, Amanda, we don't know if it's her.'

But Amanda could hear the doubt in his voice, the same

fear that was tearing her apart. 'Should we call the police?'

Dave hesitated. 'But Amanda, what exactly do we tell them?'

'About Paulo and Victoria lying about getting off the boat and Sally taking off.'

Dave ran his hands through his hair. 'Look, I know how this sounds, but... given my history, if I call in another missing woman and it turns out she's fine, just angry and avoiding contact...'

Amanda saw the pain in his eyes, and she reached for him.

'Let's wait and see what they find out,' he said. 'Try calling Sally again tonight, and try her parents again. If there's still nothing, we'll call the police. At least then we'll have given her a full day to make contact.'

It was a long time before Amanda calmed enough to think.

She straightened and pulled away from him, her composure returning as she thought about it. 'It can't be Sally. It's alright, it's just a coincidence. If it was Sally, her parents would have been notified.'

Chapter 27

Thursday, August 21.

Dave's house.

Two sleepless nights had left Amanda hollow-eyed and jittery. She'd lain beside Dave, listening to the sounds of the night—the rustle of wind through sugar cane, the distant call of a night bird, the creak of the house settling.

Each time she'd closed her eyes, she saw Sally's face as it had been in that last proper conversation before the extended charter trip. Excited, glowing with the adventure of it all, completely trusting. The guilt was eating Amanda alive.

Amanda picked up her phone for the hundredth time that morning, checking for messages that never came. She'd called Sally's parents again, but had only reached their voicemail. 'I keep thinking about that text she sent. About not trusting them. What if she found out something? What if they—'

'You need to eat something,' Dave said quietly, placing a plate of scrambled eggs in front of her. She'd been sitting at the kitchen table for over an hour, staring at her untouched coffee as it grew cold.

'I can't.' Amanda pushed the plate away. 'What if—'

'Don't torture yourself with what-ifs,' Dave interrupted gently, though she could see the worry lines etched deep around his eyes. 'We're going to sort this out today. As soon as you eat something, I'll call Detective Whitfield.'

She put her hands over her face and began to sob. 'I've got a really bad feeling about this.' Dave was beside her in an instant, pulling her into his arms.

'Hey,' he murmured against her hair. 'She'll turn up.'

Dave made the call twenty minutes later, his voice steady as he explained the situation to Detective Whitfield. Amanda listened from the kitchen table, her hands wrapped around her cold coffee cup. 'I can be there in twenty minutes,' he said. 'We'll meet you at the station,' Dave replied, but Amanda was already shaking her head.

'I'm not going,' she said as soon as he finished the call.

Dave frowned. 'Amanda, you need to be there. You're the one who knows Sally best, who spoke to Paulo and Victoria.'

'I can't face it.' Amanda's voice was barely a whisper. 'Sitting in some sterile room, answering questions about Sally like she's already...' She couldn't finish the sentence. 'What if they ask me things I can't answer? What if I say something wrong and it makes things worse for her?'

'You won't—'

'I keep thinking I should have seen something, I knew Paulo was a liar. I invited Victoria to join us. I left Sally alone with them.' Amanda's voice cracked. 'I can't sit there and tell a detective how I failed my best friend.'

Dave sat down beside her, taking her trembling hands in his. 'This isn't your fault.'

'Then why does it feel like it is?' Tears spilled down her cheeks. 'I need to stay here, in case she calls. In case she...' Amanda trailed off, knowing how irrational she sounded. 'I know she's never been here, I know she doesn't even know where you live, but I can't shake the feeling that if I leave, I'll miss something important.'

Dave squeezed her fingers. 'You're scared,' he said gently. 'That's normal.'

'I'm terrified,' Amanda admitted. 'And I know I'm not thinking straight, but I can't handle sitting in a police station right now, answering questions about Sally in the past tense like she's already gone. I just... I need a few more hours to hold onto the possibility that she's okay.'

'Alright. I'll go alone first and give them the basic facts. But you know they'll need to speak with you soon.'

'I know,' she whispered, fresh tears falling. 'I just need to not fall apart completely before then.'

Chapter 28

Thursday, August 21 - Victoria.

Dave's farm.

The old cane shack sat hidden amongst a grove of melaleuca trees, barely visible from the road that wound past Dave's property. Philippa crouched beside the grimy window, peering through a hole in the hessian sack covering the window at the distant figure of Amanda pacing on Dave's veranda. The Troop Carrier was parked out of sight behind the shack; Paulo had studied Google Maps and found a back track into Dave's property along a creek.

'He just left, and she's getting restless,' she said, letting the curtain fall back into place. 'Pacing along the verandah.'

Paulo looked up from where he sat on an overturned crate. 'Good. Let her panic. It makes people sloppy.'

The shack stank of mildew. Spider webs draped the corners, and something had died in the walls recently—the sweet, cloying smell of decay hung in the stifling air. But it was perfectly positioned, less than half a kilometre from Dave's cabin, with a clear view of their comings and goings.

'I still think we should have taken her yesterday,' Philippa said, settling onto a mouldering couch that released a cloud of dust. She wrinkled her nose in disgust, thinking of all the sacrifices she'd made over the last weeks to get what she deserved from her father. The cramped cabins, basic accommodation in backpacker hotels, the crude company, the constant pretence—all of it necessary to claim what was rightfully hers.

She hated her father for putting her through this. His stupid second marriage to that greedy woman half his age and her horrid children, his selfishness in changing his will, cutting her inheritance in half. What she had done was the right way to get what she deserved. Ten million pounds was a fraction of what would have been hers by birthright.

Her thoughts drifted to Sally, and she wondered briefly if the stupid bitch had texted Amanda before she'd come up to the deck. Not that it mattered now—Paulo had thrown her phone overboard with the rest of her belongings.

Paulo was an idiot, but he'd been useful. Soon, though, he'd become a liability too. After they'd sorted Amanda, there would be one final loose end to tie up. The Brazilian had served his purpose, but he knew too much. She'd already decided how to handle that problem.

Philippa felt no remorse for any of it. Sally's death, Paulo's planned demise, whatever they'd have to do to Amanda. She was Lady Philippa Fairchild, and she would not be cheated out of her inheritance by anyone.

'Patience, *querida*.' Paulo's accent was more pronounced when he was worried, the Brazilian lilt wrapping around the English words. 'Everything in its time.'

Philippa smiled. She'd known Paulo was a player when they'd hooked up in Noosa, but he'd surprised her. His background was different to the story he told everyone.

'The payment should go in today, but we still have to stay out of sight,' she said, more to convince herself than him. 'Daddy's already transferred the initial payment to prove he's serious. Then ten million pounds, Paulo. Once we collect that and disappear, we'll never have to think about any of this again.

We just have to get another vehicle. They'll be looking for us and the Troop Carrier.'

Paulo's laugh was low. 'You think this ends with the money? You think we just walk away?'

Something cold crawled up Philippa's spine. 'What do you mean?'

'There are witnesses now. People who can connect us to Sally. People who have seen our faces, who know our names.' His dark eyes found hers across the dim room. 'Loose ends need to be tied off.'

'You think Amanda knows something?'

'Possibly. If Sally contacted her. She's not stupid, and neither is her sailor boy. They'll start asking questions. Making connections.' Paulo stood. 'Better to clean house completely, don't you think?'

Philippa stared at him, truly seeing him for the first time. The charm, the supposed regret about Sally's death—it was all window dressing.

'Sally was an accident. She fell, and then—'

'No,' Paulo said softly, stepping closer. 'I saw you with the knife. And now we finish it my way. It was not the head wound that killed her.'

Chapter 29

Thursday, August 21 - 9.00 a.m.

Bec - Pandanus Point Station.

I woke to sunlight streaming through unfamiliar curtains and the distant sound of waves breaking on the shore. For a moment, I lay still, smiling at the ceiling as memories of the night before drifted back. Todd's hands, his whispered words, the way he'd looked at me when all his careful walls finally came down.

I reached across the bed, expecting to find warmth, but my hand met only cool sheets.

'Todd?' I called out, sitting up and listening for sounds from the kitchen or bathroom. The house was silent except for the gentle sound of the waves on the sand.

I pulled on a robe and padded to the kitchen, trying to push away the growing unease in my chest. On the counter, propped against the coffee machine, was a folded piece of paper with my name written in Todd's careful handwriting.

Bec,

I'll call you. There's been a development. I'll see you at the station.

And Bec, sorry about last night. I overstepped the mark.

Todd

I stared at the note, reading it twice, then a third time. The words hit me like a physical blow. Overstepped the mark? After everything we'd shared, everything he'd told me about Megan, about his fears—after the tenderness, the connection, the way we'd held each other—he thought he'd overstepped the mark?

I sank onto a kitchen stool, the note trembling in my hands. How could I have read the situation so wrong? The vulnerability in his voice when he talked about being terrified to care again, the way he'd looked at me like I was something precious—had I imagined all of it?

The rational part of my mind, the detective part, started analysing. Todd was running scared. Last night had meant something to him, probably more than he was comfortable with, and his first instinct was to retreat behind professional boundaries. Classic emotional avoidance behaviour.

But knowing that didn't make it hurt any less.

I showered and dressed mechanically, trying to shift my focus back to the case. We had a job to do. We had a body to identify and three backpackers to find, and my wounded feelings were insignificant compared to that. Todd was right to prioritise the investigation.

Wasn't he?

By the time I drove to the station, I'd managed to construct a fragile wall of professional composure. Whatever had happened between us or whatever Todd thought had happened would have to wait. We had work to do.

Trevor greeted me at the front desk with his usual cheerful smile. 'Morning, Detective. Big day ahead by the looks of things.'

'Morning, Trevor. Is Todd still here?' I'd parked out front and hadn't spotted his SUV.

'Yes, he's been here since about six.'

I nodded and headed towards the incident room, passing Constable Reeves in the corridor. She barely acknowledged me, her usual sullen expression even more pronounced than usual.

The incident room was buzzing with activity. Bradley sat at one of the desks, looking agitated, a cup of coffee steaming beside a stack of reports. He glanced up as I entered, but didn't speak to me.

Todd was on the phone at the far end of the room, his back to me, shoulders rigid with tension. He didn't turn around, didn't acknowledge my presence, and something cold settled in my stomach. This was going to be even more awkward than I'd anticipated. He finally ended his phone call and turned around. Our eyes met for a split second before he looked away, his expression carefully neutral. Professional. Distant.

When he finally spoke, his voice was expressionless.

'Bec. Good, you're here. We've had some developments.'

'What kind of developments?' I asked.

'The fabric caught on the boat has been confirmed as a match with the sarong the victim was wearing, so the body came off the *Lady Windward*.' Todd said, his voice steady and professional, though I could see the strain around his eyes. Whatever had happened between us last night, he clearly regretted it. 'Most importantly, the DNA results came back an hour ago. Our victim has been identified. Sally Walker.'

His phone buzzed with a text, but he ignored it for now. 'And another development. There was another ransom call last night. Phillipa Fairchild spoke to her father again. I've heard the audio. Begging him to pay the final instalment.'

'Any indication of where she is yet?'

'Yes. They've triangulated the last call to within a hundred kilometres of here.'

I stared at him. That niggling feeling that had been tugging at me for the last few days finally solidified into an idea.

I spoke slowly. 'Give me a minute.' I walked across to the incident board and looked at the photos of the three charterers. 'Yes! I know what's been bugging me.'

Hurrying to my desk, I clicked my fingers impatiently as I logged on and then Googled Phillipa Fairchild, and images of a society event filled my screen. I zoomed into one: a charity gala in London from six months ago. In the background of one photo, almost hidden behind a champagne flute, was a young woman with distinctive cheekbones and arctic-blue eyes staring at the camera.

'Lady Philippa Fairchild,' I read from the caption. 'Daughter of Lord Fairchild, notable for her absence from the family's traditional charity commitments this year. Look, Todd.'

He walked over to my desk and stared at the image. 'Yes, that's her. What are you thinking?'

'Look at the eyes and her facial structure. They're the wrong colour, but look at this.' I opened the case file and zoomed in on Victoria Chandler's photo.

'Dark hair and brown eyes.' Todd leaned closer.

'Could be. Similar bone structure, right age.'

'Run them through the facial recognition.' His voice was restrained, but I could sense his excitement.

As the program opened, my phone rang. The caller ID showed a number I didn't recognise.

'Detective Whitfield.'

'Detective, this is Dave Hewson. I need to talk to you.'

'Of course. How soon can you be here?'

'Twenty minutes.'

'Dave Hewson's coming in,' I said as I pulled up the facial recognition software. 'He wants to talk to us.'

'Good.'

I uploaded the two photos side by side. Victoria Chandler—short black hair, brown eyes. Philippa Fairchild—blonde hair, staring coolly over the champagne glass.

The software churned through its analysis, mapping facial features, measuring distances between eyes, and calculating bone structure. I held my breath, knowing this could be the breakthrough we desperately needed.

The results flashed up on screen: ninety percent match.

'Yes!' I shouted, pumping my fist in the air.

'Well, I'll be damned.' Todd let out a low whistle, setting his coffee down on the desk.

'Ninety percent match. Victoria Chandler is Philippa Fairchild.'

'Well done, Bec.' He beamed at me. 'Jesus, this is huge. A fake kidnapping worth ten million pounds, and somehow poor Sally was caught right in the middle of it.'

I felt that familiar surge of triumph that came with cracking a case, but it was tempered by the grim reality of what this meant. 'Now we know why she was killed. She must have stumbled onto the scheme somehow.'

'Poor kid never stood a chance.' Todd's voice was cold. 'These bastards have been planning this from the start. *Lady Windward* must have been used as a base. That's where the calls have been coming from.'

'Either stumbled on, or was involved in it,' I suggested.

'Do some digging, see if they knew each other in the UK.'

I stared at the screen, at those two faces that were unmistakably the same person. 'She fooled everyone, Todd. Playing an Australian girl on holiday while she set up her fake kidnapping. The passport thief. She did a good job of substituting the passport photo.'

'Dyed hair and contacts.'

'And good tech skills, or she paid someone to do it.'

'Well, she won't be fooling anyone much longer.' Todd squeezed my shoulder and then quickly pulled back. 'This is solid gold, Bec. Forensics will back it up, but this facial recognition match gives us everything we need to issue warrants. Now we have to find her.'

'She must be working with someone. The male voice,' I said. 'Paulo?'

'Or maybe more than one. Let's get to work. I'll call forensics and London.' Todd headed back to the desk he'd been using all week.

Dave was as good as his word. Trevor appeared in the doorway fifteen minutes later.

'Dave Hewson's here to see you, detective.' His voice held concern.

'Show him to my office, thanks, Constable Tickle.'

Todd nodded and followed me down the hall to my office. Dave was sitting in the visitor chair, his shoulders hunched, his hands clasped tightly in front of him on the small interview table. The fluorescent lights cast harsh shadows under his eyes, emphasising the lines on his face that had deepened over the past few days.

'Thanks for coming in, Dave,' I said, leaning forward slightly. I quickly introduced Todd. 'You said you needed to talk to us?'

Dave nodded, taking a deep breath. 'It's about Amanda. She picked up Paulo and Victoria from Mission Beach this morning.'

Todd straightened in his chair. 'She what?'

'They called her, said they needed a ride. Claimed they'd left Sally at Tully Heads yesterday and that she didn't want to come back.' Dave's voice was steady, but his knuckles were white where his hands gripped each other. 'Amanda went to get them.'

I exchanged a sharp look with Todd. 'Dave, that's impossible.'

'What do you mean?'

Todd leaned forwards. 'Dave, I assume you know the *Lady Windward* was scuttled and found on Monday morning. There's no way they could have left Sally at Tully Heads yesterday if their boat was already destroyed.'

Dave's expression was grim. 'I know. That's why I'm here.'

I felt my stomach clench. This was the part of the job I hated most. 'Dave, the body that was retrieved by *Hookers*. I'm sorry to tell you it's been identified. It was Sally.'

Dave's head dropped into his hands, his shoulders shaking slightly. When he looked up, his eyes were bright with unshed tears.

'Oh God. Amanda... Amanda's going to be devastated.' His voice cracked. 'She's been blaming herself, thinking she should have stayed with Sally, that she abandoned her.' He wiped his eyes with the back of his hand. 'This will destroy her.'

Todd's voice was careful, professional. 'Dave, we need to understand the timeline here. When did Amanda last see Sally?'

'When she left them at Cardwell. On Friday.' Dave straightened up, something shifting in his expression. 'Look, there's something else you need to know. Amanda and I... we're in a relationship now. It started when she came on my boat at Noosa. She's not part of whatever this is. She met me at the pub on Friday night, and she's been at my place since then.'

I nodded, making a note. 'We understand that, Dave. But right now, we're very concerned about Amanda's safety. Victoria Chandler isn't who she claims to be.'

'What do you mean?'

Todd slid a photograph across the table. 'Victoria Chandler is Lady Philippa Fairchild. She's been running a fake kidnapping scheme worth ten million pounds. We believe Sally may have discovered something about it.'

Dave stared at the photo, his face draining of what little colour remained. 'I'm not surprised. She was strange when she was on my boat with Amanda. So, Amanda's just walked into—'

'A very dangerous situation. Where's Amanda now?' I asked urgently.

Dave's face went ashen. 'At my farm. By herself.' His voice dropped to a whisper. 'Oh shit.'

'We'll go there now,' I said, standing up. 'But we need to move fast.'

Todd was already on the radio. 'Control, this is Detective Inspector Davenport. I need immediate backup to proceed to a rural property. We have a potentially dangerous situation involving wanted suspects.'

'Jesus,' Dave said, on his feet now too. 'She said they'd gone to Cairns.'

'They haven't,' I said. 'They'll be lying low because we've got a BOLO—that's a "be on the lookout"— for the Troop Carrier.'

'Dave, you're coming with us, but you stay in the car when

we get there. They've already killed once.'

As we ran out to the patrol car, my mind was racing through worst-case scenarios. If Paulo and Victoria—Phillipa—were there, Amanda was in danger.

Chapter 30

Thursday, August 21 - 10.00 a.m.

Dave's farm.

Amanda had another coffee when Dave left and tried to keep herself busy. She'd done a load of washing and was at the clothesline behind Dave's house when she heard voices. She peered around the corner of the house, and her blood turned to ice.

'Put the phone away.' Paulo was striding along the road, Victoria trailing behind, looking at her phone. They were coming from the back of the property, not the road. Why were they at the back of Dave's land? They were supposed to be in Cairns.

Something was wrong.

Her first instinct was to run, but where could she go? The small house sat in a clearing surrounded by walls of sugar cane that stretched for acres in every direction. Dave's family's house was three kilometres away, and Dave was at the police station.

She ducked around the other side of the house, her heart hammering against her ribs. Maybe they hadn't seen her. Maybe they'd just look around and leave if they couldn't find her. But even as the thought formed, she knew it was wishful thinking. The washing basket on the ground filled with wet clothes announced her presence to anyone who cared to look.

Amanda pressed her back against the rough timber wall, the rough-hewn wood digging into her shoulder blades through her thin cotton T-shirt. Her breath came in short, sharp gasps that seemed impossibly loud in the mid-morning stillness. The familiar sounds of the property—the rustle of cane leaves, the distant lowing of cattle, the hum of insects—suddenly felt menacing.

She tried to think rationally, but Sally's last text message kept flashing through her mind: *I heard them talking about something bad too, and I don't trust either of them.* What had Sally overheard? What had she discovered that made her frightened enough to text in the middle of the night?

The crunch of footsteps on the gravel was getting closer. Her palms were slick with sweat as she fumbled for her phone, but her fingers felt thick and clumsy. No signal bars. Of course. Dave had warned her about the dead zones around the property.

A bead of perspiration trickled down her cheek despite the cool shade behind the cabin. She could taste copper in her mouth—the metallic tang of pure terror. Every muscle in her body was coiled tight, ready to bolt, but her legs felt like water.

She closed her eyes and tried to steady her breathing, straining to hear over the thundering of her pulse. The footsteps stopped. The silence stretched taut as a wire, and Amanda held her breath until her lungs burned.

Her mind raced through her options, each one more hopeless than the last. The sugar cane might provide cover, but it was also a maze that could trap her. The road from here led nowhere but deeper into Dave's property. And even if she could somehow get to Dave's landline inside, who would she call? What would she say? That she was afraid of two people she'd travelled with and who were supposed to be her friends?

The police. She could call the station. Dave was there. He'd back her up.

But as the voices came closer, she knew with bone-deep certainty that Sally's fears had been justified. Whatever these two were involved in, whatever Sally had discovered, Amanda knew she had to pretend she knew nothing. To save her life.

She stepped slowly away from the back of Dave's house into the sun, and the heat beat down mercilessly on the tin roof above her; sweat pooled at the base of her throat. Her white T-shirt would stand out like a beacon if she tried to run across the open ground to the cane fields. Every choice led to the same terrible conclusion.

She was trapped, and they were coming for her. Voices reached her. Paulo's accented English and Victoria's low voice, though they were too far away for her to make out words. Footsteps crunched closer, moving towards the front of the house. Then they went onto the front verandah, and the screen door opened.

A couple of minutes later, it slammed shut, and footsteps walked along the front veranda again.

Amanda crept along the back wall, trying to get close enough to hear what they were saying. She pressed herself against the weathered timber, her T-shirt sticking to her skin. Maybe she could get under the house and hide. There was a gap around the eastern side of the house where Dave had installed a pressure pump.

'She's not here,' Victoria was saying, her voice tight with frustration.

Amanda frowned, pressing herself closer to the wall. It was Victoria's deep husky tones, but it sounded totally different. She sounded *English*. Not just English—but posh English. The kind of accent Amanda had heard in period dramas, all clipped consonants and elongated vowels. The voice of someone who'd been educated at expensive schools, who'd grown up on country estates owned by wealthy families.

This wasn't the easy-going drawl of a country girl from Broken Hill. Where was the broad Australian accent Victoria had used when they'd chatted about sheep stations and mining towns? The casual "yeah, nah" and "no worries, mate" that had peppered her speech since they'd met.

Amanda's mind reeled as she tried to process what she was hearing. People didn't just lose their accents. You might pick up inflections from other places, but your core accent—the one formed in childhood—stays with you. Unless...

Unless you'd been faking it all along.

The realisation hit her like a physical blow. Victoria Chandler, the supposed country girl who'd bonded with Sally over stories of small-town life and big-city dreams, was a lie. Everything about her—the casual clothes, the easy familiarity with Australian slang—it was all an elaborate performance.

But why? What kind of person invented an entire identity, perfected a foreign accent, and maintained the charade for weeks? And more importantly, what had happened to the real Victoria? Had there ever been a real Victoria?

Amanda's breath caught in her throat as Sally's text flashed through her mind again: *I heard them talking about something bad too, and I don't trust either of them.*

Sally must have figured it out. Somehow, Sally had discovered that Victoria wasn't who she claimed to be. And now Sally was missing, and this woman—whoever she really was— was here at Dave's property, speaking in her real voice because she thought no one could hear her.

The cultured English accent continued, discussing something in clipped, efficient tones. 'You find her. I've got to go back now and check if the money's been transferred. And then find us a car and we can get out of here.'

'His truck is gone,' Paulo replied.

'Yes, he drove out. I already told you that. But the washing is still in the basket. She's here somewhere. You deal with sweet little Amanda, and then when he gets back, get rid of him, too. Take his ute and come and get me. I am not spending one more night in that hovel.'

'I will.' Paulo's voice carried that edge Amanda had heard at the mangroves, the hint of something cold beneath the charm. 'I'll find her. Go and check the money. We finish this now. Before she talks to anyone else.'

Amanda's breath caught in her throat. They were here to get her.

Panic filled her, and she looked around desperately, weighing her options. The cane fields offered the only real cover, but once she was in there, she'd be running blind.

'Hello, *querida*,' he said softly. 'We need to have a conversation.' Paulo appeared around the corner of the house, silhouetted against the bright morning light, his smile as charming as ever. But his eyes were flat, predatory, and there was something in his right hand that caught the light like steel.

'Where is she?' Amanda's voice cracked with desperation. 'Where's Sally? What did you do to her?'

'Poor little Sally.' Paulo stepped towards her, his expression shifting from friendly to dangerous. 'Wrong place, wrong time. Such a shame.'

'You killed her.' It wasn't a question.

'She complicated things. We had a business arrangement to complete, and Sally found out.' Paulo shrugged as if discussing the weather. 'Sometimes these things happen.'

Amanda felt bile rise in her throat. 'Business

arrangement?'

'Oh, *querida*, you really don't understand, do you?' Paulo took another step closer, and Amanda could see the knife now—a long, thin blade like a filleting knife. 'Our friend Victoria, she's not quite who she pretended to be.'

'I know. I heard her speak,' Amanda said, trying to sound braver than she felt. 'What are you doing?' Her voice was husky and shaking, and she took a step back

Paulo's eyebrows rose. 'Our dear friend Victoria is Philippa Fairchild, daughter of a very wealthy English lord. And her daddy is paying a very large sum of money to get his precious daughter back home safely.'

Amanda stared at him, pieces clicking into place. 'But she's not kidnapped. She's working with you.'

'Very good!' Paulo's voice held genuine admiration. 'Philippa wanted money—her father has been rather mean to her since he remarried. It's what she is entitled to.'

Amanda felt sick. 'So, she faked her own kidnapping.'

'Exactly. When we met in Noosa, she was looking for someone to help her with the ransom demands. And she paid well.'

'Dave will be back soon; the police know all about you.'

'Dave hasn't been gone that long. We've been staying in his wonderful accommodation down the back. Very thorough of him to go to the police.' Paulo's smile disappeared. He lunged forward to grab her, and Amanda backed away, but he was faster, his hand closing around her wrist like a steel trap.

'Let me go!' Amanda struggled against his grip, but he was stronger than his lean frame suggested.

'I'm afraid I can't do that.' Paulo's voice was almost

apologetic as he pressed the knife against her throat. 'You understand, Amanda, it's nothing personal. Just business.'

The steel was cold against her skin, sharp enough that she could feel the sting of the cut. Amanda went very still.

'Good girl,' Paulo murmured. 'Now, we're going to take a little walk. Into the cane fields, where we can have some privacy for our conversation.'

'What conversation?' Amanda managed to whisper.

'The one where you tell me exactly what Dave is telling the police, and then...' Paulo's smile was genuinely regretful. 'Well, then I finish this.'

He began to drag her towards the cane, the knife never moving from her throat. Amanda stumbled along, her mind racing. Once they were in the cane fields, she'd be completely at his mercy. The dense stalks would muffle her screams. Fear filled her with determination. There was no one to hear her; she had to get away by herself and make her move now, before they left the house yard.

As he dragged her, Amanda suddenly threw her weight backwards, hoping to catch Paulo off balance. But he was ready for her, his grip tightening painfully on her wrist.

'None of that,' he said mildly, pressing the knife harder against her throat. A warm trickle of blood ran down her neck. 'Save your energy for our walk.'

They stepped out into the blazing morning heat, and Amanda's last hope died. The cane fields stretched endlessly in all directions, a green maze that could hide anything.

And somewhere in that green wilderness, Paulo intended to kill her.

She stifled a sob, thinking of Sally and wondering how she had felt. And wondering what Paulo had done to her.

She blinked; this whole situation was surreal, but she was in danger.

Her life, her future.

'Move,' he commanded, pushing her towards the nearest row of cane.

Amanda stumbled forward, the thick stalks closing around them like a living wall. Behind them, the house disappeared from view, and with it, any chance of rescue.

Chapter 31

Thursday, August 21 - 10.30 a.m.

Dave's farm.

The sugar cane towered above Amanda like green cathedral walls, each stalk thick as a man's arm and taller than two people standing. The leaves rustled with every movement, creating a constant noise that would mask any sound she might make—or any sound Paulo might make hunting her.

Her neck throbbed where the knife had nicked her, the cut shallow but stinging with sweat and fear. Paulo's grip on her wrist was like iron as he forced her deeper into the fields, following what might once have been a drainage channel but was now barely visible between the dense rows.

'You know, querida,' Paulo said conversationally, as if they were taking a pleasant stroll, 'I almost regret this. You're quite beautiful, and under different circumstances... if you'd ever shown any interest in me...' His grip tightened. 'I could never understand why you didn't look at me like all the other girls did.'

Amanda didn't respond. She was counting steps, trying to memorise the path they were taking, watching for any opportunity to break free. The cane grew in precise rows about two metres apart, but the spaces between were choked with grass and weeds that caught at her ankles.

'Sally fought too, at the end,' Paulo continued, his voice taking on a dreamy quality. 'Such spirit.'

Amanda's stomach lurched, but she forced herself to keep listening. Every word was evidence, something she could use if—when—she got out of this.

'But there's nowhere to run on a boat, is there? Especially not when it's anchored off a deserted island.' Paulo's grip tightened. 'Much like here, really. All this cane looks the same. Easy to get lost. Easy to disappear.'

They'd been walking for about ten minutes when Paulo suddenly stopped. Amanda looked around, seeing nothing but endless rows of cane stretching in every direction. No landmarks, no sense of which way led back to the cabin.

'This will do,' Paulo said, releasing her wrist and stepping back slightly. But the knife remained pointed at her, and his dark eyes never left her face.

Amanda rubbed her wrist, trying to restore circulation. 'The police know about you. About Philippa. Running won't help you now.'

'Perhaps. But eliminating witnesses will certainly help.' Paulo tilted his head, studying her like a scientist examining a specimen. 'Tell me, what exactly did you tell them? What do they know about our operation?'

'Everything.' Amanda tried to sound more confident than she felt.

Paulo's smile faltered slightly. 'Clever you, and clever police. But not clever enough to stop us before now.'

'They've contacted Interpol. Your faces are all over Europe by now.'

'My face, perhaps. But Philippa... well, she has resources. Money talks, even to police.' Paulo shrugged. 'And dead witnesses can't testify.'

Amanda saw her chance. While Paulo was talking, confident in his control of the situation, she suddenly broke to her left, crashing through the cane towards what she hoped was north, towards the road.

Behind her, Paulo cursed in rapid Portuguese. She heard him plunging through the cane after her, but the thick stalks worked in her favour, slowing him down as much as her.

Amanda ran blindly, branches whipping at her face and arms, the ground uneven beneath her feet. She could hear Paulo behind her, closer than she'd hoped, his breathing steady and controlled. He was in better shape than she was, and he knew it.

She burst through into a clearer row and immediately veered right, trying to confuse her trail. The sun was almost directly overhead now, making it impossible to determine direction with any certainty. Every row looked identical—green walls stretching endlessly in both directions.

A root caught her foot, and she stumbled, going down hard on her hands and knees. The impact knocked the wind out of her, and she lay gasping for precious seconds before forcing herself back to her feet.

'Amanda!' Paulo's voice echoed through the cane, maybe a little to her left, but seeming to come from everywhere at once. 'There's nowhere to go, *querida*! These fields stretch for kilometres in every direction. Save yourself the effort.'

She ignored him, pressing deeper into the maze. Her lungs burned and her legs felt like rubber, but she kept moving. Behind her, the sounds of pursuit continued—the snap of breaking cane, the rustle of disturbed leaves.

Then, suddenly, silence.

Amanda froze, crouching between two massive stalks, trying to control her ragged breathing. Where was he? Had she lost him, or was he being more careful now, stalking her instead of chasing?

Minutes passed. The sun beat down mercilessly, and sweat

poured down her face, stinging the scratches left by the cane leaves. Mosquitoes found her immediately, drawn by the scent of blood and fear.

A slight movement in her peripheral vision made her turn her head slowly. Nothing. Just the gentle sway of the cane in the breeze.

Where was he?

Which direction was he moving in?

Amanda forced herself to think. Paulo was experienced at this; he had killed Sally. He would be systematic, methodical. He would expect her to panic, to run blindly until she exhausted herself.

So, she did the opposite.

Moving as quietly as possible, Amanda worked her way towards what she hoped was the eastern edge of the plantation. If she could reach the road, flag down a car...

She was creeping between two rows when she heard it—a low whistle, tuneless and casual. Paulo, signalling his position or maybe just amusing himself. The sound came from her right this time, maybe ten metres away.

Amanda altered course, angling away from the whistle. Her mouth was dry as dust, and she would have killed for a drink of water. How long had she been running? It felt like hours, but it was probably only ten or fifteen minutes.

The cane began to thin slightly, and Amanda felt a surge of hope. She was reaching the edge of the plantation. Through the stalks ahead, she could see open ground, grass burned brown by the Queensland sun.

She was almost to the edge when she heard the voice close behind her.

'I know you're here, Amanda.'

Amanda's blood turned to ice. Paulo was close—very close. Maybe ten metres away, hidden by the cane but definitely tracking her.

'You're doing well. Better than Sally did. But this game ends now.'

Amanda dropped to her belly, crawling beneath the canopy of cane stalks. The ground was rough against her stomach, full of rocks and broken stalks, but it was the only cover available.

'I can smell your fear,' Paulo continued, his voice moving slowly through the cane. 'It's quite intoxicating. The adrenaline, the desperation. Sally smelled the same way at the end.'

Something slithered across Amanda's leg—something thick and muscular and very much alive.

The touch sent terror through every nerve ending in her body. Her breath caught in her throat as she felt the weight of it, the alien smooth scales sliding against her bare skin just above her ankle. Her mind screamed at her to move, to run, to do anything except stay frozen in this hellish tableau, but Dave's warning echoed in her memory: *If you see a taipan, stay perfectly still. They strike at movement.*

She bit her lip so hard she tasted blood, forcing herself to remain perfectly still as the venomous serpent made its way past her hiding spot. Every instinct in her body was screaming at her to move—run, kick, scream—but she fought against her instincts and stayed statue-still.

The snake paused directly in front of her face, and Amanda found herself eye to eye with something prehistoric and utterly lethal. Its head was larger than she'd expected, triangular and perfectly designed for delivering death. The taipan's scales gleamed like polished bronze in the filtered sunlight, each one distinct and beautiful in the most terrifying way possible. Its eyes were black and alien, showing no recognition of her humanity, no mercy—just the cold calculation of a perfect predator.

Dave had shown her a photo on his phone just days ago, warning her about the most venomous snake in Australia. 'Their venom can kill in thirty minutes,' he'd said matter-of-factly. 'Taipans are aggressive, but they usually only strike if they feel threatened. If you ever see one, don't move a muscle.'

The snake's tongue flicked out, tasting the air mere inches from her face. Amanda could smell it—a dry, dusty scent. Her heart was hammering so hard she was certain the vibrations would alert the creature, but still, she didn't move. Sweat beaded on her forehead and trickled down her spine, but she might as well have been carved from stone.

The taipan's head swayed slightly, as if considering her. Amanda felt her vision starting to blur from holding her breath, and she forced herself to take the smallest possible inhalation through her nose. The snake's attention seemed to sharpen at even that tiny movement, its head tilting with predatory interest.

Please, she thought desperately. *Please just go away.*

For a moment that stretched like eternity, they regarded each other locked in a standoff that would determine whether she lived or died in the next few seconds. Amanda's legs were beginning to shake from the strain of staying motionless, and she could feel a muscle in her calf starting to cramp.

Then, as suddenly as it had appeared, the taipan continued on its way, its bronze coils flowing like liquid metal as it disappeared into the deeper cane just a few metres away. Amanda's eyes tracked its movement until she could no longer see the lethal curves of its body, but she could still hear the soft scraping of scales against dead grass.

She waited, counting her heartbeats, feeling the sweat cooling on her skin as the adrenaline slowly began to ebb. One hundred beats. Two hundred. The muscle in her calf was screaming now, and she knew she couldn't stay frozen much longer.

Amanda didn't move until she could no longer see any movement, then slowly, carefully, began to rise from her hiding place. Every movement was deliberate and controlled, as if she were moving through water. The taipan was far enough away now, she hoped, coiled somewhere in the thick undergrowth where it belonged.

Her legs felt weak as she straightened, the delayed shock of the encounter making her dizzy. She'd come within inches of one of the most venomous creatures on the planet and lived to tell about it. The realisation made her want to laugh and vomit at the same time.

But as she stood, a twig snapped under her foot.

The sound seemed to echo through the cane field like a gunshot.

'Found you,' Paulo said, his voice much closer than she'd expected.

Amanda bolted, crashing through the cane towards where she hoped the road was. Behind her, Paulo cursed and gave chase, no longer bothering with stealth.

'You can't run forever, Amanda!' he shouted.

He was gaining on her, his footsteps pounding through the cane. She burst through into a slightly clearer area and veered left, but Paulo anticipated her move.

He lunged forward, his hand reaching for her shoulder—

The taipan struck without warning.

Paulo's scream echoed through the cane fields, high and agonised. Amanda spun around to see him clutching his forearm, the snake retreating into the undergrowth. Its fangs had found their mark just above Paulo's wrist, and already she could see the puncture wounds beginning to swell.

'*Merda*!' Paulo staggered backwards, his face going pale. 'It bit me! The fucking thing bit me!'

She stood frozen, torn between the instinct to help and the knowledge that this man had intended to kill her.

Paulo looked at the bite, then at Amanda, his eyes wide with a fear she'd never seen before. 'Taipan,' he whispered. 'That was a taipan. I'm going to die.'

The colour was draining from his face rapidly now, and his breathing was becoming laboured. The venom was working fast—faster than Amanda had imagined possible.

'Help me,' Paulo gasped, falling to his knees. 'Please, Amanda. Call for help.'

Amanda backed away, her heart hammering. 'Like you helped Sally?'

Paulo tried to stand but couldn't. His legs wouldn't support him anymore. 'Amanda, please. I'm dying.'

'Yes,' Amanda said quietly. 'You are.'

She turned and pushed through the cane stalks, leaving Paulo to face the same merciless fate he'd dealt to Sally. Behind her, his cries for help grew weaker and more desperate until the sound of rustling cane swallowed them entirely.

Amanda waited until she could no longer hear him before allowing herself to breathe properly. She was maybe ten metres from the edge of the plantation now. If she could get out of the cane, she might be able to see the road, and figure out which direction led to help.

Her legs were aching by the time she broke out of the cane. Her eyes widened as lights flashed on the road near Dave's house. A police car was parked at the front, with Dave's ute behind it.

Chapter 32

Thursday, August 21 - 11.15 a.m.

Dave's farm.

Two police cars kicked up clouds of dust as we roared down the dirt road towards Dave's house. My knuckles were white where I gripped the steering wheel, Todd silent beside me as we both focused on the sprawling landscape ahead. Endless walls of sugar cane stretched in every direction, their green stalks swaying gently in the breeze—a maze that could hide anything or anyone.

The farmhouse came into view, a modest timber structure sitting in a small clearing like an island in an ocean of cane. Everything looked deceptively peaceful, but my gut was telling me otherwise. We'd radioed for backup, but it would be at least twenty minutes behind us. Whatever was happening here, we were on our own. Todd and I were in the first car, and Trevor was in the paddy wagon behind us. Dave was following in his ute.

I slammed on the brakes and was out of the car before the engine had fully stopped, Todd beside me in seconds. Behind us, Dave jumped out of his ute, his face etched with desperate worry.

'Stay there, please, Dave,' I called out sharply, drawing my weapon. 'We know what we're doing.'

Todd was already moving, his service pistol drawn and ready. I turned back to make sure Dave was following my instructions—the last thing we needed was a civilian rushing into a potentially deadly situation. He stood by the car, every muscle in his body tense, but he stayed put.

The property was eerily quiet. Washing fluttered on the old-fashioned prop clothesline behind the house, and I could see that the front door stood wide open—never a good sign in the tropics where people were careful about snakes and heat. The silence felt wrong; it was too quiet.

'You go round the back,' Todd said quietly, his voice carrying just far enough for me to hear. 'I'll go through the house.'

I nodded and moved carefully around the perimeter, my boots silent on the packed earth. The sugar cane pressed close to the clearing here, creating natural blind spots that made my skin crawl. Anyone could be watching from behind those green walls. My weapon felt reassuringly solid in my hands as I swept my gaze across every shadow, every possible hiding place.

The back of the property was as empty as the front. No signs of struggle, nothing to indicate what might have happened to Amanda. But a washing basket full of wet clothes told a story—Amanda had left in a hurry.

God, I hoped they hadn't taken her in the Troop Carrier.

'Nothing around the back,' I said as Todd and I met at the front of the house, both shaking our heads.

'Same here, but...' Todd paused, running a hand through his hair. 'The interior's quiet, but someone was there not too long ago.'

'What do you mean?'

'There's a half-eaten sandwich on the kitchen counter. And there's a cup of coffee gone cold.'

I felt a chill run down my spine.

'Detective?' Dave called to me.

I turned. He was hurrying across from the ute, his head

turning from side to side as he scanned the cane fields.

'I just saw something up behind that shack about half a kilometre up that road,' he said, pointing towards a barely visible structure in the distance. 'I'm sure I saw somebody move.'

My pulse quickened.

'Okay, but you stay behind us. Bec, take us up there,' Todd directed. 'Trevor, walk with Dave and be vigilant.'

We moved along the dirt track, the sugar cane towering above us on both sides. The morning sun slanted through the stalks, creating a shifting pattern of light and shadow that played tricks on the eyes. Every rustle of leaves, every creak of bamboo-like stems made us pause and listen. The air was thick with the sweet, cloying smell of growing cane.

Dave stayed behind us with Trevor, as instructed, but I could hear his ragged breathing, the way his boots scuffed slightly on the gravel as he watched our careful advance.

The abandoned shack—an old workers' cottage, according to Dave came into clearer view as we approached, its corrugated iron roof glinting dully in the sun. Windows stared blindly out at us, some with glass missing, others covered with what looked like old sacking. It was the perfect hiding place—close enough to watch the main house, isolated enough that screams wouldn't carry.

A bloodcurdling scream tore through the air, so primal and frightened that it seemed to freeze the blood in my veins. We both stopped dead in our tracks. The sound had come from the cane fields just ahead of us, maybe fifty metres away.

'Jesus,' Todd breathed.

Behind us, Dave made a strangled sound of anguish.

Was that Amanda?

Without a word, we took off, running along the edge of the sugar cane, pushing past dense stalks that slapped at our faces and grabbed at our clothes. The cane was taller than us, creating a green wall that muffled sound and disoriented our sense of direction. Leaves swiped at our arms, and the sweet dust made it hard to breathe, but we pressed on, following the echo of that terrible scream.

A figure stumbled out of the cane about twenty metres ahead of us, moving like someone in shock. It was Amanda—clothes torn, hair wild with bits of cane leaf, but alive.

'Amanda, I'm here,' Dave yelled, his voice cracking with relief. He took off towards her.

A vehicle screeched to a halt on the roadside, and figures emerged as Amanda ran towards Dave.

'Help!' she called out, her voice hoarse from running. 'In the cane fields! Paulo Santos—he was chasing me, but a snake... a taipan bit him. He might still be alive.'

Dave reached her, and she collapsed into his arms just before Todd and I reached her.

'Amanda? Are you hurt? Did he—'

'I'm okay,' she whispered. 'Dave, he killed her. He killed Sally. He told me they did. It's Victoria, and she's not Victoria, she's someone else. I think she's in the shack at the back.'

Dave pulled her against his chest, and Amanda sobbed into his shoulder.

Behind us, police officers were already heading into the cane fields, following Amanda's directions to where she'd last seen Paulo.

Chapter 33

Thursday, August 21-1.30 p.m.

Mission Beach Medical Centre.

Amanda sat on the edge of the bed in the examination room, wincing as the nurse cleaned the cuts on her arms with antiseptic. Dave hadn't left her side since the paramedics had brought her in, his hand resting protectively on her shoulder.

I watched them from the corridor, feeling a familiar pang of something I couldn't quite name. Relief that the case was wrapping up, yes. But also, something deeper—a hollow ache that had nothing to do with the investigation and everything to do with the mess I'd made of my personal life.

'The detective wants to speak with you,' the nurse said, her voice gentle. 'But only if you're feeling up to it, love.'

Amanda nodded. I knew she wanted to get it over with—to get the story out of her system while it was fresh in her mind.

I stood in the doorway, feeling as wrung out as Amanda looked. I'd offered to come and speak to Amanda. The truth was, I needed some distance from the station where Todd was with his colleagues from Cairns. From the job, from the woman I'd become since the night before with Todd.

God, if I could rewind that evening, I would. In a heartbeat. Somehow, last night, the professional boundary we'd maintained since we first worked together last year had simply... dissolved.

When one drink had led to another, then his hand on my arm, his mouth on mine, and before I knew it, we were tangled together in a way that changed everything.

The worst part wasn't the sex itself—that had been good, too good, which made everything more complicated. The worst part was the aftermath. The way Todd wouldn't meet my eyes this morning. The stilted conversations, the careful politeness, where once there had been easy banter. We'd lost something precious last night—our friendship, our partnership, the comfortable dynamic that had made us such an effective team.

Amanda was staring at me, and I focused on the present.

'Amanda, I'm sorry to bother you, but I wanted to check how you're coping and see if you felt able to give us a preliminary statement.'

'I'm fine,' Amanda said, though her hands trembled like leaves in a storm. 'Detective, is it true what Paulo said? About it being a fake kidnapping?'

I kept my expression bland, falling back on professional composure the way I always did when my personal life threatened to intrude. At least here, with Amanda and Dave, I could focus on something concrete—their pain, their need for answers, their search for meaning in senseless tragedy. It was easier than confronting the damage I'd done to the one relationship that had anchored my life.

'I'm afraid so. Philippa Fairchild orchestrated her kidnapping to get ten million pounds from her father. Paulo Ramirez was the hired muscle to help her carry out the scheme.'

Dave's hand tightened on Amanda's shoulder. 'Christ almighty. All of this carnage for money.'

Looking at them—the way Dave instinctively protected Amanda, the way she leaned into his strength—I felt that hollow ache inside deepen. They'd found something real in horrible circumstances. Meanwhile, I'd managed to destroy the most important relationship in my life over one night of weakness.

I settled into the chair across from them, notepad at the ready. 'Amanda, I know this will be hard, but can you tell me what Paulo said to you today? About Sally, about Victoria, as you knew her?'

For the next hour, Amanda spilled everything she could remember. Paulo's cold confession, his clinical description of the fake kidnapping scheme, and how Sally had stumbled onto something that could have brought their scheme crashing down. I scribbled notes methodically, occasionally pressing for details but mostly just absorbing what they said.

As she spoke, I found myself thinking about courage—Sally's courage in standing up to dangerous people, Amanda's courage in surviving what she'd been through, even Dave's quiet courage in loving someone who'd been through trauma. It made my cowardice seem even more pathetic. I didn't have the courage to face Todd properly yet.

'He said Sally uncovered Victoria's scheme,' Amanda said, her voice cracking like old timber. 'That she was going to blow the whistle on them. So, they silenced her permanently.'

'She had courage,' I agreed quietly, meaning every word. 'And that courage, along with yours, has guaranteed that Philippa will pay the full price for what she's done.'

Meanwhile, I couldn't even work up the nerve to have an honest conversation with my partner about one night that shouldn't have happened.

Dave leaned forwards, his jaw tight. 'What's next? For Philippa?'

'She'll face charges for conspiracy to defraud, kidnapping, and murder. The fake kidnapping might have been her brainchild, but Sally Walker's death makes this a murder charge.' I closed my notepad with a snap. 'She'll be behind bars for the rest of her life.'

At least justice would be served in this case. At least Philippa would pay for what she'd done, unlike the mess I'd made of my personal life, which seemed to have no clear resolution.

Tears rolled down Amanda's cheeks, and Dave put his arm around her for support. 'How can I ever face Sally's mum and dad?'

'They're on the way to Cairns now. They want to meet you—you were the last person to see their daughter, apart from her killers. That connection will be precious to them, but it's up to you, Amanda.'

'I don't know if I can. Not yet. Dave, what do you think?'

'None of this was your doing,' Dave said quietly, reading the self-blame written across her face.

I envied the certainty in his voice, the way he could absolve Amanda so completely. No one could do that for me, because what I'd done—sleeping with Todd, ruining our friendship—had been entirely my choice.

'Wasn't it? If I never dragged her on this cursed trip, if I never introduced her to Paulo—'

'Then Philippa would have found some other lamb to slaughter when her scheme was threatened,' I interrupted, my voice cutting through her guilt like a blade. 'Amanda, Sally died because she had the spine to stand up for what was right. The only person with blood on their hands is the one who ordered her death. And we need proof of that to charge Philippa with murder.'

The irony wasn't lost on me—here I was, offering absolution to Amanda while drowning in my self-reproach. But that was the job, wasn't it? To help others find their way through trauma and loss, even when your own life was falling apart. To solve other people's problems while making a hash of your own.

As I prepared to leave them to their healing, I wondered if Todd and I would ever find our way back to what we'd once had. Or if some mistakes were simply too big to undo, and some friendships too fragile to survive.

Chapter 34

Thursday, August 21 - 3.30 p.m.

Pandanus Point Police Station

Paulo Ramirez was dead, killed by a taipan bite whilst pursuing Amanda through the sugar cane fields. His body had been recovered half an hour ago, but it had been too late for him, the venom having done its swift and lethal work. Whatever he knew had died with him.

In Interview Room 2, Philippa Fairchild—the woman Amanda had known as Victoria Chandler—was providing to Cairns CIB senior detectives what her lawyer termed "a full and frank confession." She had refused to speak until her lawyer arrived from Cairns.

'She's admitted to everything,' Todd said. 'But she's claiming it was all Paulo's idea from the start—that he manipulated and coerced her into going along with it.'

'What's she giving us?'

'She says Paulo came up with the idea in Noosa when she told him about her family problems, and convinced her the fake kidnapping was foolproof. She said he'd done it before in Brazil. Claims he threatened her when she tried to back out.' Todd's voice carried scepticism. 'According to her, Paulo masterminded the whole scheme and she was just a terrified accomplice who was in too deep to escape.'

'Do you believe her? I asked.

'Not a word of it. She's one very cool customer.'

A familiar tightness gripped my chest. One young woman died, and now the surviving conspirator was painting herself as another victim. 'And Sally's murder?'

'She's adamant that Paulo killed Sally when the girl became suspicious. Says she begged him not to hurt her, but he said they'd gone too far to turn back.' Todd's expression was grim. 'Convenient that the one person who could contradict her story is dead.'

Through the glass, Philippa looked nothing like the confident woman Amanda had described. Her designer clothes were wrinkled, her makeup smeared, and her hands shook as she held an unlit cigarette. Every few minutes, she broke down crying, insisting she was as much a victim as Sally, that Paulo had controlled and threatened her throughout the entire ordeal.

'She's claiming she feared for her own life,' Todd added quietly. 'Says that's why she couldn't save Sally or contact the police.'

'Any word from the search teams on Dunk Island?' I asked.

'They found what we think are some of Sally's belongings about an hour ago. Buried in a gully on the north side of the island, along with camping equipment and supplies from the *Lady Windward*.' Todd's expression was grim. 'Also found the spot where they camped after scuttling the boat. Looks like they were there for a couple of days, waiting for the ransom to be paid.'

I nodded, making notes. The case was coming together with depressing clarity. Philippa had faked her own kidnapping, recruited Paulo with the promise of millions of pounds, and then murdered Sally Walker when she'd threatened to expose the scheme.

'What about the Brazilian authorities?'

'They're interested in Paulo's background, but there's no

evidence of any previous crimes. Seems this was his first venture into serious crime.' Todd's voice carried a note of relief. 'At least we don't have to worry about other victims.'

A knock on the door interrupted us. Trevor peered in, looking harried.

'Ma'am, Sally Walker's parents have arrived. They'd like to speak with someone about what happened to their daughter. And the media's got wind of the fake kidnapping angle—we've got news crews asking about the Lord Fairchild connection.'

I closed my eyes. Now the process began: interviews, statements, and media management. And at the centre of it all, two families whose lives had been shattered—one by loss, the other by betrayal.

'What about Amanda Priestley and Dave Hewson?'

'Still with the paramedics. Miss Priestley's got some cuts and scratches, and she's pretty shaken up, but physically she's fine. We'll interview her properly once she's had a chance to recover.'

'Right. Todd, can you handle the Walker family? I want to speak with Amanda before the lawyers take over completely.'

Chapter 35

Friday, August 22 - 9.00 a.m.

Pandanus Point Police Station.

It hadn't taken long for the media to descend on Pandanus Point like a plague of locusts. I pushed through the crowd outside the police station, ignoring the microphones shoved in front of me, and shouted questions about the "Fake Kidnapping Murder" and the "Lord's Daughter Scandal."

'You solved the crime, Detective Whitfield,' a strident voice called.

I put my hands up and pushed my way through the crowd.

Inside, the station was busy but manageable. Phones still rang constantly, but without the urgency that had created the tension before the mystery was solved. The case was now a straightforward domestic murder and fraud.

The station was also very different today. Todd was waiting by my desk. The events of the week had put our personal complications on the back burner, and I was finding it much easier to act normally. 'Any updates on the Bradley situation?' I asked.

His expression brightened slightly. 'Actually, yes. I got a call from Brisbane this morning. Remember that efficiency review we were considering against him? Well, word got back to Bradley, and rather than face the formal proceedings, he resigned. Effective immediately. They decided to let the Katja Mueller stuff stay buried; she has asked for privacy. The one thing we're looking at more closely is whether he's behind the social media smear campaign against Dave Hewson. If we can prove it, charges could be laid. Proving it will be the tricky part, though; tracing anonymous accounts and getting the platforms to release data requires jumping through a lot of legal hoops.'

'Really? What does that teach us? It's okay to do it and get away with it?'

'I know what you mean. Thirty years of complaints and transfers, but it has finally caught up with him. It's not the clearance Dave deserves, but it's something. And it means there's going to be a new sergeant position opening up here in Mission Beach.'

The word had already spread through the station. Trevor Tickle was beaming, and Constable Reeves had greeted me at the front counter as though I were a long-lost friend. The smell of disinfectant wafting down the corridor was a pleasant change from the cigarette smoke and mould.

'The Crown Prosecution Service is sending someone up from Brisbane this afternoon,' Todd added. 'And Lord Fairchild's solicitors want to discuss the return of the ransom money.'

'What about Philippa?'

'Her lawyer's trying to negotiate a plea bargain. Fifteen to twenty years in exchange for full cooperation and a guilty plea to manslaughter instead of murder.' Todd shook his head. 'Claiming Paulo was the real mastermind, that she was manipulated and coerced. And that he was the one who stabbed Sally and threw her overboard.'

I looked at the files on my desk. 'The evidence doesn't support that.'

'No, it doesn't. The planning, the bank accounts, the initial contact with Paulo—it all leads back to her. She orchestrated this whole thing.' Todd sat down across from me. 'The prosecution's not interested in any deals. They want the full murder charge.'

A surge of satisfaction ran through me. 'That's something, at least.'

A knock on my office door interrupted us. Trevor looked around. 'Someone to see you, ma'am.'

Amanda Priestley stood behind him, looking pale but composed. Beside her, Dave Hewson hovered close.

'Amanda, I wasn't expecting to see you today. How are you?'

'I'm okay. We called in because I wanted to give you this,' Amanda said, holding out a manila envelope. 'I wrote down everything I could remember about Paulo and Philippa. Conversations, behaviour, more that might help with the prosecution. Right from the beginning at Noosa.'

I accepted the envelope with a smile. 'Thank you, this will be very helpful. Are you staying in town for a while?'

'Yes for a few more days. Dave and I are going to Brisbane next week, then to Cirencester for Sally's funeral. And Dave can meet my parents. After that...' Amanda glanced at Dave, who smiled encouragingly. 'After that, we're coming home.'

'To Pandanus Point?'

'To Pandanus Point,' Amanda confirmed. 'This is where I belong now.'

I watched them leave, trying not to be envious of their happiness. There was something hopeful about their determination to build a life here, to not let Philippa and Paulo's greed and violence define their lives.

Chapter 36

Three Months Later – early December.

Bec - The Salty Dog Hotel.

I was off duty, sitting at the bar in The Salty Dog when Amanda and Dave walked in. The pub was decorated with tinsel and fairy lights, and a garish red tinsel Christmas tree. The sound of laughter drifted across the road from the beach. Amanda looked different—happier, more settled. They both did.

Philippa Fairchild had been refused bail and remanded in custody at Townsville Women's Correctional Centre. Her elaborate fake kidnapping scheme had collapsed completely when faced with the evidence of her planning and Amanda's testimony. Lord Fairchild had publicly disowned his daughter and donated the ten-million-pound ransom to a foundation established in Sally's memory. His finances hadn't been in as bad a state as had been put about.

The foundation provided travel safety education and support for families of victims of violent crime. It was a small comfort for the loss of Sally's bright spirit, but it meant her death wasn't entirely meaningless.

Todd had mentioned that he might call in on his way north from Innisfail, where he'd had a meeting with the local area command. I wasn't going to hold my breath, but I'd said I'd be at the pub. I'd been sitting on my second drink for over an hour now and was about to give up.

It was pathetic how I snatched every crumb of his attention; I was a grown woman, with a great career and one failed relationship behind me. I needed to get over this obsession.

I watched Amanda and Dave make their way to the deck, and their contentment was obvious. They had been through hell together, but they had come out the other side stronger.

As I walked onto the deck, I heard Dave's voice carrying across the space.

'Amanda Priestley,' he said, and I realised he was down on one knee, 'will you marry me?'

'Yes,' Amanda said, laughing through her tears. 'Yes, absolutely yes.'

The pub erupted in cheers and applause. Someone started singing 'Waltzing Matilda,' and soon the entire deck was singing along, voices mixing with the sound of waves and the cry of seagulls.

I hung back, not wanting to intrude on their moment, but I couldn't help smiling. Amanda looked out over the water, towards the invisible horizon where Sally's journey had ended and her own had truly begun. Philippa Fairchild's greed had destroyed one life and shattered several others, but it hadn't destroyed hope. Their love had found a way to grow in the aftermath of tragedy.

My heart thudded as a familiar car rolled up and parked outside. I swallowed and took a deep breath when Todd stepped out.

He looked tired, the intensity of the past few months having carved new lines around his eyes. I'm sure I looked the same. His jacket was slung over his arm, and he made his way through the packed pub with quiet determination. Todd looked like someone on a mission.

'That's me done,' he said when he reached me at the edge of the deck carrying two beers. 'Meeting over, final reports submitted, evidence logged, witnesses debriefed. Philippa Fairchild is officially someone else's problem now.'

I nodded, not trusting myself to speak immediately. I'd known this moment was coming—Todd's transfer back to Brisbane had been approved weeks ago, effective immediately after the case concluded. But knowing something and being ready for it were two entirely different things.

'When do you leave?' I asked, my voice steadier than I'd expected.

'Flight's at two tomorrow. I've got a few things to sort out in Brisbane, then a week's leave before I start with the Major Crime Squad.' Todd studied my face. 'What about you? Any word on the promotion?'

'Inspector Davis called this morning. They're creating a new Detective Sergeant position here in Mission Beach, covering the whole northern coastal region. Apparently, our success with this case has convinced them that the southern region needs more permanent CID presence.'

'And?'

'And they've offered it to me.' I managed a small smile. 'Subject to completing my Detective Sergeant's qualification, which they'll fund.'

Todd's face lit up with genuine pleasure. 'Bec, that's fantastic! You've earned it, absolutely earned it. This case wouldn't have been solved without your work.'

'It was a team effort,' I replied automatically, though I felt a warm glow at his praise.

'Bollocks. You made the connections, you did the facial recognition work that identified Philippa, and you coordinated the investigation. Don't undersell yourself.' Todd's expression grew serious. 'You're going to be a brilliant detective, Bec.

Pandanus Point is lucky to have you.'

We sat in comfortable silence for a moment, the unsaid words hanging between us. Across the deck, the celebration continued, but it felt distant now, like watching life through glass.

'Todd,' I began, then stopped, unsure how to continue.

'I know,' he said quietly. 'No need to say it. I'm sorry for the way I've been.'

I felt my cheeks burn with embarrassment. 'You don't need to apologise. We've tried to keep things professional—'

'You did keep things professional. You were brilliant throughout this entire case, and your personal feelings never interfered with your judgment.' Todd's voice was gentle but firm. 'But Bec, you know why this can't work, don't you?'

I nodded, not trusting my voice. I did know. Megan.

'It's not that I don't... care about you,' Todd continued, his words careful and measured. 'What happened between us that night... it wasn't a mistake. It was real, and it was wonderful, and it scared the hell out of me.'

My heart clenched at the memory—the tenderness, the connection, the way everything had felt so right until he'd pulled away the next morning.

'Then why?' I whispered.

'Because I'm not ready,' Todd said simply. 'Megan's been gone two years, and I thought I was healing, thought I could move forward. But when I woke up next to you, all I could think about was how guilty I felt. How wrong it seemed to be happy again when she's...' He trailed off, unable to finish. You need someone who can give you everything—their whole heart, their whole future,' he continued. 'Someone ready to build something together from the ground up with you. I'm still carrying too much baggage from my past to be that person for you.'

'What if I'm willing to wait?' I asked, hating how desperate I sounded.

Todd's smile was heartbreakingly gentle. 'That's exactly what I'm afraid of. You're thirty-one, Bec. You shouldn't be waiting for a broken man to put himself back together. You should be living your life, finding someone who can love you completely from day one.'

I closed my eyes, fighting the tears that ached behind my eyes. Even that night when we'd finally given in to what had been building between us for a long time, if I was honest, I'd sensed Todd's hesitation, his fear. The way he'd held me so carefully, as if I might break—or as if he might.

'I feel like such an idiot,' I whispered.

'Don't.' Todd's voice was sharp with pain. 'Don't you dare feel like an idiot for being brave enough to feel something real. For being brave enough to help me feel alive again, even if only for one night. Do you know how precious that was? How much I needed it, even if I couldn't handle it afterwards?'

I opened my eyes to find Todd watching me with an expression I couldn't quite read.

'When Megan first got sick,' he continued, 'I thought I'd have years to prepare for losing her. The doctors were optimistic at first. But cancer doesn't follow anyone's timeline, and by the end...' He shook his head. 'I promised her I'd move on, find happiness again. But promises made in hospital rooms and promises you can actually keep are different things.'

I stared at him, seeing the grief in his eyes for a love that even death couldn't take away.

'What I'm trying to say is that you shouldn't be like me.

Don't hold back, don't wait for the perfect moment or the perfect person. When you find someone worth fighting for, fight for them. When you find something worth risking everything for, take the risk.'

We sat facing each other in the bright afternoon light, two police officers who had shared something intense, temporary and irreplaceable. I wanted to memorise this moment—the way the sunlight caught in Todd's grey hair, the familiar scent of his aftershave, the sound of waves and distant laughter.

Todd took my hand in both of his, his grip warm and firm.

'Friends,' he said quietly. 'We can be friends, Bec. Always.'

I squeezed his hand, accepting the olive branch for what it was—both a gift and a boundary. 'Friends,' I agreed.

Todd released my hand and leaned back, creating distance that felt both necessary and painful.

'Take care of yourself,' he said. 'And Bec? Congratulations on the promotion. You've earned it.'

He walked back to his car without looking back, and I stood watching until the taillights disappeared around the bend in the road. I wouldn't let myself cry. This afternoon, I'd go for a long walk on the beach and let it all out.

Chapter 37

Christmas Eve.

Tully.

I returned to the station to collect my things and lock up. The building felt different then, quieter somehow, as if Todd's departure had taken some essential energy with it.

By the time I finished the final paperwork, it was past dinner time, and my stomach was growling. I could have grabbed something from the café in town, but suddenly I found myself craving something more substantial. Something that felt like home. And with Christmas Eve upon me, there was only one place I wanted to be.

The drive to Tully took about twenty-five minutes, winding through cane fields. I had only made this journey once before, with Todd, when my parents had first moved here a few months ago. They'd been to see me at Mission Beach a couple of times in the last three months.

My parents lived in a modest weatherboard house on the outskirts of Tully, surrounded by the garden Dad had been establishing since their move. As I pulled into the driveway, I could see the transformation Mum had wrought—fairy lights twinkling in the hibiscus bushes, a wreath of frangipani hanging on the front door. Through the kitchen window, I caught glimpses of movement and the warm glow of Christmas lights.

'Bec!' Mum emerged from the house before I had even turned off the engine, wiping flour-dusted hands on her apron. 'What a lovely surprise. We weren't expecting you today.'

'Hi, Mum.' I hugged her, breathing in the familiar scent of

her floral perfume and baking, but now mixed with the rich aroma of roasting pork and Christmas spices. 'I finished the case today, and I thought... well, it's Christmas Eve. I wanted to come home.'

I reached into the car and pulled out two wrapped presents, carrying them towards the house. 'Mum, would it be okay if I stayed the night? I know it's last minute—'

'Oh, Bec!' Mum's face lit up like the Christmas tree I could see glowing through the front window. 'Of course you can stay! It'll be just like Christmas when you were a little girl. I have a room ready for you—I was hoping you'd come.'

Dad appeared in the doorway, his reading glasses pushed up onto his forehead, a tea towel slung over his shoulder. 'We've been following your case in the local paper. Quite a result.'

'It was,' I said, stepping inside and immediately stopping in wonder. Mum had transformed their new house into a Christmas wonderland. Garlands draped the doorways, candles flickered on every surface, and in the corner stood the most magnificent Christmas tree I'd ever seen. When I was growing up, Dad had dismissed Christmas decorations as frivolous.

I placed their presents under the tree. 'Mum, this is incredible. The house, the tree—it's beautiful.'

'I wanted our first Christmas in the new house to be special. The move has given us a whole new life,' she said, beaming with pride. 'And that smell? Yes, it's roast pork. I'm doing all the cooking today so I can relax tomorrow. I was hoping you'd come—that's why I got your favourite.' She glanced over and lowered her voice as Dad walked down the hall. 'And your dad is a different man.'

'But, Bec, what a lovely surprise,' he said, accepting the

hug I offered him.

For the next hour, I told them about the case, editing a lot of it out. They both listened with the mixture of pride and concern they had shown for my career since I joined the police force.

'And Todd, your partner?' Mum asked eventually, offering me a mince pie still warm from the oven. 'Will he be staying on?'

I felt a familiar tightness in my chest. 'No, Mum. Todd's gone back to Brisbane. New assignment.'

'I see,' Mum said gently. 'Was he... were you...?'

'We were partners,' I said firmly. 'Good partners. Good friends.'

Dad cleared his throat. 'Well, work relationships can be complicated. The important thing is you did good work together.'

'We did,' I agreed, grateful for his matter-of-fact acceptance.

Later, as we sat on the back veranda watching fruit bats wheel overhead, the smell of roasting pork drifting through the open door, Mum broached the subject I had been avoiding.

'Have you thought about what comes next, love? After all this excitement?'

'Actually, yes.' I set down my wine glass and turned to face my parents. 'They've offered me a promotion. Detective Sergeant, based permanently at Pandanus Point. I'd be covering the whole northern coastal region.'

My parents' faces lit up with pride and excitement.

'Bec, that's wonderful,' Mum exclaimed. 'A Detective Sergeant at your age—that's quite an achievement.'

'It is,' Dad agreed. 'And the Cassowary Coast is a lovely

area. Close enough that we can visit regularly, but far enough to give you some independence.'

I smiled, feeling some of the tension I had been carrying begin to ease. 'I was thinking... *if* I take the job, I might look into buying a place up there. Maybe something with a bit of land, room for a garden. I've been living in rentals since I first moved to Brisbane, and it's time I had a proper home.'

'That sounds perfect,' Mum said warmly. 'What kind of place were you thinking?'

'There's an old farmhouse on half an acre between Pandanus Point and the station; it's been on the market for months. It needs work, but it's got good bones. And it's right on the edge of the sugar cane fields, with views out to the water.' I could picture it clearly—the weathered timber walls, the wide veranda, the potential to be turned into a good place to live. And it would be an investment if I moved in the future.

'Half an acre?' Dad asked. 'I could mow for you when you get too busy.'

'Thanks, Dad.' Our relationship was getting better each time I saw him.

Mum smiled. I knew that Dad and I getting on was making her life a lot easier. 'Pandanus Point? That's where that young couple ended up, isn't it? The ones from your case?' she asked.

'Amanda Priestley and Dave Hewson, yes. They're staying on, getting married, I heard.' I smiled, remembering Amanda's transformation from terrified witness to the confident woman who had decided not to go home to England.

Mum reached over and squeezed my hand. 'Sometimes the best relationships are the ones that have weathered hard times, love. They know how to stand strong.' She met my eye, and I smiled, knowing she was talking of her personal journey with Dad.

As the afternoon wore on and our conversation drifted to local news, I felt myself relaxing properly for the first time in weeks. There, surrounded by the unconditional love and wisdom of my parents, the Christmas decorations twinkling around us, and the promise of tomorrow's celebration ahead, the disappointment of Todd's departure began to feel manageable. Not forgotten, but placed in perspective.

I thought about what he'd said—about not holding back, about taking risks when something was worth fighting for. Maybe he was right. Maybe it was time to stop playing it safe, to build something of my own instead of waiting for the perfect moment or the perfect person.

'Mum, Dad?' I said suddenly, interrupting Dad's story about the neighbour's escapee chickens. 'I think I'm going to take the promotion. And I will put an offer in on that house.'

'That's good,' Dad said quietly. 'Taking charge of your own life.'

As we moved inside to check on the roast and set the table for our Christmas Eve dinner, I found myself thinking about the future with something approaching excitement. Todd was gone, and that still hurt. But I was still there, still building something meaningful for myself.

Later that night, lying in bed, I could hear the quiet sounds of my parents moving around, talking as they put the final touches on tomorrow's preparations. Somewhere out there, Amanda and Dave were planning their wedding and building their life together in the aftermath of tragedy.

And somewhere, in a weathered farmhouse at Pandanus Point, Detective Sergeant Rebecca Whitfield might just find her new home.

The case was closed, but my story was just beginning.

Did you enjoy Shadows on the Shore?

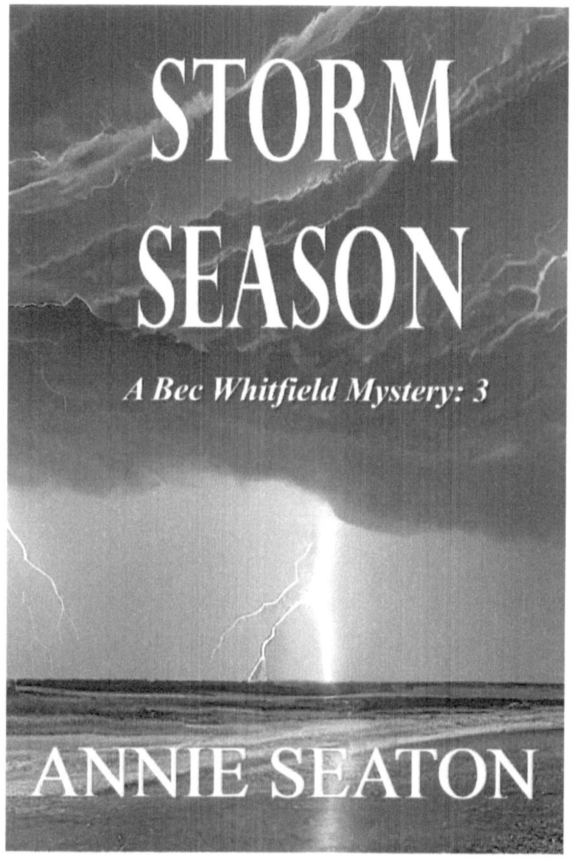

Storm Season… coming Jan 2026

Perfect for fans of Jane Harper and Candice Fox

Shadows on the Shore

A Detective Bec Whitfield Mystery: 3

Detective Bec Whitfield thought she'd found paradise in tropical Mission Beach—and maybe even love with charming local developer Jake Morrison. But when Cyclone Meredith threatens the coast, emergency preparations uncover a twenty-year-old secret buried in concrete.

The skeletal remains belong to Marcus "Moondog" Sullivan, a former Sydney property developer turned environmental activist who vanished in 2004 during heated battles over coastal development. Marcus had made powerful enemies on both sides of the conservation debate, and someone wanted him silenced permanently.

As Bec investigates, the case becomes uncomfortably personal. Jake's construction company was involved in the building where Marcus was found, and her new boyfriend grows increasingly evasive about his past. When Detective Todd Davenport arrives from Brisbane with warnings about Jake's reputation, Bec finds herself caught between two men and a web of corruption that reaches far beyond Mission Beach.

With the cyclone bearing down and evacuation orders imminent, Bec must solve a murder that exposes decades of environmental crime and political corruption. But the closer she

324

gets to the truth, the more she realises that Marcus Sullivan died because he threatened to expose secrets that powerful people will kill to protect.

In a race against time and the storm of the century, Bec will discover that some foundations are built on lies—and that choosing the wrong person to trust can be deadly.

Pre-order links:

eBook: https://books2read.com/u/385z76

Print: https://annieseatonstore.ecwid.com/Storm-Season-Preorder-January-2026-p758091512

Also by Annie Seaton

Daughters of the Darling

From Across the Sea

Over the River

By the Billabong (2025)

Beneath Still Waters

A Bec Whitfield Mystery

Bowen River

Shadows on the Shore

Storm Season

Duckinwilla Days

Coming Home

Secrets and Surprises

Wishes and Whispers

Chasing Dreams

New Beginnings

All Together Again

Home to the Outback *(2025)*

Lucy

Angie

Jemima

Annie Seaton

Isabella

Porter Sisters Series

Kakadu Sunset

Daintree

Diamond Sky

Hidden Valley

Larapinta

Kakadu Dawn

Others

Whitsunday Dawn

Undara

Osprey Reef

East of Alice

One Summer in Tuscany

Four Seasons Short and Sweet

Follow the Sun

Ten Days in Paradise

Deadly Secrets

Adventures in Time

Silver Valley Witch

The Emerald Necklace

A Clever Christmas

Christmas with the Boss

Shadows on the Shore

Her Christmas Star
The Emerald Necklace

The Augathella Girls Series
Outback Roads
Outback Sky
Outback Escape
Outback Wind
Outback Dawn
Outback Moonlight
Outback Dust
Outback Hope
Boxed Sets
Augathella Girls 1-4
Augathella Girls 5-8
Augathella Short and Sweet Series
An Augathella Surprise
An Augathella Baby
An Augathella Spring
An Augathella Christmas
An Augathella Wedding
An Augathella Easter
An Augathella Masquerade Ball
Boxed Set
Augathella Short and Sweet 1-3

Annie Seaton

Sunshine Coast Series

Waiting for Ana

The Trouble with Jack

Healing His Heart

Sunshine Coast Boxed Set

The Richards Brothers Series

The Trouble with Paradise

Marry in Haste

Outback Sunrise

Richards Brothers Boxed Set

Bondi Beach Love Series

Beach House

Beach Music

Beach Walk

Beach Dreams

The House on the Hill Boxed Set

Second Chance Bay Series

Her Outback Playboy

Her Outback Protector

Her Outback Haven

Her Outback Paradise

Boxed Set

The McDougalls of Second Chance Bay Boxed Set

Love Across Time Series

Come Back to Me

Follow Me

Finding Home

The Threads that Bind

Love Across Time Boxed Set

Bindarra Creek

Worth the Wait

Full Circle

Secrets of River Cottage

A Clever Christmas

A Place to Belong

Hearts in Harmony

Acknowledgements

As always, I've been supported by many people in the writing of this book, and I would like to acknowledge them here.

To the many friends I have made in the writing world over the past fourteen years, who constantly support me on my journey. I often say I have found my 'tribe', and I value the daily contact with like-minded people all over the world. Again, a special mention and thank you goes to my dear friend, critique partner and editor, Susanne Bellamy, and to my wonderful proofreaders: Roby Aiken and Kristen Woolgar.

To my loyal readers, who contact me by mail and on social media to tell me they enjoy my stories. To the members of my Annie Seaton Readers Group (Facebook group), a huge thank you for your interest and support.

If I had known when I began writing that I would gain such a loyal reader base, I wouldn't have believed it! Without readers, there would be no need for stories!

It would be impossible to write without support in your personal life:

To Ian, the love of my life and my research partner, as we travel this magnificent country seeking stories each winter. I could not do this without you. My driver, my chef, my bringer of wine, my fisherman, and my husband of fifty years.

To our children and their partners and our grandchildren: thank you for your love and support.

Again, my love and appreciation go to my wonderful aunt, Maureen Smith, who not only supports me but supports so many Australian writers through years of reading, loving and sharing their stories. Sadly, Aunty Maureen can no longer read due to failing eyesight.

And to you, the reader: thank you for choosing this book. I hope that when you read my story, you love it and talk about it, and that maybe you will want to visit this wonderful part of Australia.

I would love to hear from you.

Drop me a line at annie@annieseaton.net

Reviews on Goodreads and eBook sites are always welcome and much appreciated!

eBook links:

https://www.annieseaton.net/books.html

Print Store:

All books are available in print at Annie's store:

https://annieseatonstore.ecwid.com/

Awards

2023: Winner of the long contemporary RUBY award for *Larapinta*

2023: finalist in the Australian Romance Readers Awards for *Kakadu Dawn,* the sixth and final book in the Porter Sisters series,

2018 and 2020: finalist for the NZ KORU Award

2017: Winner Best Established Author of the Year 2017 AUSROM

2016, 2017, 2018, 2019: Longlisted for the Sisters in Crime Davitt Awards

2016: Finalist in Book of the Year, Long Romance, RWA Ruby Awards for *Kakadu Sunset*

2015: Winner: Best Established Author of the Year AUSROM